ARMENIA'S FINGERPRINT

Dear Pat ~

You've been a friend, colleague, and guide of mine for almost three decades. Now, I have a chance to thank you for always being there for me.

Thanks also for being a long-time CSF member and for reading my family's story.

Much Love + Respect —

Bruce Badrigian

ARMENIA'S
FINGERPRINT

A Family's Fight Against Genocide During WWI

BRUCE DAVID BADRIGIAN

Badrigian Family: Bruce, Rose, Tess, Nancy,
and Keeland ~ March 2002

ISBN: 0996963502
ISBN 13: 9780996963503
Library of Congress Control Number: 2015919868
Bruce Badrigian, Morro Bay, CA

DEDICATION

When my Armenian grandmother came to live with us in our small space on the bottom of a 3-decker house in Worcester, Massachusetts, I was just a young child. During those formative years, she often referred to me with a nickname which I thought was a term of endearment—-one she fondly used in reference toward her oldest grandchild. Much later, after she had passed, I mentioned the term to my father and asked him its translation in English. He looked at me... smiled, and as he walked away, he said, "Oh, that...it means cabbage head, but don't worry —— she loved cabbage."

For my many transgressions during my turbulent youth, I dedicate this novel to my Armenian grandparents who suffered greatly, yet persevered, so I would be able to one day write this story.

On my mother's side, I shall always treasure my childhood memories thanks mostly to my mother, Elaine Badrigian. She gave birth to five children by the time she was 26, and with my dad working three jobs his entire life, the child-rearing responsibilities fell mostly upon her-—whew!

Also, helping to raise me were my grandparents Elsie (Kowalski) and Clifford Keeland Robbins, Uncle Clifford Robbins, Uncle Kenneth Robbins, and a host of relatives mentioned below (it truly does take a village….).

To my wife -— for her skillful illustrations within these pages which she completed while teaching art to her public school students. Thanks to her patience, understanding, and love, I finished this novel while recovering from my illness while she worked full-time *and* raised our children.

My wife…my life….my balance…my love.

To my son Keeland for being an inspiration to me as he continues to fight fires up and down California as a member of the brave Cal Fire Firefighters and for the family of Morro Bay Firefighters who helped to mentor him (especially Captain Todd Gailey). Thank you, my only son, for being my right arm.

To my daughter Rose whose heart pushes her toward becoming a doctor (hopefully, one without borders) —- may your stunning aquiline profile (displayed on the front cover of this novel) forever symbolize the beauty of many hybrid Armenians whose historic blending of the races continues to produce photogenic eye-appeal. That said, may your outer beauty always be aptly eclipsed by the truer beauty of who you are on the inside.

To Tess, my youngest and last child, for whom I owe much gratitude for her patience toward my many idiosyncrasies. May your winsome sense of humor and dedication to your physicality be two of the many touchstones that will serve you and others well in the future. Your laughter brings me more joy than you will ever realize until you are blessed with children of your own.

To my extended family, friends, and students who taught me much more than I ever could express —- thank you for taking the time to know and understand my best intentions. Despite my faults, you stayed the course. By believing in me, <u>you</u> empowered me to believe in myself.

Finally, to these familial individuals who inspired me by loving me unconditionally: Diane and Joseph Badrigian-Krosoczka, Wayne and Andrea Badrigian, Debra Badrigian, Susan Badrigian-Langlois, Derek and Anna Langlois, London Mae Langlois (my great niece newly arrived), Garret Langlois, Elayne Badrigian, Leigh Badrigian, Wesley Badrigian, George Jr. (Gigi) Anderson, and Mary Badrigian (age 90 and still going....).

In memoriam of the following souls now gone—but not forgotten:

Kachadoor Badrigian	56
Isgouhi Mary Badrigian	71
Simon Joseph Badrigian	50
Elizabeth Badrigian	68
David Michael Badrigian	0 (still-born)
James Robert Doud	78
Dominic Riolo	18
Robert (Bob) Dougherty	85
Patrick Reilley	28
Seamus Reilley	32
Watchtang Botso Korishelli	92
Josefa Davi-Nolan	58
Joseph Krosoczka	64
Nancy Helen Filmer	90

꙰

Death hath no hold over those who lived for the betterment of others. Their lives shine like a beacon of eternal light illuminating the way for others—-one person at a time. BB

꙰

ACKNOWLEDGEMENTS

My sincerest thanks to my good friend and fellow teacher Jack Harris for calling me out of the blue and offering to help me move out of my classroom of 33 years with his big red truck. Aided by some nearby Morro Bay Fire-Fighters (some who where former students of mine), the transition was made. Thanks Jack…for rekindling our friendship and for being the first person to read my rough manuscript and provide valuable feedback.

An eye-appealing thank you to photographer Willie Kessell who artfully photographed my daughter Rose and allowed her portrait to be part of the book's creative cover. Thanks also to CreateSpace's gifted and talented Cover-creating Team.

I would also like to thank my colleagues on The Curriculum Study Commission (past and present) for their tutelage and inspiration (especially John Cotter, Ernie Karsten, Thelma Worthen, Leo and Deborah Ruth, Tom Gage, Miles Myers, Steve Weinberg, Joan Owen, and Marcia Russell).

Professionally, my career was enhanced by my colleagues from SLCUSD and SLCTA (especially Superintendent Dr. Eric Prater, Terry Finegan, Concho Crotzer, Jim Nett, Laurie Johnson, Paul Orton, Tom Boyle, Deb Pagan, Debbie Heck, Rose Fowler, Jim Quesenberry, Kathy Greer, Jana Bragg, Gayle Goodman, Katherine Kirby, Carol and Rich Gunther, and all the SLCTA executive board and site reps).

My special appreciation flies on tireless wings to all my Armenian brothers and sisters of all ages who openly and honestly shared with me their ancestors' trials and tribulations.

With sincere thanks, I humbly bow to my West and East Coast families (the Badrigian and Doud clans)—-the Badrigians for loving me always and the Douds for warmly welcoming me into their family— three thousand miles apart, but together in heart. Also, special thanks to my Mother-in-law Meridee Doud and Charlie & Annie Doud.

For their never-ending hospitality, encouragement, and support, I humbly bow to my McCloud, CA friends and neighbors.

Educationally, my genuine appreciation goes to all my students from Mission College Prep, Morro Bay High, Cuesta College, Cal Poly, and the University of LaVerne. Each of them made me a better teacher, better person, and a more reflective person as I grew older.

Other relatives, mentors, and friends (past and present) who knowingly or unknowingly helped me include the following individuals: Dan Andrus, Dennis Baeyen, Dennis Bailey, Lois Baldwin, Poppy Barnes, Roy Barrett, Marilyn Baty, Beryl & Sid Bennett, Kathy Benson, Bob Chapman, Columbus Park Crew, Craig and Jane Combs, Nick Combs, Ed Conklin, Concho Crotzer, Lanny Coulston, Bobby Cunningham,

Joe Curran, Ida Cruz, Eileen Daniels, Matt Davantzis, Michaela Doud, Jaci Downer, Ray & Patti Duff, Anna Erickson, Buddy and Lois Erickson, Bill (Cross-Country Walker) Fairbanks, Nancy Filmer, David Foster, Natalie & Lew Gamarra, Jaci & Judy Graham, Carol & Rich Guenther, Rose & Kathy Haroutunian, Michael Hartwell, Dr. Ed Hayashi, Father Ed Holterhoff, Eileen Houston, Max Jarrell, Richard (Doc) Johnson, Cheryl Joseph, Diane Kirk, Kitzman Family, Harleigh Knott, Ron La Barre, Dave & Lori Leary, Jack Leary, Joy Love, Mike Lynch, Noel Manchester, Megan Manley, Bill & Bernadette Martony, Scott & Lori Mather, Tamra & Jim McCarthy, Judy Meradian, Nattalia Merzoyan, Tony and Dayna Mininni, Julie Minnis, Eghosa Obaiza, Fred Paap, Perry Pedersen, Kristen Pelfrey, Charlie Perryess, Ray Philpot, Gene Pratt, Paul Proko, Jim Quesenberry, Chris Ray and my Maverick Brothers, Marcia & Phil Reardon, Terry Reed, Larry Reilley, Kathleen Reilley, Kaitlin Reilley, Charlie Reilley, Susan Robbins, Mike Robbins, Pamela Robbins, Doug Robbins, Alexis Ross, Susane Rotalo, Heather Richey, Marcia Russell, King Schofield, Elaine Smith, Eddie Soutra, James Squire, Dr. Andrea Tackett, John Tanionos, Hut Taylor, Laura Tremblay, Cindee Varni, Dr. Patrick Vaughan, Mila Vujovich-La Barre, Tom Weinschenk, and Steven (Huck) Williams (my first friend in Cayucos, CA — 1971).

EPIGRAPH

There is something special about Armenian eyes that defies description. Some say such eyes reveal the essence of one's soul, but I say they are more like the portals in the body of a ship——- a spiritual craft——- one which God has allowed us the free will to control. I hope someday to prove myself worthy of such a holy trust.

Bruce David Badrigian

INTRODUCTION
BY BRUCE DAVID BADRIGIAN

Laughter is the soul's own fingerprint. After all, a person's individual expression of verbal joy becomes a window of revelation—the essence of one's true self revealed. The novel you are about to read takes into account a people whose undeserved suffering reveals an inner strength so spiritually strong-willed it allows future Armenians (like my grandparents, parents, myself, and my children) the opportunity to experience peace, happiness, and yes—even laughter—once again. Being the first nation state to adopt Christianity, Armenia became God's first acknowledged human fingerprint on Earth; as a result, Armenians are doubly blessed—first for their spiritual vision and again for their steadfast faith.

While reading this novel, you might ask why a second generation hybrid Armenian would devote so much of his time to write a narrative where imaginations are stretched and hopes are inspired? My answer is simple—my Armenian ancestry haunts my heart more than any other lineage. Let me explain. As I grew older, I wondered how many unrecorded events of Armenian bravery...how many noble acts of courage...how many sacrificial acts for others were erased by a nation led by malevolent leaders determined to end Armenian history? Therefore, I created a fictional family (based on familial stories and researched facts) to represent the many families whose stories were never told. I used my grandparents' first and last names, but the story remains one that I created and revolves around two courageous teenage sisters. When circumstances beyond their control test their faith, inner strength, and ability to survive, they quickly learn the meaning of life...and death.

The events that follow illustrate and celebrate Armenians' meritorious commitment to life in the face of unjustifiable extermination. While this novel may be classified as historical fiction, the main events described (albeit hard to imagine) are based on eye witness accounts. This story is a covenant to my ancestors—one that evolved over sixty-four years of gradually accumulated pride. One that perhaps explains my own miraculous survival.

Diagnosed in early 2012 with Pancreatic Cancer, a team of doctors (headed by Dr. Hobart Harris of UCSF) performed a nine hour Whipple surgery and removed half of my pancreas, part of my stomach, my gall bladder, and the duodenum. A new hole was made in my stomach and the upper intestine attached using titanium staples. No food or water passed through my lips for more than thirty days. Complications followed, yet 30 days later...I left the hospital with tubes in my nose, mouth and both sides of my stomach. Miraculously, and with the skillful help of a team of talented surgeons, doctors, nurses, and medical staff, I am fortunate to be one of the less than 5% who survive pancreatic cancer for more than five months. Thusly blessed, I chose to use my recovery time to write this story for my children, so they will never forget what their ancestors and millions of Armenians sacrificed and suffered to make their lives possible.

Within these pages, the reader will find many descriptions based on varying accounts and situations told to me by others of Armenian descent. Many other actual accounts are numerous and can be found through diligent research online and in books written by Armenian survivors or their gifted progeny. The seriousness of these memories carry the day... for despite the vile efforts of Turkish leaders, these truths were passed down from Armenian elders to their children, and hopefully, one day—to their children's children—for the truth must be told regardless of the pain of memory or the specificity of ghastly details portraying the depths of depravity into which mankind can devolve. The first-hand accounts that follow describe the sordid acts no human should ever inflict upon another as well as the inspirational actions of courage that defined a generation of Armenians.

Sadly, many stories of Armenian opposition were snuffed out by the Turks (the "victors" write the history). So, as you turns these pages, I can only hope you will maintain an open mind to my vision of what happened behind the scenes. I believe in the likelihood of these possibilities and other similar unrecorded events, and I justify my belief on the Armenian spirit of faith-based strength, stalwart fortitude, willful strong-mindedness, and heroic resilience.

Some of my ideas stem from early accounts overheard by me when such conversations took place between my father and his mother (Isgouhi Yepremian-Badrigian). Unfortunately, my Armenian grandfather died before I was born. Although, I remember my father telling me that when his father rode on a donkey, his feet would drag on the ground. Children remember the strangest things about their parents.

During the early 1900's, my Armenian grandmother, her first husband, and their three young daughters lived in Western Armenia (now Eastern Turkey), but their lives were pauperized when the Turks continued their plan to eliminate all Armenians. Isgouhi's husband (his first name is lost) was killed fighting the Turk's attempts to take his home.

Isgouhi had to flee with her three young daughters wearing only the clothes on their backs. Over the course of a few months, without any help and no father for protection, her three girls starved to death (at least, that is the account Isgouhi reluctantly shared—the reality may have been much worse—as was the case for many young girls who were taken by the Turks). Isgouhi was near death herself when an Armenian man found her, nourished her, and somehow managed to gain passage for both of them on a ship traveling to America. During the arduous boat ride, this man (Kachadoor Badrigian, from Harput, Turkey) protected and lovingly nursed her back to health. When they passed their physical and mental tests at Ellis Island, Kachadoor and Isgouhi (Elise in English) were married. During the following years, they were blessed with three children—two girls...and finally—a third child...a boy.

That baby boy became my father.

Later, my father (Simon Joseph Badrigian), and my father's two elder sisters, Elizabeth and Mary, shared their memories of my Armenian grandparents. These stories and others found through personal research (books, novels, historical accounts, Armenian friends, etc.) dove-tailed together to create the following novel.

Many of the encounters described originate from actual self-witnessed accounts courageously shared publicly. I owe a great deal of gratitude to each of these survivors, for they unflinchingly shared harrowing, painful memories for all of us to read...for all of us to remember, and for all of us to never forget. That said, my story remains a work of fiction. I use my Armenian grandmother's name for the mother, for I never knew her as a teen. My own daughters serve as archetypes for Diana and Alisia, and my own father served as the archetype for Kachadoor. Finally, the witnesses who shared their stories are the true heroes, for they bore the burden, and...did so...their entire lives.

These sources inspired me to create a story based on truth and steeped in suffering. As a result, what follows is a compilation of facts embroidered by a storyteller on a mission to share a time in history that weaves a tale worthy of anyone's consideration (especially anyone with even a drop of Armenian blood running through his/her veins).

Lastly, this novel will help people understand what happened to an historic nation of proud Armenians. It will also champion those who miraculously survived the horror of a heart-wrenching holocaust despite despicable and inhumane efforts to annihilate and destroy all Armenians. Clearly, that attempted genocide failed—we, the descendants, are still here! We, Armenians of all types, colors, mixtures, and hybrids, carry on our lineage with sincere respect for those who saved us, for those who died for us, and for those who, risking everything, finally found the freedom they earned and we enjoy.

Within the pages of this novel, I hope to offer what did occur, and what might have occurred as Armenians fought back against deception, deceit, and the overwhelming numbers of those former Muslim friends and neighbors who were too easily swayed by heartless bigotry, religious intolerance, jealousy, suspicious insecurities, and distorted leaders who demanded the murder, rape, and annihilation of anyone who did not believe in Allah. By refusing to accept the doctrines of a twisted interpretation of a religion that over-ruled human decency and produced an indifferent cruelty towards fellow humans never witnessed before by the modern world, Armenians placed themselves directly in front of megalomaniacal Turkish leaders who manipulated, deceived, and betrayed their own people's history—leaving behind a wake of shame and infamy.

Hopefully, the honest, intelligent Turkish youth of today will express the goodness in their hearts and demand that their country apologize and accept responsibility for its ancestors' crimes. Only then—can Armenians try to forgive. The United States of America can also help this cause by recognizing and using the correct term for this horrible historic action (as have many other honest and brave countries) and use its most accurate terminology—**Genocide.**

During the year 2015— the 100th Anniversary of the Armenian Genocide, a new Pope was elected. Pope Francis was born in Buenos Aires, Argentina on December 17, 1936. His birth name was Jorge Mario Bergoglio. Pope Francis chose his papal name in honor of Saint Francis of Assisi (known for his love of all animals). Francis is the first Jesuit pope, the first from the Americas, the first from the Southern Hemisphere, and the first non-European pope since Syrian Gregory III in the year 741—some 1,272 years earlier. He is renowned for his Christ-like humility and humbleness. Many Christians believe he embodies new hope, new direction, and a new attitude that may truly transform the church and once again inspire millions. He has been expressly pro-active in the following: helping the poor, concern for the environment, criticizing the inequality of wealth, and for calling to task those who stand in the way of a better life for future generations.

In April 2015, Pope Francis was the first Pope to publicly use the G-word (referring to the Armenian Genocide). No sooner had his words been made public, Turkey's president, Recep Tayipp Erdogan, began his bullying tactics and suggestive threats by "warning" Pope Francis not to use the word *Genocide* again.

Such a warning carries serious historical implications. Many Armenians still remember back to May 13th, 1981 when Pope John Paul II was seriously wounded in St. Peter's Square by Turkish assailant Mehmet Ali Agca?

Below is a special report taken from the <u>New York Times</u>.

ROME, Thursday, May 14, 1981 -- Pope John Paul II was shot and seriously wounded yesterday as he was standing in an open car moving slowly among more than 10,000 worshipers in St. Peter's Square.

The police arrested a gunman who was later identified as an escaped Turkish murderer who had previously threatened the Pope's life in the name of Islam. The Pontiff, who was struck by two pistol

bullets and wounded in the abdomen, right arm and left hand, underwent 5 hours and 25 minutes of surgery in which parts of his intestine were removed.

According to Wikipedia, the Pope was struck four times, and suffered severe blood loss. Ağca was apprehended almost immediately by the Vatican's head of security, an alert nun, and several brave people in attendance. Agca was later sentenced to life in prison by an Italian court.

The Pope later forgave Ağca for the assassination attempt. The criminal was pardoned by Italian president Carlo Azeglio Ciampi at the Pope's request and was deported to Turkey in June 2000.

The president of Turkey's threat reveals Erdogan's own insecurity and despotic style of leadership. Perhaps the good people of Turkey should "warn" Erdogan not to threaten the Pope or anyone else. After all, Turkey's history of shameful violence against helpless people is more than well documented by a wide array of international sources; it is an open book, and... it... speaks... volumes.

Despite these threats, Pope Francis found the courage to speak the truth so honestly that all the world took notice of the Armenian genocide as well as the continued persecution and killing of Christians today. I can only hope the United States of America and other countries will follow Pope Francis' example and find the moral strength to stand up to Turkey's unjustifiable threats of retaliation.

Today, scholars and historians estimate that between the Greeks, Assyrians, and the Armenians who were killed by the Turks, the number of dead would be around three million. No one has ever been punished for these crimes. Perhaps, that is why this particular genocide has been referred to as "the forgotten genocide".

That said, let the reader understand that due to the cruel content within these pages, one should be forewarned that some of the descriptions or illustrations may shock or offend certain readers.

This novel chronicles the story of one fictional Armenian family, but it was inspired by my Armenian grandmother who survived the Armenian Genocide. I am a second generation Armenian whose grandparents were Armenian and whose father was a first generation American-born Armenian who married my mother (ancestral names Robbins/Kowalski) who was English and Polish; my pedigree is melting-pot American.

With regret, I have not yet visited Armenia to water my ancestral roots, nor am I writing with the experiential base of those who have carefully and skillfully detailed the historical timelines and specifics of the Armenian genocide—these individuals (such as the Balakians and others) are truly the Armenian scribes and historians who deserve to be read widely and repeatedly. As these individuals inspired and informed me, hopefully, this novel will inspire others to seek out these Armenian scribes and their factual, historical writings. I simply share what I have learned, heard, and felt over the past six decades and now offer my story to you.

Many thanks go to my family, friends, and students who encouraged me to write down my story.

This is it.

Kachadoor and his wife Isgouhi (in back), Mary, Simon, and Elizabeth (in front). The above picture is the only known photo of my grandfather; unfortunately, he died before I was born.

Chapter 1

ARMENIAN HISTORY ~ A FATHER'S PERSPECTIVE

A sudden, surprisingly brisk wind blew the tiny, feathered nest from its semi-secure footing high in the sun-baked branches of the gnarly oak tree as the alarmed fledglings fluttered helplessly to the ground—no parents to protect them, they were quickly laid bare to the cruel forces beyond their control. Still, Nature's offspring often overcomes the greatest of odds; thus was it back then…and so it is…even today.

Winter reluctantly receded and gave in to the resurgence of spring and its much anticipated explosion of brightly-colored valleys bordered by verdant hillsides, patch-worked forests, and burbling streams. Clearly, God smiled upon all living things with their vital beauty bearing witness to His wondrous work.

In 1902, Diana turned four years old, her younger sister had just turned three the month before. Their mother, Isgouhi (Elise or Elizabeth in English), taught her young daughters self-discipline by assigning them the simplest of chores beginning at an early age. The sisters learned quickly the unspoken understanding of responsibility and contribution to an entity larger than oneself. Later, that understanding would grow to include neighborhood, community, village, city, and country.

As the girls entered their teen years, Mother shared her skills in sewing, cooking, cleaning, and reading. She made sure her little ones understood the importance of learning a wide array of skills. Isgouhi created an environment which included books, writing tablets, informal tutors, and many mentors throughout her girls' young years. She wanted her offspring to be smarter, stronger, and healthier than her. She devoted her time, energy, and life to her children, so they would prosper greatly in theirs.

On the other hand, Father (Kachadoor Badrigian), encouraged his daughters to sharpen their skills in more physical ways. His methods were unorthodox and unusual; however, the near twins were delighted to comply. Therefore, as the two sisters approached their teen years, both learned to run long distances without stopping, to ride horses and respect animals, to build strength and stamina through physical activities, and develop mental discipline through yoga and meditation. These exercises often contained competitive elements, but the celebration of living within a healthy, strong body took precedent over simplistic competitions. Each girl learned to defend herself; at first, with just hands and feet—but eventually, they were introduced to archery. Father did not believe in guns; his strength came from fitness of mind and body.

When the girls watched their father pick up his long bow and throw his leather quiver over his shoulder, they felt as if they were watching a gifted warrior preparing himself for some spiritual rite. The young girls could not understand completely his dedication to perfection but were nevertheless fascinated by the possibilities. His hands caressed the smooth wood as he carefully bent the bow...flexing its curvature to slip the bowstring into its rightful place—notched at the very end of the half-moon crescent. With the pressure released, the string grew taught and twanged softly when he plucked it lightly with his forefinger and thumb.

Kachadoor hand-crafted all of the targets he employed: bulls-eyes with straw backing, old leather jackets or patches, and even moving targets. Diana liked the moving targets the best because she was needed to pull or push to begin the movement. Diana would pull on a long piece of rawhide attached to a target roughly simulating a deer or other animal. Father would almost always hit the target within the critical kill zone—explaining that one should always kill mercifully and that all animals had certain kill spots or "targets within the targets".

He further shared his spiritual philosophy of hunting— "All that is killed must be used for a purpose. Never kill for thrill or challenge. Rather, kill for food or clothing or protection—never for pleasure; it is a sin. Everything and every person has a purpose—all part of God's infinitely wise design." To Kachadoor, nature was God personified. Thus, when his oldest girl first witnessed him kill a deer, her precocious intellect allowed her to understand when he bowed respectfully over the freshly slain buck and placed his large hand over the animal's still beating heart. In her rapidly developing mind, she realized he was offering a prayer of thanks to this magnificent animal for giving up its life to nourish her family.

As the sisters entered their mid-teens, Diana would share her youthful enthusiasm with her sister, for Alisia looked up to Diana and hung on every word. Unlike other sibling rivalries, Diana rarely took advantage of her little sister, for she sensed their special bond early on. Even when playing chess, Diana offered her enough pieces to make the game one of fair play. Father would say, "Your sister will one day be your best friend in the world, so always focus on building her confidence; make her as strong as you, for her strength will be your best ally some day."

As the girls grew older, Diana would beg mother to allow her to stay and help father in his leather shop. The smell of leather, wood, sawdust, and earth combined to transport her to another time and place inhabited by fairies and elves. Her imagination ran amok as father would occasionally look up from his work and smile to see her creating scenes with her younger sibling by making little figures out of leather scraps and kindling wood. Her father was a blacksmith, cobbler, leather-worker, wood-carver, and teacher. He loved to use his hands as well as his mind.

"Learn to read and write—use your brain—for your back will wear out sooner than your mind. Just remember—there will be times when only physical strength will save the day. So, do your exercises, go for your runs, hikes, and walks. Sitting...well, sit only when you must, and then try and think of a way to get moving again. Now, move <u>yourself</u> to bed!"

With a shriek, the girls scrambled away from his outstretched arms as he chased them to their rooms. The two young girls thrived in such a loving home, but they did (as do most children) occasionally take their parents for granted. Unconditional love and support are essential building blocks, yet most young people never realize the true importance of such underpinnings until they grow older and see that not everyone has been blessed with that same crucial foundation.

In the girls' bedroom, his story continued....At bedtime, either mother or father would read or tell their sleepyheads a story; these tales delighted the sisters as they drifted off to sleep in their separate single beds ready to enter a dreamland filled with endless possibilities.

As the years passed, the girls continued to listen and learned from their father and mother the ancient history of their Armenian ancestors.

"For three thousand years or longer, an established, close-knit Armenian community had flourished inside the expansive region of the Middle East bordered by the Black Sea in the North, Mediterranean Sea in the West, and Caspian Sea in the East," began father. "These ancient times were ruled by Greeks, Romans, Byzantines, Persians, Arabs, and Mongols. During these repeated invasions, the Armenian people fought for their homeland and died side-by-side as they faced one overwhelming enemy after another. Nevertheless, Armenian pride and cultural identity never faltered; rather, these persevering souls adapted as does the Willow tree to the wind—for forces that are beyond one's control can only be endured by exercising patience and flexibility. By bending, the Willow survives the wind and does not break.

While enduring these hard times, the snow-capped peak of Mount Ararat became an inspirational symbol for many Armenians, and by 600 BC, Armenia (as a nation) manifested itself into being. Following the advent of Christianity, Armenia became the first nation to accept this new religion with its philosophy of forgiveness and humility as its national religion. Such an unorthodox commitment took extraordinary devotion and undying faith—especially in such a hostile environment for those who believed differently from the masses.

As the years slipped by, an exceptional era of peace followed as Armenians successfully enriched their culture with the creation of a distinct alphabet, an artistic wave of literature, art, trade, and a remarkable style of architecture. Around the 10th century, Armenians founded the city of Sofi. This city grew to be the new capital city and became known by the nickname The City of a Thousand and One Churches."

Father gently moved a strand of hair covering one of Alisia's eyes.

"Does this history make you tired my little one?"

"No Father, tell me more, but make it into a story—I <u>love</u> your stories!"

He smiled patiently and continued to weave the complex history of Armenia into a chronological tapestry—one that his girls could understand—and more importantly, one they would always remember.

He stroked Alisia's temples as Diana yawned and turned toward her dad. He continued....

"Well, in the eleventh century, the Turks first invaded our Armenian homeland. We again were overwhelmed by the sheer numbers of them.

We remained polite, kept to ourselves and tried to be good neighbors. Of course, the Armenian people embrace peace over war; we celebrate forgiveness, enlightenment, and honor...and since Christianity embodied the best of these virtues, it was soon worshipped by our people. However, some Muslim Turks resented our belief and looked upon us with distrust and disgust. After all, their religion seemed a direct antithesis of ours. Their Koran demanded that they annihilate unbelievers—a concept foreign to us, but eventually many Turks would use these sayings to rationalize their murderous ways.

That said, the Turks were a determined people, and soon their numbers grew vast. Eventually, we were surrounded by those who would easily be convinced to turn against us. Thus began several hundred years of rule by Muslim Turks, and a period of unjust treatment for the Armenians.

By the sixteenth century, Armenia had been absorbed into the vast and mighty Ottoman Empire. At its peak, this Turkish empire included much of Southeast Europe, North Africa, and almost all of the Middle East. However, by the 1800s, the once powerful Ottoman Empire was in serious decline."

"What happened Father? Why did their numbers decline?"

"Excellent question my inquisitive daughter— in the late 1800's, much of Europe began to refer to the Ottoman Empire as 'the sick man of Europe' because it refused to evolve socially, ethically, and politically. Its backwards views towards women, education, and equality for all people separated it from its more progressive neighbors. Its corruption in government and its inhumane treatment of minorities finally moved Europe to demand the Ottoman leadership treat its Armenians fairly and without discrimination.

Unfortunately, this criticism had the opposite effect. The Ottoman regime of Sultan Abdul Hamid II arrogantly viewed such suggestions as 'imperialistic intervention' and a direct threat to its sovereignty. Instead of exercising compromise, understanding, and fairness towards all, it responded harshly and viciously. In 1896, the Sultan began a quick-moving, deceptive, and deadly campaign in which hundreds of thousands of Armenian were slaughtered.

Now, here we are two decades later, and I am afraid the Turks are not done with their acts of hatred toward Armenians."

"Why do they hate us so much? Did the Armenians hurt their people?"

"No, my dear, although, we were <u>always</u> different than the Turks; we existed peacefully for a long time despite our religious differences. Yes, they treated us unfairly and discriminated against us for petty reasons. However, instigated by the Turkish government, a wave of nationalism swept through the country and hatred, jealousy, and fear reigned supreme. Many Armenians resented and resisted this unfairness.

On the other hand, for centuries, the Ottomans had fiercely refused to accept technological progress. Meanwhile, the nations of Europe championed and encouraged innovation; in doing so, they became industrial giants. Subsequently, the Turkish armies who had once been virtually invincible—now lost battle after battle to modern European armies. The Turks remained stuck in their own sanctimonious and self-righteous views.

All other people who did not believe as they did were going to hell, so the close-minded Turks stubbornly refused to listen to new ideas. As a result, they were left behind economically and creatively as the world changed.

As their empire gradually crumbled, formerly subject peoples including the Greeks, Georgians, Serbs, and Romanians achieved their long-awaited independence. Unfortunately, the Armenians and the Arabs of the Middle East remained stuck in the backward and nearly bankrupt empire, now under the autocratic rule of Sultan Abdul Hamid II. The

Armenians, however, would not leave their land—'never lose your land' became an age-old edict passed down from father to son."

"Why Father? What is so important about the land?"

"This land, my child, will always be the womb of our people. It is the sacred soil watered by our ancestors' blood, sweat, and tears as they made the ground fertile and rich with their labor and love. This is ancient, earthy dirt that our mothers seeded, and the hallowed ground where we buried our venerable ancestors—no, we would not leave without a fight...three thousand years is too long...." Father rubbed his eyes; he stretched a bit and shrugged his broad shoulders.

The girls rested their heads in their father's lap as he patiently continued the storied history.

"By the 1890s, young Armenians began to press for political reforms— reforms that were long overdue. It is often the youth who are in the vanguard of such protests— unafraid to demand something from justice and move the feet of the oppressors. They were calling for a constitutional government, the right to vote, and an end to discriminatory practices such as special taxes levied solely against Armenians just because they were Christians. Isn't it always the youth who cry out for change— the youth who take the risks?" His sagacious head slowly bowed as he looked at his sleepy girls... "the youth who too often pay the ultimate price?"

His square jaw tightened as he continued—

"The despotic Sultan responded to their pleas with brutal persecutions. Between 1894 and 1896 over 200,000 inhabitants of Armenian villages were massacred during widespread pogroms (widespread massacres) conducted by the Sultan's special regiments. These were dark times for our people.

Nevertheless, I want you to know this: your ancestors survived horrific treatment because they knew they must. Their inner strength manifested itself through the Father, Son, and Holy Spirit— which is why you should never renounce your faith. This is why you often hear your Mother exhort, 'Jesus, Mary, and Joseph—please pray for us!'

Today, Jesus Christ remains the exemplary role model we strive to follow.

Despite our efforts, we were vastly outnumbered, but we persevered by bonding together. We are of the Hye (meaning—of the Armenians, similar to to the *ian* or *yan* endings of Armenian surnames representing "the son of"—Hye meant you were special...you were Armenian); we would not go away, and we would not abandon our Armenian brethren. This is our way. We were Christians and paid in bitter blood for our beliefs.

Eventually, the Sultan grew old and the young 'wolves' restless. As the ancient Sultan became slow and ineffective, the Turkish nationalists known as the "Young Turks" forced the old Sultan out. The year was 1908, the Young Turks were ambitious junior officers in the Turkish Army who had ideas of their own. They quickly made dramatic changes. At first, Armenians in Turkey were hopeful, albeit naive, with this sudden turn of events and its possibilities for a friendly and fair future. Well-attended, ethnically mixed public rallies were held. The Turks and Armenians both were calling for freedom, equality, and justice—sadly, this would not be justice—not for the Hye.

Before long, our dreams were dashed when three of the Young Turks seized full control of the government via a coup in 1913. This triumvirate of Young Turks, consisting of Mehmed Talaat, Ismail Enver and Ahmed Djemal. These three villains deceitfully employed dictatorial powers and diabolically crafted their own megalomaniacal plans for the future of Turkey. They wanted to bring together all of the Turkic peoples. Their plan was to expand the borders of Turkey eastward across the Caucasus all the way into Central Asia. Such a zealous move would create a new Turkish empire with one language... and—one religion.

However, there remained a conundrum beyond their intellectual grasp. A problem that needed solving. When one sees every problem as a nail, every solution calls for a hammer. They became a hammer—and we—the Armenians— became the nails—much like Christ's nails in His hands and feet, we were soon deceived, hobbled, and ravaged without pity or compassion by a people we no longer recognized.

Our historic homeland of Armenia lay right in the path of their plans to expand eastward. Also, on that land was a large population of Christian Armenians totaling some two million persons, making up about 10 percent of Turkey's over-all population. Following thousands of years of tradition, these Armenians were amazing horsemen, artists, intellects, tradesmen, craftsmen, farmers, inventors, teachers, politicians, priests, etc. They were also a tight-knit, loving people united by their faith and loyalty to one another. (*Such loyalty would serve them well when they migrated to other countries throughout the world.*) These God-loving, creative, intelligent people were your ancestors."

"I know many were tortured and murdered, but Father, how many over the years were killed?"

"It is difficult to know my dear Diana, but the killing continues even today. This is why I have trained you to protect yourself with your small bow, and one day I will leave my bow to you—my oldest child. As my father trained me, I now train you, and <u>you</u> will train <u>your</u> children to protect themselves—to not be victims ever again—to fight against injustice, and to challenge those who treat them unfairly. Better to die on your feet, than to live on your knees. We kneel only to God."

The sun set softly behind the green-gold hills beyond the modest small home.

Father continued by candlelight, "Also, with the Young Turk's agenda, there was a rapid rise in Islamic fundamentalist extremism throughout Turkey. Christian Armenians were once again labeled as infidels (non-believers in Islam). Anti-Armenian demonstrations were instigated by young Islamic extremists who embraced violence against Armenians. Shamefully, our own government allowed these racist protests. The Turks blamed the Armenians for their state of misfortune. During one such outbreak in 1909, two hundred villages were plundered and over 30,000 persons massacred in the Cilicia district on the Mediterranean coast. Throughout Turkey, sporadic local attacks against Armenians continued unchecked over the next several years."

"But why father? Why don't the Turks like us?"

"You ask questions, I ask myself—how old are you? Well, my young teen sweetheart, I can only say that most people always fear what they do not understand. Of course, there were clear cultural differences as well between Armenians and Turks. The Armenians had always treasured its educated communities despite its external pressures from the Turkish empire. Armenians were the professionals within the Ottoman society: the businessmen, lawyers, teachers, priests, bankers, architects, tin makers, cobblers, musicians, wine-makers, engineers, merchants, doctors, and skilled craftsmen. Also, they were more open to new scientific, political, and social ideas from the West (Europe and America). Children of wealthy Armenians went to Paris, Geneva, or even to America to complete their education.

By contrast, the majority of Turks were illiterate peasant farmers and small shop-keepers. Leaders of the Ottoman Empire frowned on formal education of the masses—especially for the women. Thus, institutions of higher learning could not be found within their close-minded empire. The various megalomaniac and despotic rulers throughout the empire's history had valued sycophantic loyalty and blind obedience above all. Their uneducated subjects had never heard of democracy or liberalism and thus had no inclination toward political reform. Conversely, this was not the case with the better educated Armenians who sought justice, fair representation, and social reforms that would improve life for themselves and Turkey's other minorities.

Thus, as a deviously deliberate plan, the Young Turks cleverly decided to honor the virtues of simple Turkish peasantry at the expense of the Armenians. They did this in order to capture peasant loyalty. They exploited the religious, cultural, economic, and political differences between Turks and Armenians. Soon enough, the result the ruling Turks sought (the deliberate extermination plan) eventually came to be— the average Turk came to regard Armenians as strangers among them. Neighbors became enemies and jealousy reared its ugly head as prejudice became its crown of thorns. Still, remember this my child— not all Turks hated us. Some remained our friends and challenged the authorities; unfortunately, these good people were dealt with severely by the Young Turks, and some of our true Turkish friends (the best of the Turks) lost their lives trying to defend us against this great injustice. We remain in their debt to this day.

And so, my little one, that is why we are persecuted even today, but never fear, for we are a strong and smart people who will not be forgotten by our most wise and merciful God. Now, off to bed with you both and don't forget to give me my goodnight kisses, for their magical properties insures me a restful night—I love you."

That night remained burned indelibly into his girls' memories.

Despite Kachadoor's wisdom, and even though he suspected danger lurked around the corner, the steps he intended to take to move his family from harm's way did not materialize in time. Perhaps, it revolved around his strong connection to the sacred lands, but whatever prevented him from acting sooner, tragically narrowed any hope for escape. Death and destruction were closer than he realized.

⌒⌒⌒

After dinner on the next day, Kachadoor and his family again heard the sound of loud speakers declaring that all Armenian men should report to the government building before sundown. Despite the repeated demand, father refused to leave our house, yet Mother could recognize his anxiety. "I do not respond to their demands; I am not their dog."

Father walked across our wooden floor and pointed to a flag of Armenia prominently displayed on our wooden wall. "This is what I am loyal to" and he looked at us sternly to make us understand—"The red color of our flag represents the sacrifice and blood of the many Armenian soldiers who died in various struggles in both past and present. The beautiful blue color stands for hope and aspiration for the progress of Armenia, and the color orange is symbolic of the fertile lands of Armenia. Yes, I am proud of what our flag represents, and that is why I wear its colors." He smiled broadly as he spread his arms like a giant condor and displayed his favorite shirt—the one Mother made for him from fine cloth woven together skillfully blending bright red, blue, and orange in a display of patriotic brilliance.

Mother laughed, "You resemble a giant rainbow moving across our humble home. Why don't you calm down and put our girls to bed?"

The burly man froze at his wife's words, and slowly his head turned to his daughters. His wide eyes narrowed to slits as the corners of his lips lightly turned upwards.

Suddenly, he moved like lightning across the room and grabbed up his two girls and began kissing them (as he did everyday) and saying, "Did I tell you I love you today?" The startled girls cried out in protest and pretended to be bothered as they repeatedly yelled—"no!"

Father grinned mischievously, "Well, I do!" He then began repeatedly kissing whichever one he could catch as she tried to push him away laughing and squirming in his large hairy arms.

Once, mother asked him if he had ever wished for a son. His head signaled no, but his hesitation sent another message. Every father secretly wishes for a son...<u>and</u> a daughter. Nevertheless, he remained a happy man. Kachadoor Badrigian chose to be happy to work, happy to be alive, and happily in love with his wife and children who adored and respected him as a loving husband and father.

After kissing his girls goodnight, Kachadoor hesitated for a moment, his back to the girls' beds. Their soft breathing reassuring to his ears. He turned slowly to gaze one last time upon his twin-like girls. As his contented, weary body leaned against the wooden frame of the small room, he could smell the hand-hewn wood surrounding him, the perfumed fragrance lingered on the still moist hair not yet dry from mother's washing, and he began a silent prayer to himself asking God to help him be a good father and a better husband.

As the moon peeked protectively into the small room, a luminescent ray sliced its way in between the wooden slats of the window and rested lightly on the foot of the girls' beds. At that moment, Kachadoor's mind opened and he understood—

The most substantive and significant act a father can do for his children is to unabashedly and openly love their mother.

⌒⑂⌒

Chapter 2

A LOSS OF INNOCENCE ~ A TIME TO FLEE

February 1, 1915—The Badrigian family members bowed their heads in prayer to the one and only Christian God who would always be their strength and salvation. As mother shushed the sisters, father began grace with his own version of the Lord's Prayer:

> **Our Father whom art in Heaven— hallow be Thy name**
> **here on Earth as it is in Heaven.**
>
> **Thank you for giving us another glorious day**
> **to do your will and strengthen our souls…**
> **and for providing this blessed food**
> **to nourish our bodies.**
>
> **We thank you for forgiving us our many trespasses,**
> **and, by doing so, teaching us to forgive**
> **those who trespass against us.**

**And thank you God for your only begotten Son—Jesus Christ
and his Mother Mary— full of grace….
and for allowing Them to help and guide us away
from the many temptations that often distract us….**

**And finally, for delivering us from evil…
not just now…but also at the time of our deaths…
for we know, oh Lord, that all the power that is within us…
and all the glory that this world can offer…
stems from you—our Lord…our Father.**

Amen.

Kachadoor usually worked on Sunday despite it being the day of Sabbath. He simply said God would understand his actions, and he did not concern himself with what others thought about him. Isgouhi took her daughters to church faithfully and never complained about father's absence.

Isgouhi's black hair was worn long and often braided. Shards of gray streaked her black tresses and each plait weaved a unique pattern of ebony and silver. Her eyes were chocolate brown galaxies that seemed to look into her daughters' eyes with patience and understanding. She did not smile as much as Kachadoor, yet her warmth surrounded the whole family like the hand-woven comforters and afghans that protected the family from winter's biting breath.

The sisters followed their mother's tradition of practicality and neatness; however, their physical regimens involved physical exertion, focused energy, and coordinated muscle movement—such devotion steeped in discipline toned their youthful bodies. They became athletic, graceful... filled with kinetic energy that begged to be challenged, exercised, or released in some manner or form. Both parents understood this and found creative outlets that stretched their abilities and strained their growing muscles.

For example, when Diana became proficient at archery, her father added another layer of difficulty—asking her to hit the targets while on horseback. When she met that particular request, movement provided a higher bar—soon, she could hit the target with her horse at full-stride—her strapping legs securing her core to the galloping form as her knees guided the animal beneath her toward the target. This added challenge renewed her enthusiasm and piqued her curiosity; soon, Alisia wanted to try, and both girls willingly extended their practice time—laughing and playing together as sisters are apt to do when they are happy and content.

⌒⋙

Despite the bellowing commands from the loudspeakers, Diana's father again refused to report to the government building. He said that he was too busy to follow orders from those who treated his family unfairly. Later, Diana's parents heard that all the men were piled into trucks and transported to a nearby town. They were told they were going to an important meeting in a nearby town—one where their presence was much needed.

Later, Diana learned what happened to the transported men. The truth found its way back via a few fleet-footed survivors. They told how once they were a good distance from town, the Turkish Army approached a lonely area alongside the road. The Armenian men were told to get out and take a rest. As the old men sat sullenly on the flat rocks, the young Armenian men paced nervously like trapped jungle cats—something was amiss. Suddenly, the Turks turned into executioners and rained down bullets that tore into brothers and fathers, cousins and friends.

The younger men screamed at their heartless assassins and some ran headlong into the smoking guns and piercing bullets in a futile effort to reach the authors of such a heinous crime. Some of these young men were shot several times but refused to die until their bloody hands embraced the throats of the surprised killers. One Armenian man (despite wounds to his upper legs and stomach) made it to one of the youthful Turks and with his two strong arms clasped his hands on both ears of the shocked youth and pressed his thumbs into the wide eyes of his murderer and pressed hard until the crushed eyes sunk into the young murderer's brain. Armenian and Turk died together—their arms intertwining awkwardly as they fell to the ground—blood of one mixing with the blood of the other.

Regrettably, most of the Armenian men died looking into the scared young eyes of Turkish youths too ignorant or too zealous to realize their sins against humanity. Others ran for their lives, but most were killed or wounded and left bleeding. A few escaped into the trees and disappeared into the safe refuge of the forests they knew so well. They would be the harbingers of truth—so the rest of the Armenian population would know the brutal facts. These Armenian escapees (some only teens) would live like wild animals until they were able to fight and seek revenge. Many shed their boyhood quickly and became the men known only as Freedom Fighters.

Hatred reigned supreme; it marked the beginning of a nightmare that would last many years.

As Diana slept, her dreams took her back in time. She winced at images of her people crying out for mercy, she shuddered as Armenian churches burned and tears wet her pillow as her prophetic vision penetrated the holy walls and stained glass windows to see the screaming women and children huddled together, wide-eyed and fearful. Like a sleepwalker stuck in a nether world between imagined reality and mind-bending hallucinations, Diana drifted from one scene to another until a large familiar weight rested gently upon her shoulder and began to shake her upper body.

"Wake up my child, we must prepare ourselves." Kachadoor stood, looked down at his oldest daughter. *What will come of her now? Where will we go?* He turned and left the room. Isgouhi had already packed items from the kitchen. "We will need many provisions; I will get them from the shed. The Turks are still a village away, but word has it they will be here tomorrow. We must leave this morning."

Isgouhi nodded her head and resumed her preparations. What the loving couple did not know was the Turks had split their forces to move more quickly. While one group stormed the neighboring village the other skipped over it to surprise Kachadoor's village.

The soldiers were only moments away.

Kachadoor was often referred to as "Father" by his children and wife just as Isgouhi was referred to as "Mother" as a sign of great respect.

Father spoke to his family roughly and told them they were in danger and must flee immediately and find refuge elsewhere. With fear for his family's safety painted grotesquely on his face, he suddenly, for the first time, looked old to his children.

While Kachadoor gathered supplies (what does one bring under such circumstances?) from the far back shed, the first of the arriving soldiers came to Kachadoor's home. Does anyone ever expect the unexpected?

The family, hurriedly packing essential items, looked up in despair when four soldiers suddenly kicked in the front door and entered quickly with guns pointed in the girls' faces. Their concerted actions must have been repeated many times for they were a well-oiled, diabolical group of cutthroats bent on death and destruction. These gendarmes wore blood-lust expressions on their faces and bloodstains on their soiled uniforms. Words lost their meaning as the invaders' body language left no doubt of purpose.

The hellish scene transpired in a flash. The soldiers apprised the situation without hesitation. The men presumed that Father had been taken yesterday with the other men and boys. Their expressions reflected lust laced with hatred—a bizarre expression the girls would never forget. Diana was sixteen and her sister just turned fifteen. Diana protectively reached for her father's bow by the fireplace, but in the confusion, she was too slow—paralyzed by these blood-thirsty men now in the kitchen of their once peaceful home.

Without a word, the first soldier grabbed Diana from behind, another ripped through her thin cotton dress with a firm jerk; the assailant's dirty nails scraped her clean white skin leaving long red streaks. The first Turk (who was unusually tall) bent down and whispered threateningly in her ear.

"Do not struggle or resist. Embrace me freely and let me enjoy your body. Do everything I say, and bring me great pleasure. If you do this and satisfy each of us completely, we will leave your little sister and mother untouched, and you all will be set free."

Diana froze—her mind as numb as her body as she tried to comprehend the meaning of the heated words half-whispered in her ear as the soldier squeezed her breasts hard from behind her. Together, the men quickly stripped away the rest of her torn clothing and underwear as Alisia watched in horror shaking and sobbing as a different soldier held her by her hair. Less than a minute had passed. With a sudden jerk, Mother twisted away from the short, stocky soldier holding her and attacked the tall soldier with fists of fury and tried to scratch out the eyes of the offender molesting her oldest daughter, but the butt of a rifle smashed into her skull, and she dropped to the floor with uncharacteristic carelessness—blood began to seep from her forehead; a small vermilion pool formed on the wooden floor. Diana gasped and tried to twist away, but the soldier's grip tightened dangerously around her throat—she gasped for air—paralyzed with fear, Diana did as she was told without comprehending what the man wanted.

Tears ran down her cheeks as she screamed out her pain into the suffocating hand over her mouth. She looked down at her mother's body with red/black blood rivulets trickling around her forehead and face. Diana could no longer hear the laughing and grunting demands of the soldiers. The man's body melded with hers and tore at her insides. Her screams were muffled again by the dirty hand held tightly over her mouth. Time seemed to be suspended as she felt herself leave her body behind as she was manhandled and brutalized—her innocence ripped from her young body while seeds of hatred were planted permanently in her mind's memory and beyond.

In minutes, the perpetrators were spent, they left her bleeding—a naked, shaking heap. As the short soldier strode toward the door, new soldiers entered with guns pointed. The tall one, holding Diana's long black hair, yanked her head up, and said with a laugh, "She is well-trained now; she will do anything you ask."

Adjusting their uniforms, they picked up their guns and made ready to leave the grisly scene behind. The new soldiers pulled Diana up to her feet and gawked at her nakedness as they forced her over the kitchen table. Two of the other soldiers began to strip Alisia of her clothes when

Diana broke away in an effort to protect her younger sister and screamed at the assailants until her throat cracked.

⌒⌒

On the back-side of their property, Kachadoor struggled with the load of supplies as he tried to carry all the items in one trip, but when he heard Diana's blood-curdling scream—he dropped everything he was carrying except for one familiar item…. Kachadoor's legs where a blur despite the sickening feeling deep in his stomach that somehow he had miscalculated the danger to his family.

A shoulder-induced explosion suddenly shattered the door as it burst open separating itself from its hinges. As the soldiers looked up, a knife flashed threateningly in Kachadoor's large hand. His burning eyes surveyed the scene in a split-second—he moved like a huge angry tiger crouching low with flashing eyes moving from prey to prey.

The attacking Turks were clearly surprised; they thought all the Armenian men in the village had been taken away and killed. Suddenly, they looked upon this angry beast with such fear that their movements were delayed; thusly frozen in place with fear, the one trying to hold Diana suddenly felt his head jerked back violently as a razor-sharp blade cut a deep red line a few inches below his jutting jaw. The sound of blade-on-bone creaked eerily as it moved swiftly from one ear to the other. The smoking hot blade continued its wide arc to the next soldier who aimed his gun shakily in Kachadoor's direction—but the shot went wide narrowly missing Father's fierce face, and this time the blade found its home deep in the black heart of the assailant. His dirty white shirt slowly turning crimson before he hit the floor.

A warm liquid ran down Diana's back as she squirmed away from the falling body and reached out to draw Alisia to her side in a protective embrace.

Two villains remained in the kitchen—the nearest one tripped over Mother's prone body as he attempted to jump on to Kachadoor's wide back. Father felt the smaller man against his back when a sudden prick of cold steel entered his hot body just behind his broad shoulder. The assailant's knife tore open the red, blue, and orange shirt as it ripped into Father's back. Kachadoor cringed, bent his knees and lunged backward smashing the smaller man against the wall—the soldier's broken body crumpled to the floor. Meanwhile, the taller one tried to pull up his pants and go for his rifle at the same time; he tripped in his haste and Kachadoor plunged his steaming knife into the culprit's heart and twisted it with Herculean strength. Father's knife remained in the chest of the second gendarme, so without a pause, he spun back around to the first soldier and forcefully threw him head-first into the fireplace splitting his skull against the steadfast stones. The third would-be-killer rushed Father recklessly, but Father swiftly lifted the fire-poker by the fireplace and crushed his skull with a force that scared his own girls.

The final assailant was already out the door with his pants half-up and shirt flailing behind him, but father's movements seemed lightning fast as he bolted after the fleeing man. With a natural grace, he swept up his bow and fitted it quickly with an arrow; he stood tall in the doorway and his broad shoulders blocked out the early light as the twang of the string could be heard clearly, and the sudden end to the soldier's cries for help proved father's aim was true. Father turned and faced his stricken family, his face and hands crimson, his eyes wide and alert, and shouted,

"Run! Take your mother! Run to the forest! Go hide!"

He suddenly dropped to his knees and lifted mother to a sitting position—she was awake but still dazed, and his hand shook a little as he hurriedly wiped the blood from the side of her head. He gripped her shoulders tightly...on one knee and through tear-streaked eyes looked deep into her soul—now, only you can save our children.

"Run—my children! Run! Others are coming—I love you!"

Father pulled mother up, gently pushed her toward the back door, and turned back to the front door as the previous molesters burst through with guns blazing, but another arrow flew straight through the throat of its surprised victim. The next was met head on by the hairy beast who used to be the girls' father. His bow dropped from his hand and clattered to the floor, but none would be allowed to pass...for the enraged red, blue, orange clad guardian of the threshold held back the rush of murderers.

Mother stepped toward father for a moment, then stopped.... She quickly picked up a few items and a packed bag as she pushed Diana and her sister out the broken door toward the forest. As Diana looked back, other soldiers were trying to get through the doorway over the rising pile of broken bodies—father's red hands a blur—pounding, tearing, ripping— blood everywhere.

"Run!" Run for your life!" he shouted over his shoulder and at the top of his lungs. "Run!"

Diana would hear this last utterance of her father for the rest of her life.

⌒⌒

And run they did—like the wind...and that same wind dried their tears as lungs gasped for more oxygen, but <u>still</u> they ran—small feet finding the familiar goat paths they walked all their lives and now followed desperately to find temporary salvation.

Screams for help echoed throughout their town as they stopped to catch their breath and pull on some clothes that mother had grabbed at the last minute. The soulful cries for help from their neighbors and cousins below sent chills through their bodies and froze their hearts more than the wind's icy nip biting into their flesh.

Darkness began to envelope the triad and their steps slowed as their vision failed to ascertain the path clearly. Mother directed them to some nearby bushes and told them to crawl under the low-hanging branches and be still. The screams slowly began to fade out as the stars peeked out from behind dark clouds—the half-crescent moon shyly set slowly into the black hills... ashamed of what it had just witnessed.

Chapter 3

FATHERLESS CHILDREN ~ TEARS IN THE RAIN...

Sleep became a stranger—and soon the rising sun peeked at the family's first day without a father—shock, disbelief, and stunned silence. Dark clouds angrily smothered the rising sun before its rays could warm the grief-stricken triad. The tiny family huddled together shaking and sharing tears. BA-BOOM! A thunderous rumble echoed forth as the girls clung tighter to Mother. Seconds later, lightning bolts unzipped the gathering gloom parting the blackest clouds to allow heaven's tears to wash away the human ones below.

Salty tears and heaven sent rain…look the same…a sorrowful blessing… a second baptism… a metaphorical metamorphosis—nothing will ever be the same…tears in the rain.

The pain between Diana's legs became eclipsed by the torturous agony in her heart. She continued to hear the Turks' vile taunts….."The seeds we've planted in you will make your children hate you. Death to all Armenians!" shouted one of the soldiers as Mother and her two daughters fled. The small family hid in the forest nearby their village while the girls watched over their mother and carefully tended her head wound with the rain captured from leaves, direct pressure, and their own saliva. Diana bandaged Mother's head with strips of her shirt-sleeves.

That night, as bats flitted helter-skelter through the darkness picking off one insect after another, Diana dreamed of her father's open-eyed, bloody body staring through the family's doorway that he had made with his own hands—to a heaven only he and God could see. The dreams... now nightmares, drifted away as sleep finally...mercifully... laid her exhausted body low. Mother soon followed, and then Alisia—and one-by-one— each survivor's brain shifted finally into therapeutic oblivion.

Sleep, sweet sleep, the death-like state that mends minds, soothes psyches, and rebuilds broken bones and torn muscles. Where the unconscious meets the semi-conscious, and dreams battle nightmares for control of one's mental faculties—that strange nether-land where we regenerate our energies and set free our souls to search for higher meaning—the land of nod where one finds peace...or...poignant pain.

Not knowing the future, the two sisters could only dream of a time and place where freedom ruled the day and fear would be buried by righteous justice. Such a dream they dared to dream, and with that daring soon would come the trials and tribulations that would decidedly test the strength in their arms, the faith in their hearts, and the grace in their souls to a degree heretofore never witnessed nor told.

Chapter 4

OUR FLAG ~ OUR FATHER ~ OUR FAITH TESTED...

The sunlight filtered through the trees as Diana moved a low-hanging branch to reveal her sister huddled against their mother—her head resting peacefully on her mother's knee. A small wisp of a bird perched delicately on a parallel branch above them. It sang a brief song before flittering skyward and disappearing into the morning sun. As Diana watched the tiny bird fly upward, she was stunned momentarily by the blinding brightness of the early morning sun. Blinking through watery eyes, she remembered one of her last conversations with her father.

It occurred when she began to doubt herself and her abilities—tired of her equestrian training and archery practice—she broke down...tears streamed down her face. Her father felt his daughter's pain as he sat down beside her. When her sobs subsided, he placed his large hand on the middle of her back and said he also felt frustrated at times, but always remembered what his mother had told him... *God will take care of you if you take care of yourself. You are never alone with your problems.*

Every night when you lay your weary head down to sleep, turn all your worries over to God and know in your heart that He will be up all night looking after you. When you awake in the morning, share His love with others knowing you are loved. Diana felt a comforting calmness come over her as she looked down upon her mother and sister still in a deep slumber leaning against one another—the dappled sunlight just beginning to play with their eyelids.

Diana, being first to rise, stoked a little fire as she sat alone remembering the evil events that brought them into the forest—this was not a bad dream. She would not wake up and be back in her loving home; her life had truly changed—her childhood was over. Diana revived Alisia with a few drops of water from the dew collected on nearby leaves. Her mouth was dry...her stomach hurt from hunger. Mother hugged her precious girls to her, and they, in return, washed her face with warm tears.

Mother's dress was torn and bloody—her body bruised and discolored. Her swollen head throbbed in pain. She could still hear the high-pitched screams ringing in her ears from the night before—barely human, piercing the night as the carnage continued throughout the village. She knew then, without looking, that her extended family, cousins, and friends were being slaughtered, but there was nothing she could do but take her teen daughters and try to escape the massacre. Nevertheless, guilt hung its heavy head on her heart, and she could only sigh and move on....

As the bereft family left, they climbed to the summit of the highest hill and looked back on their small town. The people looked like ants scurrying around. In reality, they were Turkish families already moving into the Armenian homes. Turkish peasants readily dragged out the Armenian bodies and moved in their own families—into the loving homes of the murdered Armenians.

Mother surprised her daughters by taking out of her bag an old pair of binoculars (one of the items she had carefully selected and placed in a rucksack and hastily grasped before they ran from their defiled house). As her girls asked solemnly for a turn to look back at the devastated village, she hesitated... but then relinquished the black glasses to Diana—realizing there would be little she could protect her daughters from now.

Looking down, Diana spied the activity of the Turkish peasants who scrambled through the bloody streets and homes searching frenetically for Armenian treasure. Heart-broken, she focused the glasses and witnessed the Turks move into the blood-stained homes of those surprised victims who now were being told to form a line. Soon, under guard, they began to walk out of the town carrying whatever they could manage. She was about to hand the binoculars back to her mother but as she looked back toward their home, she saw a large mound just outside their front yard—as her eyes strained, she could barely make out the shape of a twisted body. While she could not see its face, she could make out the blood-stained colors of the Armenian flag on the shirt covering the fallen figure—"Father!"

⌇⌇⌇

Mother gently turned her children from the hideous scene below and led her children toward the familiar forest where they had hunted and practiced archery. Isgouhi looked back over her shoulder—a sinking feeling in her heart—I *will never see my home again. Good-bye my sweet husband; you were all I could have ever wished for.*

The small family followed the twisty paths they knew well— once safely hidden in the trees, they thought about their friends walking on a dusty road moistened by the tears of innocent victims—a people slaughtered by their own government. A people whose only crime was their belief in one Christian God.

⌒⋙

Where was this almighty God now?

Chapter 5

A MOTHER'S LOVE ~
A FATHER'S LIGHT ~

February 4, 1915—As birds take flight when danger looms near, the three women fled on foot as the sun set behind the hills of their once cherished valley.

The crisp evening air penetrated the several layers of clothing. Shivering, the three scanned the countryside searching for some shelter from the cold. Alisia's sharp eyes caught a flash of white dart across the darkening shadows of the sparsely treed area—a rabbit? She followed its direction; straying a bit from Diana and Mother. There it was again, its white head staring at Alisia—she stepped forward and as the ball of fur disappeared in a white puff of talcum— a lightly worn path appeared ahead; Alisia followed it. There in the distance—the peak of a roof. Alisia called to her mother and Diana. As the three approached the elfin structure cautiously, Mother spoke first, "No one has been here for a while." She pointed out the fine undisturbed dirt in front of the entrance. "Let us go inside."

The abandoned rural home showed signs of a struggle, but no Turks moved in here—too far from the town perhaps. As they scoured the house, Alisia spotted a piece of leather under one of the beds. It was pressed up against the wall, and she had to crawl on her belly to retrieve the dusty item. When she unrolled the leather, its contents fell to the floor—two small bone-handle knives. She picked up the knives placed them back in their makeshift pouch and sought out the others to show them what she found.

Diana and Mother searched the kitchen, but its cupboards were bare except for a few items: a pan for cooking, a few plates, an old wineskin with stale water inside, an oily tarp, two dirty blankets, and a bag of rags. The rags looked to be the family's clothes that were ready to be thrown out or used simply as cleaning rags. Nevertheless, they had buttons, and the girls needed warmth, so they made them fit by tying ends together and scavenging for pieces of leather or cloth or a needle and thread. Now, everything became a precious commodity…a matter of life or death.

The next morning, they prayed together and thanked God for providing them shelter. Mother considered going north to Van to seek out her sister, but she knew Turkish presence prevented such a plan. Instead, they spent one more night sheltered in the Lilliputian-sized cabin combing it for more "treasure". That night, they slept together for warmth and—comfort. The house was cold and probably dangerously close to the invading Turks, but Mother thought it best to take the chance—it was bitter cold outside. Mother woke early and simply watched her daughters as they slept…. When they woke, she pointed them southwest towards Shatakh. The five layers of "new" clothes offered protection, so moving forward generated much needed heat.

The dawn brought frozen dew—drooping iced branches hung overhead when they stepped outside. The icy-wet frost sparkled like diamonds shooting prism rays of light back toward the rising sun. "We must keep moving— we must stay ahead of those who will cause us more harm." Mother led the way….

Mostly recovered from her head wound, Isgouhi set the pace—encouraged her girls to keep their weary feet moving. Alas, the paths were rocky and treacherous and difficult to traverse quickly; the girls wondered where they were going with no food, little water, and tattered clothes. Rags tied tightly to their feet for warmth and protection—kept falling off, and soon their toes were numb. Mother instructed her girls to suck on pebbles to stave off the incessant pangs of hunger and thirst that haunted them—food was scarce— roots, grasses, berries, were not available—the ground too hard. Mother knew they must find food and water soon.

〜〕☆〜

God works in mysterious ways some say—the petty cobwebs man has spun trying to understand that which cannot be explained to those of little faith. And when God remains silent...right at the moment when one needs Him the most...well, those times can test the faith of the most loyal follower. Yet, prayers do sometimes get answered as was the case on this day. Breaking through a final stand of trees, the land dipped sharply and led the small family to a swift stream fed by an underground spring and melting snow. It provided water, and vegetation, and...hope. With renewed vigor, the group searched for anything to eat along its banks. Stomachs growled angrily as digestive juices did their work on the inner linings of empty stomachs. The triad scavenged some green moss along the banks, bright green algae was skimmed off the top of the standing inlets, creek beetles and other bugs provided some crunchy nutrients—protein...at last.

The light meal relieved some light-headedness and stopped the stomach aches. Clarity of mind returned, and the mid-day sun warmed their bodies.

Continuing to follow the path of the stream, the three were surprised when they came upon other dazed victims who somehow escaped. These refugees also chose to walk the rocky path along the small stream. Together, the now nomadic exiles struggled to hasten their pace—no words were needed.

Mostly women and very young children joined the small but growing group. One little boy's arm was twisted awkwardly as he held it against his chest trying not to cry. His shirt was ripped, so Diana gave him one of her layers for warmth. He looked up at her with his chocolate eyes searching, his face blackened with dirt, and she saw her father's brown eyes smiling back at her. "I will always be with you,"— they seemed to say. "I will never leave you." She shivered...as she forced a smile and kissed the boy's hand before he scampered back to his mother.

Night soon enveloped the small clan, and a blanket of fog quieted the forest where they finally found shelter. Mother huddled the girls together, and they soon surrendered to the enveloping darkness.

Before Diana fell asleep, she tried her best to remove the indelible images of Mother's unconscious body being kicked by the soldiers as they laughed and cursed her. Diana's mind replayed her father's last words....**Run, run, run for your lives!**

When one's father dies, the world changes. His sun becomes your sun; his path becomes your path made easier by his well-worn footsteps, and finally, his light shows you the way as its heavenly luminescence glows with precious memories and remains ever present, ever bright— especially during your darkest hours.

Chapter 6

FATHER'S BOW ~ MOTHER'S RETURN

In the morning, the bright sunlight found its way through the trees and on to Diana's closed eyelids. Her sensory receptors stimulated, her brain gained consciousness—slivers of light, chirping birds, subtle breeze over lips.... She thought for a moment about her last dream— her sister and she were playing with homemade puppets, laughing at each other's made up dialogue and jerky gesticulations. She pulled the blanket up higher hoping to recapture them for a while longer, but it was to no avail; she was now awake and could hear mother's gentle whispering.

"Our family must go its separate way now. Our road will not be easy, but our enemies will hunt down all the Armenians they can find, and they will find us if we remain in a large group." She looked toward the rising sun. The slightly curved lines of her cheek laced with dark brown earth— "Our lives depend on us remaining invisible...she said softly... we must move west...Your sister is already awake—c'mon Sleepy Head." Mother turned her back on the rising sun and threw her pack over her shoulder all in one practiced motion. Diana scrambled to her feet and glanced around looking for her sister. She spotted her on the edge of camp one hand holding on to a young tree as she squatted and emptied her bladder. Diana was packed and ready by the time Alisia strode up to her. They looked to the east just as Mother's back disappeared over a hill. The girls broke into a run; they'd be at Mother's side in a matter of minutes.

After they departed from the others, they walked silently. Occasionally, Mother would stop and pull a weed from the soil. She would rub the root vigorously and spit on it to remove the remaining dirt.

"Here—eat. It will taste bitter, but it contains some nourishment— eat!" Alisia took a bite, grimaced a bit, and then began chewing vigorously while she handed the other half to Diana. The girls' jaws were tired by the time the weed was masticated properly. The stringy little ball still resisted for a moment before being swallowed.

As the sun approached its nadir, they stopped in the shade of a large well-leafed tree. Mother took time to gather herself and breathed deeply as she spoke calmly and decisively.

"Now, hear me well my daughters. Your father watches and protects us from above; I feel his spirit even now—guiding us. He sacrificed his body— but not his soul! We must live—for his spirit soars above and within us." Mother's head dipped for a moment as she took another deep breath. "And remember this—he left you both a means for survival. Alisia, your namesake connotes gentleness in your nature and softness in your step, but your father also recognized your agility and quickness and tutored you daily in martial arts; you are still young, but now you must be strong—believe you can be anything you need to be, and it will be so—be ready to abandon your namesake and embrace your inner strength of resolve, and finally, be quick to defend yourself. Do not allow anyone to ever hurt you or your sister again."

Mother's eye were steel grey—deadly determination emanated from her lanky frame. She turned to her left.

"Diana, you are special to our clan because of the gift your father gave to you—a skill usually reserved only for males. Your training is not complete, but your father guides you by sending his wisdom and inviting you to inherit his skill; thus, you must be precocious—practice daily and learn to wield this weapon masterfully. Together, powerful possibilities abound. Let us not be victims again.

"Mother, Alisia and I can't fight all the Turks and Kurds. We are just two girls." Diana shook her head, and Alisia nodded and placed her arm around her sister.

"You are more than you think. The first step to doing something is believing you can do it. Together, we are going to survive this ordeal, but first you have to believe in yourself." Mother stood up, swooped up her pack and started walking.

Alisia handed Diana her pack, "We can do this together. Mother is right. You are stronger than you think." She sniffed Diana's body and frowned. "But smell isn't everything." She laughed and ran to catch up with Mother. Diana just smiled. *Some things never change.*

The sun cast long shadows and Mother gestured toward a rock outcropping. She lay her long bundle on the rocks and sat down to catch her breath.

"Mother, you have such a large bundle to carry. Let me carry it for you."

Mother smiled at her oldest daughter. "No thank you, but I will allow you to carry part of it."

Diana's eyes squinted as she peered through the flickering sunlight as the magnificent and familiar bow revealed itself from under Mother's shawl as she gently laid it at her eldest daughter's feet. There it was...her father's bow which he had promised to give her someday—"Thank you, mother;" Diana bowed to her mother—and then lifted the bow toward the sky. "Thank you, father...."

She looked back at her mother. "But how...? When...?"

Mother smiled slightly and continued..."When we fled our home, my foot found your father's bow, and I instinctively picked it up as is my habit for the three of you. I was dazed and stupefied; my habitual actions took control. It seemed to leap into my right hand as my left grasped his favorite arrows, so I tucked them under my shawl as we ran for the forest. Later, I wrapped them in an old shawl for safe keeping." She smiled as she stared at Diana. "Of course, God's grace and wisdom may have also been at play."

Mother's eyes began to water. She placed her arms around her girls pulling them into a tight embrace and as heads touched, she ardently whispered, "Now, you two must survive no matter what! Your father's foresight saw this day as a dark possibility and trained you unlike other Armenian girls who learned to play the piano or violin. No, your destiny is different! You are now protective angels invincible to those who mean us harm...for even though you walk through this Valley of Death, you shall fear no evil, for God will be your guide." Mother leaned back against the smooth rock.

In a moment, she sat back up and leaned forward. "Yet, remember in your heart—our goal is not revenge; rather, it is freedom from fear."

"Will we ever be able to be free from fear? I am afraid for all of us."

"So am I," responded Alisia.

"We've been spared for a reason. All good people fear something, yet we can overcome our fears with help from God and each other. I will be here for you, but you are the future, and our fate rests more in your hands each passing day."

The girls hugged their mother and kissed her cheeks.

"What if we are attacked again?"

Alisia stoked her mother's cheek.

"We fight...we fight for our lives...for our right to life...we fight and protect each other." Mother paused seeing the girls worried faces. "Remember— take a life only to save a life... kill only to protect the innocent, and kill only to preserve our lineage, for it is steeped in righteousness. Finally, my dearest daughters, know that in every little girl there exists a young woman...with the strength of a warrior." Mother rose and stood up straight and as her girls looked up. Mother's aquiline profile projected a firm durability— one they knew and loved more deeply with each passing day.

Mother held her head high as she motioned towards the path with a graceful gesture and sweep of her arm—time to move on.

Diana nudged Alisia as they stood up; their eyes locked. Diana's facial expression said it all—*Mother is back!*

Chapter 7

SUSTENANCE ~ SURVIVAL ~ SISTERS

After only a few minutes, Mother stopped in her tracks. When her daughters approached with quizzical expressions, she made a slight gesture toward the east. "It is time; the two of you should decide the way. I will be here as a resource, but leadership is learned by leading...so lead."

The two sisters looked at one another. Diana, being the oldest, tentatively stepped forward. Many thoughts raced through the girls' minds as they walked away from their village, from their peaceful lives, from their only known existence. The three did not stop to rest until feet hurt, legs ached, and exhaustion had its way.

Finally, Alisia tapped Diana on her shoulder and glanced back at Mother now lagging a bit behind. Diana nodded... "There is some flat ground here. We should set up camp before it is too dark." Alisia set down her pack and helped her mother with hers.

Diana proceeded to search the area for dry wood as Alisia and Mother made a clearing for the meager blankets they had in their possession. After spreading the soft pine needles that smelled of spring, they laid out the oily tarp and covered it with one of the blankets they had confiscated from the old house. Alisia lay her body down on the improvised bedding. "It is good. Come Mother, come rest here with me."

Diana soon joined them—too tired to make a fire, she dropped the wood nearby, and the three lay together for warmth as the night fell softly upon them; its dreamy weight closed their eyes and sleep had its way.

⟊⟊⟊

Morning light opened Mother's eyes. She rolled slightly feeling the ache in her joints as she separated herself from her sleeping daughters. Before long, she put the small branches and dry wood Diana had gathered to good use and a crackling fire shared its warmth with its maker. Soon, the girls joined Mother at the fire.

"I have a bit of tea we can make, but we need food. I surveyed the area, it seems safe, and a little creek runs freely nearby. Let us camp here and rest for a few days. Diana, you need to put your bow to good use, and may God bless your hunting efforts."

Diana hunted most of the morning and that evening, but her arrows missed their small scurrying targets, so roots, weeds, and a bit of bark served as dinner. More practice needed....

⟊⟊⟊

The next morning, Diana Rose early. After washing her face with a little water, she wiped down her bow, selected her arrows, and set her targets.

I must be able to shoot quickly and maintain accuracy. Being able to shoot on the fly, to hit moving targets, grace under pressure—these are all the skills Father demanded of me, and I resisted because they required hours of repetitive practice. Shame on me for not trusting his wisdom. Now, I understand; the world can be a cruel teacher, and one must be strong to survive—not everyone can be trusted, and some…mean to do great harm, so I will practice to survive; I will practice to be faster, more accurate, and… even deadly when I need to be.

Diana shivered at her last thought. *Could I ever kill another human? Isn't it a mortal sin to kill? Was it a sin for my father to kill the Turks who invaded our home? Is killing ever justified?* She shook her head and notched an arrow. *I will follow my heart, for my head confuses me.*

She remembered her father's drills, his words of guidance. "Release your arrow after you release your breath…relax your muscles so they work smoothly, in unison with your breathing." She remembered. Arrows whizzed repeatedly in search of one target or another. Diana practiced shooting from her knees, leaning against a tree, running full speed and stopping suddenly to shoot. She even learned to shoot while on the run; although, her accuracy suffered with such a challenge.

"Sister, you look like a deadly dancer. Teach me that pirouette move where you spin, drop to a knee, and release your arrow all with one motion—may God guide all your arrows!" Alisia ran to her older sister and hugged her enthusiastically.

"Go put on the rest of your clothes before you freeze, and we will practice together."

Diana looked up at the treetops. *No wind yet…a good time to hunt… must find food for my family.*

Long hikes and little nourishment melted the flesh from their bodies; meat was needed and Diana knew the responsibility rest on her shoulders. She—the oldest, her father's training, now came the time to reap what must be sown to survive.

Before Diana left, mother offered some advice and possible emergency scenarios. These included what to do if one became separated or attacked. They also decided on certain signals to communicate if they were in hiding, and finally, what to do if one of them is captured or even killed. The girls listened intently and nodded their heads in agreement.

Alisia wanted to join Diana, but it was decided that two bodies might be too noisy, so Alisia opted to search for firewood, grubs, berries, and anything else that would bring needed protein to their thinning bodies. The small creek offered much game and hope, so the family set out to hunt, gather, and search.

By the afternoon, Diana was tired, hungry, and frustrated. She had one shot at a rabbit, but the arrow flew over its head. The birds above her head chirped happily...or were they simply laughing at her inability to survive in an environment in which they thrived? She headed for the creek to get some water. The gurgling grew louder as she approached the running water from behind some bushes, but suddenly she paused as another sound entered her acute ears—a strange noise—a lapping sound mixed with a squish-squish juicy resonance as if one were pulling a boot out of a muddy river bank. She crouched down and silently peeked over the foliage—her heart missed a beat and then stopped! A large white animal with thick, wooly fur was bent over drinking from the cool river. Its legs were buried up to its knees in the soft-sucking mud as it stretched its neck to lap at the clear, cool water. The animal was almost all white—a mysterious animal for sure. It did not make sense, but that did not matter. *Meat—meat matters!*

Diana drew an arrow and notched it to the string. *God, steady my hand, clear my mind.* She pulled back slowly, and just as the animal lifted its hulking horned-head, she let loose a well-practiced shot. The arrow whizzed through the air and hit the beast just behind its lower right shoulder—its penetration deep but not quite deadly. The surprised animal tried to leap but its body just shuddered for a moment. Mightily, it struggled to loosen its hooves from the deep muck as it grunted and groaned in pain. Finally, the angry beast freed itself with a praiseworthy effort and once it found steady footing on the gravel—looked frantically for the source of its malady.

With a desperate cry that surprised herself, Diana jumped from the bushes to gain a better vantage point with a new arrow at the ready. *I must not let it run away, not when I am so close to food for my family!* Now that she was closer, she felt confident that her next arrow would find its target more easily. Yet, a sliver of doubt entered her brain—up close, the animal was larger than she thought, and as the confused beast realized she was the threat and source of its pain, it lowered its head and aimed its impressive horns in her direction. With a sudden burst of breathtaking speed, it charged towards Diana with blood streaming down its white side and foam spitting and spraying from its mouth and nose.

Diana's hands shook nervously, but she steadied them in time to fire the notched second arrow right at the head of the charging animal. It found its mark and struck the oncoming bloody form right in the forehead and directly between its two riveting eyes, but the sharp-pointed arrow simply tore a finger-length gash in the beast's head and bounced erratically off the hard skull of the maddened mass of hurtling hooves. The animal now bled from its head as well. The bloody forehead and left horn made solid contact with Diana's leaping body despite her timely defensive action and roll (a favorite move Alisia taught her during Martial Arts training). Diana avoided a frontal collision, but the beast's horn and head hit her solidly and spun her around in the air like a pinwheel; a loud cry shook her lips as she fell on her head and back with a forceful thud—dazed and dizzy, the wind knocked out of her.

As Diana raised her head, the animal came to a sliding stop as dirt and stones flew wildly from its scrapping hooves—blood now spilled into its eyes making them red and dripping crimson fluid as they blinked repeatedly looking frantically to find its enemy. In a moment, it spotted Diana's predisposed figure on the ground not ten feet away.

Diana's bow lie in the dirt out of reach, so from her knees, she frantically reached for the small knife in her belt, but her raiment had shifted; thus, she could not find its handle as she stared helplessly at the relentless beast. Again, the determined animal locked its bloody gaze on Diana, lowered its head and began its rapid forward movement.

Yet, before it could reach full speed, it was suddenly pounced upon—attacked by a flying figure that fell from the sky and landed hard on its back. The weakened animal collapsed to its knees from the sudden weight, and before it could rise again, it had been stabbed in the back of its neck several times by its ferocious attacker. With a final heaving sigh, the dauntless animal collapsed as the wiry, lean figure rolled off its back and landed unceremoniously in the dirt not far from Diana.

Time froze for a moment—only the babbling brook could be heard laughing at the spectacular scene fiercely fought on its banks.

Diana's jaw rested on her chest as she stared at the familiar figure before her—Alisia! Her face and hands were covered in crimson, eyes closed, face still, yet her chest heaved in and out. Diana crawled over to her sister's side, placed her right hand on Alisia's shoulder, she leaned over her sister's face and stared—willing her eyes to open—one eye twitched and then the other. Alisia blinked to clear her vision as her sister's face came into view above her. As she moved her still-working limbs, she smiled and held up a bloody hand to her still-amazed-delighted-shocked sister. Diana snapped out of her trance and pulled Alisia into a breathlessly tight hug as the two sisters shared a long bloody embrace. "Are you all right?" she cried. "You are covered in blood."

"It's not mine," replied Alisia brushing the gravel off her face and shaking it out of her long hair.

"Where did you come from? How? When?"

"I heard the struggle and the cries of pain and came running. All I had was my small knife that I was using to dig weeds from the ground."

The bloody knife remained in her hand as both girls looked down at it.

"Won't mother be surprised?" said Alisia with a beaming grin.

"Yes, oh God! Yes, she will be." The girls laughed and embraced again.

⌇

The stout animal was a Bezoar Ibex, mother explained. "It is essentially a wild goat that was once domestic. When farms were deserted, it turned feral." Mother examined the animal as she began the preparation. "Tonight, we will eat some of its organs while the meat cures." Looking over her battle-proven girls, she smiled… "Your father would have been proud of both of you. I wish he…." Her shoulders began to shake as her chin rested on her chest.

Both girls entwined themselves around their mother. "He _is_ with us, Mother—he always will be."

The kill signaled a key turning point for the small family; they managed to survive the first week.

Chapter 8

NIGHTMARES ~ PROMISES ~ A BLESSED KISS ~

The wild goat's organs provided much-needed protein. The blood-rich infusion of heart, liver, and kidneys revitalized the girls—their bodies seemed to immediately gain back some of the lost weight as repeated exercises developed and toned muscle.

"Sister, your strength surprises me," gasped Diana after Alisia threw her down by using Diana's own weight against her. "Show me how you did that!"

Alisia's hand clasped Diana's as she pulled her up off the dirt.

"It is a simple move, just a variation of one of the defensive moves you already know. Here…this time, you throw me." The girls continued to practice while Mother mended clothes, worked the hide of the feral goat they killed, and shaped moccasins for the girls to wear. It would be time to move soon, no one place is safe for very long.

While the girls' physical statures improved, their mental health remained vulnerable. During sleep, one's defenses are down. A mind goes where it will go, and it often revisits past incidents in one's life.

One's time asleep is where a human works out his or her problems in life. It is why one feels refreshed when one awakes—ready to take on the new day's challenges. Still, sometimes a mind has a will of its own and goes off to scary places one would rather not go, but a somnambulist has no control, so he/she must learn to deal with a psyche that remains wounded. Fortunately, Old Man Time is a great healer.

A nod to the above, but reoccurring nightmares often interrupted the sleeping figures—forcing the restless girls to relive merciless memories. These flashback occurrences would never be erased—only endured. Prayer helped ease the pain, and spiritual strength offered a way forward.

On one such night, Diana woke to find Alisia sobbing softly into her scarf. She crawled to her, and the sisters hugged. "I am sorry; I didn't mean to wake you." Alisia's body shook uncontrollably as she clung to Diana tightly and buried her head between her older sister's rising and falling breasts...her tears wet and warm on Diana's skin.

Gently stroking the nape of her sister's neck, Diana's lips lightly touched her sister's ear, "I am going to protect you, and you are going to protect me. You will be the moon...and I... I will be your sun; no one can hurt us again. I will teach you to use father's bow, and you will continue to teach me your skillful dexterity. Together...we will stay alive."

Alisia smiled up at her older sister... kissed her on the cheek... and whispered... "I love you, Di. Please never leave me. Promise me... Promise me...."

Diana's finger touched a solitary tear on her sister's cheek—raised it to Alisia's forehead and made the sign of a cross. She bowed her head and kissed the wet symbol.

"I do....I do....I promise."

⌐⌐⌐

Fallen leaves, decaying in a final display of mottled calico, formed fragrant cushions providing the sisters a temporary resting place. An owl hooted above their heads repeatedly calling for a mate. Its hopeful pleas provided background comfort as the girls huddled together for warmth...eventually... they drifted back to sleep and into a place of solace where psyches are massaged and memories buried.

Stars above watched over the huddled figures as the mysteries of life and death swirled endlessly in unseen galaxies above and beyond the imaginations of simple human beings.

A lone night lark honed perfect arcs seeking food for its hungry brood.

Chapter 9

A LESSON ~ A PRAYER ~ A BOW ~

A coven of crows cawed repeatedly over the triad—black diminishing dots disappearing gradually as they flew determinedly eastward against a milky blue sky. The small family gathered their dwindling resources: a few roots, a bag of fresh water, some bits of dried meat, and the last of the tea. The three slowly transformed from suffering victims to stealthy survivors bent on not being surprised again.

As the days slipped by, Diana practiced every dawn with her bow and arrows. The solitude and soft early light aided Diana's concentration—her skills grew sharp. Alisia watched and learned and took her turn at commanding the bow to do her bidding.

At one point, Diana demanded that Alisia shoot an arrow on the run. "Run to the target with your arrow notched and when within a stone's throw, fall to your knees and hit your target!" Alisia tried her best repeatedly but could not replicate her sister's skill.

"I can't do it! It is too hard for me!" She dropped the bow and fell to her knees. Hands at her sides and chin on her chest.

Diana approached her sister and dropped to her knees in the dirt beside her, clasped her hands together, and bowed her head.

"What are you doing? asked Alisia.

"When life knocks you to your knees, you are in the perfect position to pray for renewed strength, focus, and skill. Join me...." Diana bowed her head again...Alisia just shook her head...smiled...and joined her sister in prayer.

The girls practiced religiously. Alisia became skilled at hunting, and Diana learned how to use an opponent's own weight against him. The results encouraged early dawn and sunset practice sessions. They shared each other's skills and bonded as do twin trees in the forest.

She thought to herself— *Father's bow remains strong; its arrows fly straight. I grow stronger—more skilled. I can hunt game successfully and feed my family. Alisia continues my education in Martial Arts, and she learns quickly on our father's bow. With God's help, we will survive. Meanwhile, Alisia needs her own bow. I remember Father making bows in his workshop, but my memory of the process seems a bit faded. Be still my heart; let me visualize. I can see and hear my father. The right branch must be selected from particular trees. Oak was one of his favorites. Dead wood—better than green, live wood. I remember— length—*she spread her arms wide apart. *Yes, I remember enough—oh, yes, a slight curve— one that will determine its main features. Yes, it's all coming back to me now.* She smiled as she pointed toward the sky and bowed her head. *Thank you God for helping me to remember my well spent time in Father's woodshop...and thank you father for the gifts you bestowed upon me.*

Chapter 10

A SON ~ A BROTHER ~ AN ENIGMA ~

Empty stomachs, light heads, and fatigue haunted the family, and sometimes they found nothing to eat except for roots, bark, grass, and weeds. The girls' bodies remained slender, well-toned, and wiry from constant activity. While they did not starve, <u>other</u> Armenian children were not so fortunate.

"Beware of the starving Armenians" echoed fearful Turkish peasants. "They are desperate and will eat anything." True—many Armenians starved due to the devious plans laid out by Turkish leaders. Help from others remained a rare occurrence for fear of retaliation from the patrolling Turkish gendarmes. Many good people of other nationalities turned away in fear as well. "Too many destitute Armenians to help...too dangerous...what if we get caught...*but*... will we ever be forgiven if we simply look the other way?" Thus were the moral dilemma's for those who stood by and passively watched a genocide in action. So it was for mere individuals; so it was for entire nations.

As the small band traveled, they passed Shatakh and were close to Redvan according to a sign they saw when crossing one of the roads and disappearing again into the forest cover. Mother and her daughters disguised themselves to take on chameleon-like features. Sometimes, they would change their raiment to appear Turkish; other times, Kurdish dress was required before going under the scrutiny of the public eye. They made up stories when they would risk going into a village or town or market as to why they were traveling and where they were going if someone should be overly curious. However, suspicion of strangers, and the threat of death upon anyone helping Armenians, made the three's journey dangerous and difficult. They tried to stay off main roads to avoid the Turks and others who would take advantage of their situation. Many opportunists existed on the open road ready to exploit any Armenian refugee.

Even so, they needed food, water, and shelter—Mother's focus narrowed. She found a few edible roots, but the ground was too cold for most plants; however, some berries were already visible yet not ready for consumption. Hungry and weak, the three surreptitiously navigated the forests and valleys—mother's courage, willpower, and resolve inspired her daughters. Still, they remained wary— avoiding the roads—always fearful of the roads.

As the sun hid behind the trees, a grassy patch looked promising as a camp for the night. Diana and Alisia looked for wood and made preparations while mother searched her bag for the little food they had left. However, she froze with her hand still in the bag—a crunching sound came from the bushes behind her. She looked quickly at her daughters, but they had also heard it—Diana's hand moved to her waist belt and rested upon the bone handle of her knife; Alisia followed suit—time slowed to a full stop.

The brush nearest to Mother parted slowly, and a young boy of thirteen or fourteen emerged with Lazurus's eyes and visage. He seemed disoriented, almost other-worldy. Desperation motivated him, so now he straightforwardly approached the family.

"Please—will you help me? I am alone and hungry." He looked at the small fire, "and cold."

Mother held up her hand as she surveyed the situation. His dark hair stuck to his head. Dry blood matted the strands against his face. Dirt lined the crevasses about his neck, and his shirt had only a few buttons left. His pants were stained in the crotch area, torn and frayed at the bottom.

"Are you sure you are alone?" Mother asked suspiciously. He nodded. "Come closer boy." Mother spoke softly as if he were a frightened deer—wounded and bewildered. She nodded and caught Alisia's eye and made a gesture. Alisia fetched a small cloth bag. The young girl shared a bit of bread and water with the bewildered boy which he made disappear almost immediately. Soon, his eyes grew bright and his face gained some color.

"What is your name?" asked Alisia as she tried to surmise his age. *He looks like he could be my age, but he is so dirty it's hard to tell.*

He looked up at Alisia, paused, drank some water, and began to talk. He explained how his small family was taken late at night by the gendarmes.

"They tried to arrest my dad, but he fought hard and stabbed one of the bad men right in the face. The others chased him…he kept yelling for us to run and hide." Alisia and Diana shivered with the reminder of their own father's last words. "We ran, but I heard a rifle shot, so I looked back. My father had fallen to his knees—a bloody stain appeared on his chest. Another police officer ran up and shot him in the head with a pistol. "I wanted to help him, but I…." The sitting boy poked a stick angrily at the dirt near his feet. He paused as he wiped his nose on his sleeve. The stick fell to the dirt pointing its damaged tip at

Mother. All remained silent except for the plaintive call of a lonely owl waiting for the semidarkness to surrender its remaining light.

The boy wiped the snot on the back of his hand which then rubbed the side of his leg. "The gendarmes soon caught us without much trouble. I would not leave my mother. The next day, we walked until sunset and were tired, hungry, and too weak to run fast. My mother carried my baby sister for miles while we walked in line without food or water. There were different men who would come at night to my mother and take her away. 'Take care of your baby sister,' she would cry as they dragged her off into the darkness. When she returned in the morning—her hair messed and clothes torn—she refused to answer my questions. Instead, she rocked baby sister while she hummed softly and stared straight ahead. The next day, she could not keep up because my little sister could not walk, and my mother's feet were swollen and raw. I tried to help, but I had no shoes and my feet were bleeding."

He drank a bit more water, looked at Alisia as if to ask a question. Instead, he looked down and continued by describing the guard who came back toward the fallen family.

"An angry man yelled at my mother and waved his gun like he was going to shoot her. My little sister screamed at the top of her lungs while the soldier aimed his gun at baby sister being protected in mother's arms." He paused...not sure if he could go on.

"I heard a sudden explosion that hurt my ears and knocked me to my knees; when I looked up from the dirt, I saw the angry man with his uniform standing over baby sister. No one moved for a moment, so he touched little sister with the toe of his boot. Her tiny body fell like a rag doll from my mother's unmoving body and landed in the dirt face down. My mother..." he picked up his stick and stabbed half-heartedly at the forgiving dirt... "a black/red hole in her chest."

Tears streaked his cheeks as he shared how he ran headlong at the gendarme, but his screams were cut short when the Turk turned quickly and slapped the teen's head with the butt of his rifle.

Through blurred eyes, the youngster watched helplessly as the gendarme bent down on one knee and examined the hole in the mother's chest and now still heart. Unexpectedly, he took his open hand and grasped the mother's hoop earring and ripped it from her ear—he repeated the action on the other ear. Rising to his full height, he smirked at the stunned, wide-eyed boy, and turned away to go and join the others. The young teen again ran after the soldier who had not reloaded his gun yet, but as he raised his small fists to strike his mother's murderer, the gendarme's rifle butt smashed him between the eyes.

When he woke moments later, he crawled to his mother's still-warm body, the boy gently placed his sister's tiny body on his mother's chest and draped her arms over her dead baby. He stood…looked one more time…long…and hard…backed away a few steps…and with a sorrowful moan, he began to run at breakneck speed for the forest.

"I hid here until you found me."

Tears were in his blackened eyes, snot ran down his nose and over his chapped lips, and his skinny frame convulsed and shook with his sobs. He looked up again, blinked away the tears and then looked down as he softly replied, "Brosh—my name is Brosh. I…I thank you… for your kindness."

"Wait here," said mother as she motioned the girls to join her under a nearby tree out of earshot of this youngster. "He is alone, scared, and malnourished. If we leave him, he will not fare well. What do the two of you think?"

"I believe him. We must help him," Alisia implored glancing back at the boy now sitting in the dirt looking around as if he was unsure about being left in the open.

Diana nodded as she laid her hand upon her sister's shoulder.

"I agree," announced mother. "He will not last long without our help. Perhaps one of you can take him to the river. Bathe him, wash his feet, and clean his body; afterwards, bring him to me." Meanwhile, I will wash and mend his clothes as best I can. The two of you should look for food along the banks; now, we need food for four."

Mother beckoned him to come, and he slowly walked forward. "You may join us if you wish, but you must do as you are told and cause no trouble. Our lives are at risk, and we must help each other if we are to survive. Do you understand?"

He nodded his head, dropped to one knee, and blessed himself... sobbing softly. The group sensed that he was special, and both girls smiled at each other when he blessed himself.

Later, Mother spread a soothing balm over his feet. She massaged the cream into the deep cracks and cuts on his heels and toes. Brosh buried his head in the small afghan blanket as his body jerked involuntarily at Mother's healing touch whenever she hit a nerve or open wound.

Now we are a family of four, thought Diana; *now, I have a brother. Thank you, Papa. We shall love him as our brother, and bless you for your gift.*

Chapter 11

LOVE ~ NOT HATE ~

The sun shone brightly casting long morning shadows dappled with patches of grey and green as the four headed toward a small tributary off the Tigris River. Empty water skins bounced lightly on their sides as they moved steadily toward the ancient water source. Strangely, an Osprey flew erratically over their heads wildly flapping its wings and heading away from the river—no fish in its talons this time.

When the group finally arrived, they stopped dead in their tracks—stunned by an abnormal vision. Replacing the clear water they anticipated, a red river ran slowly by them. The small family simply stared in wonder until Diana spoke, "Wait here. Alisia and I will head up stream to take a look."

As the girls sprinted upstream, their quivers bounced slightly against the middle of their backs; the lightweight bows hung loosely in their left hands. Leather-covered feet barely touched the soft earth as the svelte figures silently covered ground with long graceful strides.

"Stay close, danger lurks nearby—I smell death." Alisia closed the gap between the two—her senses alert as she scanned the banks and bushes.

Following the path upstream, Diana stopped mid-stride. Both sisters stared at the spine-chilling scene. There lie the source of the crimson color—hundreds of dead bodies, mostly women and children, thrown into the river—the number of bodies so great that the river was forced to change its course as fleshy damns diverted the natural flow of this great river too noble to be subjected to such a disgraceful act against nature.

Some of the bodies had no heads, body parts had been punctured or cut off completely, others displayed stab wounds and/or bullet holes. The macabre setting forced the sisters to look away…and then at each other. "We are in danger here; these lives were taken recently!" Alisia placed her hand on her sister's shoulder. "We should check on the others." As they turned to go, a twig snapped behind them.

Appearing along the same path, Mother and Brosh joined the girls at the ghastly scene. Brosh stared blankly at one decapitated child before he quickly turned off the path, and bent over as his pale frame shook violently exorcising the nauseating images before him—memories of his own family's gut-wrenching demise came flooding back to him.

Diana stepped forward and held him by the back of his shirt. Mother did not go to his aid; instead, she scanned the area cautiously for the source of this mayhem. "Whomever is responsible for this monstrosity must still be close by for the blood remains sticky." She held up one of her hands—fingertips covered in dripping crimson. Looking to and fro, she warily led the group away from the main path in search of a safe hiding place.

A narrow opening through barbed brush led to a willow-covered slope of red clay and sand so gritty it rolled under their slipping feet as they made their way down into the umbrella-shaded canopy. The four sat down quietly trying to regain some degree of composure. Nature's calming influence juxtaposed with the horror woven into the youngsters' psyches married together the unusual dichotomy of this surreal scene.

The Badrigian girls were taught not to hate, for to carry such a heavy burden would poison one from the inside. That iniquitous poison would eventually work itself outward until it manifested itself into actions dishonoring a reputable person. Nevertheless, emotions ran amok inside young heads. Their only salvation providing a somewhat tenuous link to sanity revolved around their mother and their now-loved "brother". The family members clung together and waited in silence.

Finally, Diana, began softly repeating one of her father's sermons.

"When all hope appears to be lost, look up—not down.

Encourage your soul to soar heavenward—look to the eagles and hawks—let their eyes be your eyes. Send your soul upward to settle softly in the billowy clouds of comfort. Dwell not on what has been, but focus on what tomorrow may bring—remain in control of your future; it is your destiny. While others may be losing their minds, you must project calm. By doing so, the body and mind can work together to produce mysteries science can not explain. Use meditation to channel your positive energy into a life-guiding source—love. Love—not hate— is the answer."

Mother looked at her and saw her husband, and she knew he was present with them—within her daughters—within herself. Mother gazed at her oldest daughter. She knew she was witnessing a significant transformation in her daughter's evolving mind.

Diana paused, and then uttered, "Oh, my dear father—how I miss your wisdom. Yet, I believe I listen to you more now that you are gone than I ever did when you were alive. Alas, what a fool I have been! Now disaster calls upon me to awaken to the adult world, for my childhood innocence has been stolen. Revenge lives on my lips, but I hold my tongue; however, I doubt I can temper my actions. Blood will have blood! So be it—and mercy on all our souls."

Brosh listened intently—he also longed for revenge. He rocked back and forth with arms crossed over his chest—waiting. His breathing rapid and shallow, he felt Diana's energy flow into him.

Before anyone could react to Diana's lamenting promise, a rustling ahead—birds suddenly in flight—what scared them? The family froze realizing they were not the source of the birds sudden upheaval—so what was? Senses hit high alert as Mother's right arm went up sharply signaling a halt to movement and immediate silence. Something was ahead; They could sense its presence—almost hear its imagined breathing—Diana's bow was raised slowly…silently her right hand caressed her leather quiver in search of a trusty arrow. Alisia's hand covered the handle of her belted knife.

Diana peered toward the shrubbery. Her bow now ready with arrow pointed toward the solitary sound. Sun-rays pierced the clouds and illuminated the green/yellow speckled leaves—and there was another movement, slow, slight, soft—the branches reluctantly parted. A gnarly, wrinkled hand parted the branches.

An old man hesitantly stepped forward, one hand held high… the other holding back the springy branches. As he carefully stepped out from the green curtain. His grey, shaggy hair streaked with black strands fell over his face. Once out of the foliage, he stood erect and looked warily at the young family. Cautiously, with one palm still held up in our direction, his scrawny frame turned back toward the bushes—soon two young boys of nine or ten followed in his footsteps. Their eyes were dark pools of uncertainty. A moment later, a woman in her late twenties cautiously revealed herself—two little girls—tiny hands clinging tightly to the woman's ripped dress. Diana lowered her bow.

After the strangers' fears were put to rest, they were given fresh water and bits of unleavened bread which they ate hungrily. The old man began to share what he had seen with his own eyes. Diana and the others listened closely. First, he spoke of the massacres taking place along the roads and streams.

He explained how, under the guise of deportation, the Turks were rounding up thousands of Armenians and forcing these helpless people (mostly women, children, and old men) to walk to the next town. Sometimes, they were told they would meet their husbands, fathers, or sons there and be united once again. The Armenians tried to carry most of their belongings with them. Some were even allowed mules that were packed with Armenian heirlooms and family savings. Naively, some Armenians believed the Turk's lies. However, the calamity that would soon befall them would put an end to their slim hopes.

The old man explained how the deportation was ordered by an imperial edict, and it read... all deserters (another word for Armenian refugees) should be shot on sight with no trial. Therefore, the Armenian families had little choice but to comply with the well-armed Turkish soldiers. Fortunately, the old man managed to convince his family to leave the village before it was occupied.

Because this clearly prophetic old man who possessed the historical memory to sense the coming atrocities, most of his family survived, thought Alisia. She turned and gave the boys another piece of bread as the old man shared his plan to seek asylum in Egypt. He wished the family good fortune and thanked Mother for sharing the sparse food. Mother and the others watched as the small family made their way along the base of the mountains.

Once the two groups parted ways, Mother suggested we stay another day in the secretive and secluded little camp in the bushes. Brosh's' feet needed to heal a bit more before he could walk any significant distance, and it seemed the danger may have moved past them.

"What will become of them? said Alisia to her mother.

"That, we do not know, but our families are better off separated. A small group of individuals will be harder to spot than a large one—still, they have the ancient one for guidance—may their blessings continue."

The family discussed their next move. The Tigris River would need to be crossed, yet such a crossing would not be easy. Brosh added that he could not swim. Mother put her hand on his shoulder and leaned toward him. "Neither can I", she whispered. "Fortunately, both girls swim like fish. We will figure it out."

Chapter 12

ARROWS OF RIGHTEOUSNESS AND REVENGE

A Tawny Owl flew silently across the travelers' path. As Diana studied the streamlined creature, she reflected its distinctive features— *its feathers are perfectly designed to slide silently through the dusk—no warning for its prey— its talons outstretched and sharp as razors. I know of evolution, of science and its fact-based obsession…and I understand its demystifying abilities—no argument there. I do not believe the creation of an owl's feathers is a miracle; science can explain that through thousands of years of evolution—the survival of the fittest. What can't be explained is that there is something here instead of nothing—the perfect balance and rhythm of the universe and how it manifests itself in nature. That is all the proof I need that a higher power created something and made it from nothing—that is a miracle—and that is why I believe in God…and evolution.*

Man's myopic vision prevents him from seeing God's greatest creation, and that remains man's imperfection—its antidote rests in our own Free Will—God's gift to us. Our ability to choose what we want most to see… to believe…to accept in our hearts and minds. God helps those who help themselves. Man is not God's greatest creation; he is flawed. Nature remains God's greatest creation. God created it for humans to preserve—not destroy. I do not know what man will do, but I do know what I will do. I will learn from nature to be invisible...to be ready...to be lethal when I must—and to survive.

Small footprints fell silently on the soft dirt as the group proceeded west.

Mother surveyed the cloud-filled sky and tossed a bit of grass in the air observing its directional movement.

"The weather favors us; let us continue our steady progress. Soon, we will cross the Tigris River. Then, we will rest for a while."

The crossing of the Tigris proved to be easier than the family thought. There were many people crossing on boats of many sizes. No questions were asked as the steady flow of humans were moved from one bank to the next.

Once across, mother took the time to explain to the group the origins of the Tigris. "Both the Tigris and the Euphrates originate in Armenia. The headwaters there come from the mountains of Armenia and numerous tributaries help to drain the entire mountainous region. Most of the roads follow the Euphrates River because the banks of the Tigris are steep and difficult. Eventually, these mighty rivers empty into the great Persian Gulf."

The family proceeded forward as they listened, but they soon veered off the main road and headed toward the wooded area. Occasionally, they would rest outside a village—safely hidden in the woods. Two or three from the clan would cautiously enter a small Turkish village. Disguised as Turkish peasants, they would try to purchase necessary items—a knife, some rope, candles, matches, pans, fruits, vegetables, shoes, etc. Sometimes they were successful, other times they were looked upon with great suspicion and had to leave quickly. Mother's money (sewn into the hem of her dress) bought a few of the essentials, but it remained a limited source. Diana wondered how the group would survive when it was depleted.

As the four moved quietly southward, a muffled scream could be heard off in the distance. The group stopped and looked at each other ascertaining that they all had heard the same sound. Again, a loud shriek....

Diana looked at the others... "I am going to investigate; I will be right back." Before anyone could react, she set off at a fast-paced run—adjusting her bow and quiver mid-stride—soon, her lithe figure disappeared.

"Diana, be careful. We need to stay in the shadows." Mother half-whispered to herself for her daughter was already out of voice range; her face reflected the concern they all felt.

Diana had to see for herself. Her independent actions did not surprise anyone; her confidence increased every day as did her skills. Cloaked in semi-darkness, she pressed on bit by bit until she could see the faces faintly reflected in the dying glow of the setting sun. As it grew darker, she crawled closer until she found a well-hidden vantage point. Sure enough, there below lie a caravan of Armenian refugees—at rest for the night—their weary, ragged frames spread out in the dirt—exhausted.

Diana spotted the cutthroat gendarmes guarding the dwindling group; they grew careless and bold. They had posted no guards, for there was no visible threat from outsiders. The ragged group of children, women, and old people were barely alive—starving and exhausted. Family members huddled together, frightened expressions on their faces.

Besides the Turkish military guarding the prisoners, Diana identified another group of men strutting alongside the resting bodies. These swaggering men were torturers, rapists, and murderers who stole innocent lives in the night without care or mercy. These men were the "Shotas", and the Military guards were under strict orders to not interfere with their criminal actions against the Armenians. The Shotas were criminals and prisoners who were released from prison to do the dirty work for the Turks—a way for the Sultan to wash his hands of the atrocities when questioned by the world order of humane countries. He would explain to the British and Americans and the rest of the world that these bands were outlaws and ruffians—beyond his responsibility—all the while smiling out of the side of his mouth. For the most part, Europe, France, and America just nodded naively, albeit sympathetically.

In reality, these assassins made up the "Butcher Battalions" sent out to kill Armenians. Much of the old man's descriptions were right on the mark. The cruel tactics of the march were as he described.

Once the deadly caravan had come to a halt for the night, these Shotas began their abuse. The cries and screams made Diana's blood run cold...then hot, but she knew little could be done by one girl to intervene, so with sadness in her heart and anger boiling in her brain, she reluctantly turned to go.

Just then, Diana spied two Shotas at the end of the caravan confront a young teenage girl. She was being hugged tightly by her mother. The men tried to pull her away, but the mother screamed at the men and held on tightly until an unseen sword suddenly cracked her skull. Her neck snapped to the side with a loud crack and blood from the top of her head flowed over her face and onto the ground surrounding her suddenly still body like a crimson halo. Diana turned back, kneeled and continued to observe although her entire body cringed, and her stomach threatened to empty itself, but revulsion soon turned to fury as she watched the young girl fight ferociously—kicking, clawing, twisting away while her mother lie dead at her feet, but the two men eventually subdued her with brutal punches to her face and stomach. When she fell helplessly to the ground, they lifted up her slender body and half carried-half dragged her off into the growing darkness—away from the caravan.

Diana could not resist; she followed like an interloper whose fatalistic actions could not be stopped—even by the forces of self-preservation.

ᗧᗡᗢ

From behind a knoll, with a slight height advantage, she watched the struggling triad make it to a secluded area. Diana's rapidly beating heart swelled as one man restrained the young girl. His toothless grin sent blood-curdling chills up Diana's spine as she watched the other begin to strip away the girl's long dress as she kicked her legs with her last bit of strength.

Unconsciously, Diana's right hand moved automatically over her shoulder to the middle-top of her back as she lightly ran fingers over the leather case. Finally, her searching fingers felt feather guides and an oak shaft as she carefully pulled an arrow from its quiver. Beads of sweat formed above her lip as she mechanically notched the arrow and took aim. *God, please steady my hand and calm my heart, so my arrow may fly true.* A serene, spiritual calmness steadied her hand. She had become an instrument of justice long overdue. Her own rape still fresh in her mind's eye as she concentrated on the center of the chest of the man closest to her. As he separated the long dress from the girl, he stood up straight in triumph—his outstretched arms wide apart. Abruptly, his smile disappeared as Diana rose from the darkness like an Angel of Death; his eyes narrowed as he spotted the teen in a poised position ready to deliver a deadly arrow into his black heart. Alas, his brain sent its message too late; the arrow of redemption was already on its way. The would-be-rapist's mouth opened, but no sound came out.

The taut bowstring pressed tightly against Diana's upper lip as bent fingers suddenly freed the rigid line; the familiar motion sent the hand-made arrow swiftly through the cold night air. Time stopped for a moment... and then continued... as Diana's eyes stared keenly at the feathers of the arrow as they shook violently upon impact with the rapist's left upper chest. Both hands desperately grabbed at the intrusive arrow, but it remained stubbornly stuck all the way through his chest and out the back as he fell to his knees paying homage for his evil deeds.

The Shota's criminal partner in this devilish crime twirled around—eyes blazing wide with fear and hatred. He dropped the girl like dead weight, and ran like mad at the young archer, but another arrow was already in place.... This one left the taut bowstring with its tip headed for the bearded face and furrowed scowl. However, the attacker's head moved slightly to the left, so the arrow entered into the softness of his right eye and exited the back of his skull taking with it pieces of bone, brain, and blood which spurted outward like cardinal-colored tears. His body splayed awkwardly on the ground with hands outstretched and legs together—crucified! *Yes*, thought Diana—*as it should be. Glory be to God in the highest!*

Surprisingly, she felt no remorse; however, her mind reeled with questions—*who am I? My father fought back, and am I not my father's daughter?*

She stared down at her hands; they did not shake even though her heart continued to race. Taking a long breath, she moved forward to the edge of the bank and looked down into the eyes of the shaking young girl—*like looking into a mirror,* Diana thought—sliding down the embankment.

The young girl's mouth leaked ruddy rivulets out of its corners, yet only her eyes moved—staring at the Archer of Death who appeared like an avenging angel sent by God. Who was this girl—a teen like herself... wearing a sleeveless shirt tucked into black pants—and a dagger protruding from its waistband. A leather vest protected her upper body and leather bands covered her arms—a long-bow with matching quiver partially hidden by long black hair made her a striking figure, but was she real? The naked girl remained awestruck—frozen in place as Diana pulled the girl's tattered dress out of the warm hands of the near-dead body sprawled out before her and handed it to the frightened girl. The girl pulled the dress to her chest, but never took her eyes off Diana.

Diana tentatively held out her hand, but the unsure girl hesitated... shrinking away from the outstretched hand. Diana took a knee and said softly, "Be not afraid—I will not hurt you. I am of the Hye...like you; come with me and live— or... stay and die."

Wide-eyed brown pools stared as the words sunk in slowly—in a flash, she jumped up—an embrace of desperation followed as she squeezed her surprised rescuer with resilient strength.

Diana smiled slightly as the last rays of the sun reflected off the fast moving clouds—*a storm is coming.*

Chapter 13

LUSINE OF THE LIGHT ~

Diana led the still-in-shock teen swiftly over the uneven terrain using her keen vision in the deadly-silent near darkness. Soon it would be completely dark; with no moon, their progress would slow to a crawl. The struggling teen, despite her waif-like state, stayed close behind her rescuing angel—such tenacity one could only admire. *There is hope for her*, Diana mused. *Her heart beats strong despite being broken.*

As the two out-of-breath girls approached the familiar landscape, Diana paused and whistled out a well known warble often used by Alisia and herself during their childhood games of hide and seek. Diana held up her hand and the girl froze—her wide-eyes reading the abrupt, yet clear, body language. Soon, the tweet returned sounding like the twitter in her original best-bird-song imitation. Moving slowly through the brush, the two soon found the well-camouflaged family. They had been worried, so they left camp and were on the lookout for Diana's return.

Back at camp, all eyes were now on the tattered girl; her eyes glanced furtively from one person to the next. In the darkness, the family spoke in whispers. First, they learned the young girl's name—Lusine (pronounced lewseen). Soon, the following story fell from her lips as she kicked at the dirt and blurted out her grief. She was given water and a bit of bread as Alisia applied a soothing balm to her many bug bites, scratches, and cut lip. Mother handed her a blanket for warmth. With some verbal encouragement, she stoically continued. She told her sad story over time.... Speaking slowly, but with conviction—"Our town near Ourfa had no protection after the men were forced to leave—the other younger men were conscripted (mandatory enrollment) to fight in the Turkish army. The older men were rounded up to meet with Turkish officials. My father was one of the elders, so he went along to try and stop the bloodshed—to explain to the officials that we meant no harm to anyone. We just wanted to live and be left alone."

Tears streaked away the dirt under her eyes as she tried to stem her emotions. She pulled the blanket tightly around her—thankful for the softness and added warmth.

Lusine spoke haltingly but clearly— "The elders in our village were hoping to discuss the upcoming situation and possible solutions—it was all a ruse! A devious plan was set in motion, and its tentacles were more wide-spread than anyone could have imagined.

Later, rumors began to leak out and find their way back to our ears hungry for news of our loved ones. The airy words turned out to be true— the men of our town—our fathers, husbands, brothers, and priests—<u>murdered</u>.

My mother refused to leave our house despite being ordered to leave by the Turkish police. The next morning, police came to our front door and told her to leave immediately. They handed her a large bag and walked away laughing—its weight surprised her, and she almost dropped it to the floor. Once inside, my mother placed the package on the kitchen table and opened the bag—my father's bloody, decapitated head! I can still hear my mother's screams." Lusine's shoulders shook violently; her nose began leaking, and she tried to wipe away the torrent of tears.

Mother wiped her face with a clean kerchief. "Enough Lusine, you don't have to share anymore with us; it is too painful."

"Please, I want it all out, so I never have to repeat it again."

⚬⚬⚬

Lusine struggled on bravely with her story and told the family that within days, the Turkish police and soldiers came again into the town to deport the remaining Armenians (mostly women with their children still clinging to their skirts) to the next village. Time became precious as it evaporated in a rush of panic—no time to gather all their belongings before they were forced to march southward. She described how her family grabbed what they could as they were led out into the street at gunpoint. Soldiers on horseback with rifles told them to get in line and be quiet. A few days later, their military escort met with a band of strangers—later, they would learn these men were called "Shotas" or as one German officer referred to them—"scum". The Turkish police spoke privately to this motley group—but after a brief argument, the officers reluctantly withdrew.

These strangers became our worst nightmares. Diana nodded knowingly.

Lusine sipped her water, carefully trying to make it last.

Diana and her family knew of the Shotas. They were prisoners released by the Sultan and spread throughout Turkey and Armenia. These men were placed in or near areas where the Armenian deportees were likely to pass. Some estimates of their numbers ranged between thirty and forty thousand of these blood-thirsty villains bent on violence and given free reign to slaughter innocent Armenians.

Lusine continued—she painstakingly told the group how the Shotas forced the exhausted Armenians to march without rest, food, or water.

Those who fell behind (often the elderly or young children) were shot and left in the dirt. Mothers carried their children as they took their last dying steps. Some mothers were forced to choose—leaving their weakest or sickest child behind. The agony…the screams of despair…the pleas for mercy…. These plaintive cries fell upon deaf ears.

"When the mothers were too weak or too sick to walk, they were shot or simply left to die. The babies were grabbed by their legs and swung wildly until their heads smashed against rocks—saving bullets." Lusine took a long breath and let it out slowly. She looked at the others who waited patiently for her to continue.

Lusine told how she heard that some Armenians were marched into the Deir ez-Zor—a desert so unforgiving that few ever survived its inhabitable climate. She made the sign of the cross quickly thinking of the many Armenians forced to march through such a hellish wasteland and prayed she would never be in such a position.

When night finally did come, the Shotas picked through the weakened Armenians searching for young girls or mothers to drag off for their entertainment that night. One mother was raped while holding the hand of her crying child. Many of the young girls never returned. Families tried to hide their daughters by concealing them with heavy clothes and scarves to hide their faces. Still, the rapes continued and the horrors were indescribable. Some women killed themselves; others, scarred their faces to make themselves less desirable to the men preying upon them.

Lusine's story matched the reports and accounts the family had already heard. They knew this was not an isolated case. What they did not understand was why?

"How old are you?" asked Alisia. Lusine stared at Alisia for a moment.

"I am sixteen."

The family glanced at each other uncomfortably. They all thought the same—she may be sixteen, but in her present state—skinny, emaciated, gaunt—she appeared to be no older than twelve or thirteen.

Mother embraced Lusine. "Lusine of the Light—you have come to us through divine intervention; as of tonight, we accept you as one of our own. Alisia and Diana will educate and train you. You will learn to be a survivor and a precious, contributing member of our family." Mother extended her right arm and blessed Lusine with the sign of the cross. She leaned over and kissed her on her forehead. "You are now my daughter, and I shall love you with my heart and soul—know you are loved, and will always be loved by your family now in heaven, and your new family here on Earth. We will do our best to protect you from harm."

With the stars hidden, the clouds began to cry and the cool rain baptized Lusine into her new family. Scattering and shuffling, the family finally crowded together under a makeshift cover. Intermittent raindrops tapped out an informal refrain that soothed the sleepy brood.

Diana felt serene and at peace as she looked at the young girl. *Her face is wet with tears—mine with raindrops—once again, tears in the rain all appear the same—we will grow strong together. My dear new sister— may you enjoy the blessing of family once again.*

Author's note:

Countless children were killed directly and indirectly during the Armenian Genocide. Their deaths continued for years afterwards as many fell through the inevitable cracks of well-intentioned humanitarian aid.

Knowing their fate was imminent, some Armenian parents gave their children to honorable Turks who hid them in their homes at great risk to themselves and raised them as their own children by falsifying identification papers. They did this for their Armenian friends who were slain. Today, many of those "hidden Armenians" in Turkey and the surrounding areas no longer hide their heritage.

According to Raffi Bedrosyan, Hrant Dink displayed great courage when he identified one of the many "hidden Armenians". This Armenian girl was an orphan who was raised by a wealthy Turk family. The identified individual's Turkish name was Sabiha Gokcen, but her real Armenian name was Hatun Sebilciyan—orphaned in Bursa in 1915. Hatun became the first female military pilot in Turkey.

Unfortunately, this revelation was the beginning of the end for Hrant, for it triggered a massive hate and threat campaign against him by the Turkish government, the military, and the media, resulting in his assassination three years later.

Today, Hrant Dink is remembered as an Armenian hero.

Chapter 14

WHERE HAVE ALL THE MEN GONE?

Much later, time would unveil the truth— the methodical madness revealed itself when the Young Turks put forth the decree that all Armenian men of age would be conscripted or drafted into the Ottoman Army to fight for the Turks. However, by 1914, things would change. As the Ottoman Army suffered defeat after defeat, they needed a scapegoat—the Armenian people became their targets—they were infidels, traitors, and "in the way" of the grand plan—turkification of the entire region.

Rumors circulated that there were Armenian spies and traitors among the Ottoman Army; therefore, no Armenian could be trusted. After all, the Armenians, Greeks, and Georgians all had Christian leanings (as did many Russians) that flew in the face of the Muslim religion. As a result, Armenian soldiers were systematically disarmed and sent to perform the most laborious and dangerous physical tasks. These Sisyphean rituals would weaken their bodies and exhaust them—not just physically, but mentally as well.

Eventually, these labor battalions would be executed en masse per order of the Turkish officials in charge of the government. They were unarmed and easily slain with swords, shot and/or bayoneted by the Ottoman army, police, and gendarmes. Their bones still can be found scattered over Eastern Turkey and beyond.

〜〣〟〜

Author's note: **More information can be found online using the internet and searching Armenian Genocide. Also, p**hotos of tattooed (face, hands, arms, etc.) Armenian girls may be found online as well. The Turks, Kurds, and others bought and sold Armenian girls. They would then tattoo them showing everyone that these girls now belonged to them—their property to do with as they pleased. These young girls were frequently sold as sex slaves or household slaves; some were forced into prostitution.

Chapter 15

THE KILLING FIELDS ~
WATERY GRAVES ~

Diana continues to exhibit good judgment and sound leadership. Below, she describes the family's progress as well as the first-hand accounts told to her by other Armenian refugees.

Time to move our growing family. Lusine seemed strong enough to travel despite her night sweats and reoccurring nightmares. Brosh remained reserved— quiet, pensive, but always watching for danger. His boyish body had changed into a wiry version of a young man. His knife throwing skills, wood carving artistry, and dedication to archery practice were most admirable as he strove to achieve perfection. All of us strived to remove fear from our psyches and became survivalists—not just for ourselves, but for our relatives who sacrificed their lives for us to carry on our lineage.

We decided to head toward the gorges of Birejek.

The rocky path led us through archways and crevasses—good for hiding and remaining unseen. In one gorge, we met a small band of Armenians.

Like us, they were cautious, careful, and resilient survivors. Two old men, one with salt and pepper hair, the other all grey—thin, but unyielding with piercing eyes and a creased face. The others in their party included one older women who seemed to be the grandmother of a young girl about the same age as Lusine. Her parents were nowhere to be seen. The fear in the eyes of the young girl—her protective body language, screamed that she had been violated and hurt—now, untrusting of any strangers.

I shared the remnants of a rabbit I had shot earlier. The meat was cold and difficult to chew, but they devoured the scraps gratefully. I asked them about the death marches, and they shook their heads and admitted to seeing similar marches during their travels.

They also added the following accounts: "We saw marches and we hid. Eventually, we heard from other Armenians about boats being overloaded with hundreds of Armenians to be supposedly transferred to another port. In reality, they were taken out to the Black Sea far enough for no one to be able to swim to shore. Next, they were forced to jump overboard or be shot. There were also boats filled with tiny children who were being transported to an orphanage. Instead, the children were stabbed, put into sacks and thrown overboard.

The Turks watched the families drown—ignoring their watery cries for help.

They told us small groups of Armenians had escaped into the mountains and forests—some with the help of their decent Turkish neighbors who risked their own lives by trying to save their Armenian friends. Other Armenians revolted against their abusers, and while most were shot or stabbed, a few managed to escape. These survivors were trying to find sanctuary by fleeing to another country, but help was rare and many individuals could not find food; eventually, they starved to death.

The older woman finally spoke: "Our children were victims of mass poisonings and deliberate diseases passed on to our most vulnerable under the deception of disease-curing inoculations and injections.

Last week, we found children with their throats slit and tiny skulls smashed against rocks along the trail where the death marches had passed earlier, so many lives taken... too horrible to describe. Thus, we remain in the shadows as we move east. One last thing we know, our elders, priests, teachers, politicians, intellectuals—our best and brightest leaders—all rounded up and jailed. Soon, we fear they will be slaughtered as well. Our understanding of the breadth of the genocide is clear—the Ottoman Turks were determined to exterminate all Armenians." The old woman sat down slowly.

March 7, 1915— *Diana continues her story after her too busy brain refused to go to sleep.*

A solitary night lark screeched above as I tried to sleep, but too many thoughts pestered my brain. I thought about the old man and his last comments.

He shared the following observation. "In this sea of misery, there were some righteous Ottoman officials such as Celal, governor of Aleppo; Mazhar, governor of Ankara; and Reshid, governor of Kastamonu, who were dismissed for not complying with the extermination campaign. However, any common Turks who protected Armenians were killed."

"Aghlayanun maluh, alana khair getirmez" shouted the old noble Turk reminding the looting young Turks—*The merchandise of the person crying does not bring happiness to the buyer.* "What you reap now, your children's children will sadly pay for in the future."

Author's note: Those words especially ring true today in Syria, Turkey, Iran, Iraq and other countries in the Middle East.

Also, there were other minority groups (Georgians, Assyrians, Greeks, Russians, and other foreign witnesses) who, regardless of the threat of death if they were caught, helped hide as many Armenians as they could or found them safe passage across the borders. They showed them compassion and refused to be a part of this attempted genocide. Blessings on these brave individuals for their loyalty, courage, and intrepid actions.

As the old man stroked and gently pulled at his beard, he explained how Armenians were a tolerated minority in Turkey for a while.

"We paid higher taxes and had very few political rights. They subjected us to unfair and unjustifiable actions and referred to us as 'infidels'."

Diana continues to share what she learned from the old Armenian man.

The old man continued to share how in spite of these obstacles, our Armenian community thrived under Ottoman rule. He further explained the same basic tenants that my father had shared with me. This included how the Armenian people tended to be better educated and wealthier than our Turkish neighbors. Armenian women were educated and respected and allowed freedoms denied to Turkish women.

As I thought about what the old man said, I remembered the words of my own father. Father said Armenian pride and respect for those who were Hye could not be understood by most Turks because the concept of sacrificing self for others was not in their nature. I question that assertion today. The Turks love their children, their wives, their parents, but many show little tolerance for those who worship a different god.

One night, my father explained the difference between the Koran and the Bible.

"Listen to me carefully. I researched and read and tried to understand our Muslim neighbors. I read the Koran and began to comprehend essential differences. At the same time, it became clear that the <u>Bible</u> and <u>Koran</u> had much more in common than I thought. Anyone using twisted logic could unfairly pick quotes and excerpts out of context from either book and use those words to justify the most cruel actions imaginable—that, my dear, is exactly what extremists do to justify their sick actions. People with goodness in their hearts know the basic tenets of all religions: Do unto others...take care of the Earth and its animals...love and forgive others...exercise tolerance towards others who are different from you...help those in need for we are all brothers and sisters moving forward on this marvelous world we call home."

And remember I did...those prescient words...prophetic words that would later ring true during the fall of the Ottoman Army. An army led by men who rationalized the death and destruction of an entire ethnicity using lies, deceit, and cruelty based on perverted interpretations from their most holy source—the <u>Koran</u>."

Diana looked again upon the emaciated figure as her eyes blurred and burned.

When will we ever learn to stop the hate?

The old Armenian slowly ran his wrinkled hands over his weather-beaten face as he rubbed his salt and pepper bushy eyebrows. The skin on his leather face appeared creased with dirt—his hands and arms covered with paper-thin parchment skin—tough and fragile—all at the same time.

The old man thrust a boney hand forward and pointed his index finger at Diana. "These men (speaking of the Turks), whose wives were friends with our wives, with whom we shared animals, rode horses, loaned our tools, whom we thought of as our good neighbors and friends—these fellow citizens would soon turn jealous eyes upon our success. Their resentment (he paused to sip a little water through parched lips from a wineskin carried on his shoulder) was exaggerated by largely unjustified suspicions that the Christian Armenians would be more loyal to Christian governments (that of the Russians, for example, who shared a border with Turkey) than they were to the Ottoman caliphate who would eventually support Germany. While that may have eventually came to be, there was no proof, no evidence, no humanistic reason for what was to follow." *He shook his grey head vigorously as he began again....*

"*Before my Armenian priest was taken from our church, he told me he heard a Turkish man telling another Turk of his participation in a village raid.*

'*When we started the massacre, the valley and the mountain resounded with the screams and cries of those being killed. One man begged me for his life by saying he was a doctor; he only wanted to heal people. I told him to heal himself as I dug out his eyes with the tip of my dagger; next, I broke his neck with my long sword. Here is his gold watch and chain.*'

"*Repeatedly, this Turk gave praise to Allah knowing that he had earned holy praise by participating in the massacre; in his eyes, he had now become worthy of the rewards offered by their holy prophet.*

After the bloodletting, he earned his place in paradise, and all its promises and rewards belonged to him."

The others in the old man's group began to stretch out on the ground; tired and sleep-deprived, they began to spread small blankets and rugs out and close their eyes as he continued to explain how suspicions grew more acute as the Ottoman Empire crumbled.

"At the end of the 19th century, the dictatorial Turkish Sultan Abdul Hamid II—focused on loyalty above all, and infuriated by the emerging Armenian campaign to win basic civil rights--declared that he would solve the "Armenian question" (what to do about the Armenians) once and for all.

As I tell this story now, my mind wanders to previous years in my life. I would read how the bloody Sultan boasted, 'I will soon settle those Armenians,' he told a reporter in 1890. 'I will give them a box on the ear which will make them...relinquish their revolutionary ambitions.' As I later found out, sometime between 1894 and 1896, this "box on the ear" took the form of a state-sanctioned pogrom (an organized massacre of a particular ethnic group). It occurred in part due to large scale protests by Armenians (who demanded fair and just treatment and certain basic civil rights). Turkish military officials, soldiers, and ordinary men sacked Armenian villages and cities and massacred their citizens. Hundreds of thousands of unarmed Armenians were murdered. These were the first large-scale Armenian massacres.

Instead of working out a compromise based upon fairness and compassion for his own citizens, the Sultan expressed an inexplicable hatred for the Armenians—so, he chose genocide." Now, the old man leaned forward like he had just found a second wind strong enough to push him forward to finish his story.

"However, there may have been a secret reason for his animosity. Some say his mother was a young beauty whom his father seduced but would not marry. The theory is that she was Armenian, and he was ashamed of his possible Armenian heritage. Ashamed that his father never loved his mother—ashamed that he was a bastard child born of a cruel father, and destined never to know his Armenian birth mother—never held in loving arms, never cuddled, kissed, or stroked by loving hands, and having never been loved, could never know love or give love—thus, the making of a monster explained. Nothing was ever written down, so history may have erased any proof of this explanatory possibility. Nevertheless, the result produced a monster—and yes, monsters do walk among us—unrecognizable at times...disguised more often than not—yet, know this—heroes also walk among us—carrying within them an expansive courage sometimes unknown even to themselves. They are like warrior angels looking out for our best interests despite our many faults and weaknesses."

The Armenian elder looked at my bow and quiver—nodded knowingly and reached out to touch my arm to see if I was still listening—I nodded my head and he continued....

"In 1908, a new government came to power in Turkey. A group of reformers who zealously called themselves the 'Young Turks'. Unethical, conniving, and unabashedly arrogant, they eventually overthrew old Sultan Abdul Hamid and established a more modern constitutional government.

At first, the Armenians were hopeful that now they would have an equal place in this new state, but they soon learned that what the nationalistic Young Turks wanted most of all was to "Turkify" the empire. According to this way of thinking, non-Turks--and especially Christian non-Turks—were a grave threat to the new state. These 'problem people' included Greeks, Georgians, Russians, Armenians, and Assyrians. The Assyrians...the poor Assyrian women and little girls suffered a fate worse than death."

The old man looked around at the sleeping bodies. "I've gone on too long," he said as he looked at Diana. "Please forgive me."

"No apologies necessary; you have girded me for strength in battle. It is I who should thank you. Good night."

The old man nodded his head. *She makes me proud*, he thought with a yawn. The wise man paused—tired, drained, and unable to continue his historical perspective even if he wished. Diana watched him drift off with a heavy sigh that seemed to collapse his chest and slow his heartbeat.

Sleep took him peacefully as he leaned against an old rock which seemed to soften in an anthropomorphic gesture of nature's respect for the cyclical journey of all life.

Diana smiled and sighed softly to herself. She adjusted her bedroll and followed the sage's example.

Chapter 16

TO SIN IS HUMAN ~ TO FORGIVE ~ DIVINE

Diana continues her reflections by remembering the stories told by her parents and other Armenian friends.

As I grew older and could understand more complex ideas, I learned that the policy of genocide against the Armenian population of the Ottoman Empire began with the annihilation of the male population. Remove the leaders (the intellectuals, professors, lawyers, doctors, architects, businessmen, bankers, politicians, etc.), and the rest of the populace will flounder. Another step of this diabolical plan revolved around the requirement of conscription. Armenia's young men were mandated to join the Ottoman Army—no exceptions.

Once in the army and under the authoritative command of the Turkish Government, the Armenian men would be guilefully disarmed and forced to perform the most difficult and strenuous labor. These work details included preparing the hard ground for railroad tracks, but also entailed dangerous work (handling chemicals, tar, waste products, etc.)

that risked the health and safety of the budding youth of Armenia's pride and joy. Finally, underfed, weak, sick, and exhausted, the men were easily slaughtered en masse per order of their own (Turkish led) government.

Next came the humiliating searches as Armenian homes were ransacked under the guise of looking for weapons held illegally. I remember my dad hiding his bows and arrows high inside our fireplace chimney—dark and sooty—but... safe from prying eyes. Looking back, I now realize my father and mother never trusted the Turkish government. Perhaps, it stemmed from their ancestors who were also conquered, enslaved, and subjugated by foreign enemies. These suspicions became linear transferences out of which grew resilience and resentment. I remember all of this now.

༄

Author's note:

Once the Armenian villages were without any men to protect them and most of the populace's weapons confiscated, the subsequent deportation of women, children, and old men began—many of these marches headed directly into the Syrian deserts, but hundreds of different routes led into the mountains, gorges, along rivers, lakes, and even to the sea. Some of the larger deportations led to other cities seeking trains for transfer to concentration camps. The routes were often randomly selected and were sometimes not much more than goat trails. The direction did not matter for the smaller deportations as they quickly turned into "death marches". Deportation caravans mostly consisted of Armenians carrying their belongings and their babies. Some were allowed to take their horses or donkeys, but they were soon stolen from them as well as any other items of value.

Ironically, Hitler would later direct his Nazis to follow the Turk's example and move large numbers of Jews (by trains) in the same manner—to concentration camps and gas chambers). Noting that the "world powers" were slow to intervene on behalf of the Armenians, Hitler deviously improved on the Turks' methods of genocide. For example, the Nazis carefully destroyed or hid Jewish bodies—no bones and skulls spread all over the countryside—indisputable evidence for other countries to later find. Despite Hitler's heinous attempts, other countries finally intervened, but not until millions of Jews were murdered or displaced. Thus, one genocide led to another.

Today, with advances in technology, the people of the world are more aware of injustices occurring around the world. Unfortunately, genocidal acts still occur far too often. Hope lies in the youth of the world, for they must be the harbingers of peace—the ones who will subvert the deadly paradigm that allows bureaucracy and greed to cripple attempts to stop genocide as soon as it rears its ugly head.

༺ঞ༻

It is important to note, that during the Armenian genocide, many of the women were kidnapped either by Turkish soldiers, Bedouins, or Kurdish bands. Chètes and/or Shotas (criminals set free by the Sultan to murder and torture the helpless remaining Armenians) were waiting for these unsuspecting caravans. Some of the women were pressured into renouncing their religion and were forcefully tattooed on their face, chest, and hands to signify that they were slaves and simply property to be held or disposed of as their owner wished. The tattoos were meant to be clearly visible—much like a brand on an animal. Pictures of these girls and women may be found online by searching "Armenian Genocide pictures".

Armenian children were sold as household slaves or sex slaves—others were raped, tortured, brutally desecrated. Resistance meant death—nevertheless, <u>death</u> was repeatedly chosen over renouncing one's belief in God and Christianity. Brave women, old men, and even children fought fiercely defending one another despite certain death for doing so. Most of these incidents were never recorded or reported— witnesses were scarce, and the Turks would quickly bury any evidence relating to any semblance of honorable actions on the part of Armenians. History (always written by the victors) turned a blind eye....

Decades later, many Armenians would courageously share their experiences during the genocide. During research for this novel, I read hundreds of these painful first-hand accounts of what oc-curred—they remain forever etched upon my brain.

And what of the children of genocide survivors? What do they say about their parents and grandparents? They say, I am Hye; my love for those before me—who bore me—who paid in blood, so I could move forward—I shall never forget—<u>never</u>. One hundred years—and vengeance still burns within me towards those who will not apologize, will not admit, and refuse to accept responsibility for their actions. Sadly, these naysayers blindly encourage the spread of genocide and insure its continuance by their own shameful denial.

Forgiveness will always be an essential quality of the strong—but how can we ever forgive if the trespasser never admits the truth? Our most heartfelt hope lies not in the Turkish leadership, but in the Turkish youth. It is always the youth who serve as catalysts for change; thus, we count on the Turkish young people to demand their government steps up and admits the truth.

I offer the following example, after four decades of denying a dark past, East Germany sincerely apologized to Israel and all Jews for the Nazi Holocaust and accepted joint responsibility for the slaughter of six million Jews during World War II. Germany stepped up and admitted responsibility on behalf of its people for the humiliation, expulsion, and murder of Jewish men, women, and children. "We feel sad and ashamed, and we ask the Jews of the world to forgive us."

And after such holy humility, what do you think happened next?—

The Jews forgave them.

～⁊∿

"I am sorry" is a simple statement. It may or may not ring true.

"I won't do it again" is a positive promise. It may or may not ring true.

"How can I rectify the pain you suffered?"

<u>That</u>, my friend, is taking responsibility.

It <u>always</u> rings true.

～⁊∿

Chapter 17

BOYHOOD ~ TO MANHOOD

Diana reflects on Brosh's precocious development.

I remember Brosh's transformation. For the longest time, he watched and learned—silently. He learned to throw a knife and consistently stick it into a tree. He whittled little pieces of wood for hours on end— cups, bowls, whistles materialized and were put to good use. He even fashioned a rudimentary wooden hook and attached it to a line of string. His face shone with the joyful exuberance owned only by youthful first experiences when he caught his first fish and shared it with us in a Christ-like manner. Yes, he became a fisherman, a believer, and a forward-looking young man who refused to dwell on his hellish past. Instead, he chose hope over despair, smiles over frowns, and life over death. These changes occurred in a relatively short time—the restorative power of Love. I learned that when demands are made upon one whose heart beats for others' happiness, one can accomplish miraculous goals—I witnessed all of that and more occur within Brosh and became inspired by this boy forged into a man by cruel circumstance.

One day, we were gathering wood together, and I said to him, "Brosh, your talents impress us all. Do you think you could make me some new arrows?" I pointed to my quiver hanging on a low leaning branch nearby. It contained several arrows I had carefully made from select branches of Goldenrod.

He smiled and walked over to my quiver of arrows. Delicately, he withdrew one from the leather holder and examined it closely. His fingers traced its imperfect smoothness and stopped once at the tip (a bit of glass filed and scraped to form a rough arrowhead) and once at the tail. The tail sported a few stiff bird feathers glued in place for the purpose of guiding the arrow and insuring pinpoint accuracy. Next, his fingers paused at the nock (the notched end). His actions reminded me of a blind person; I could tell he was examining and analyzing the minutia, the dimensions, the subtleties—soon, he would make even better arrows. His eyes were brown/black pools with yellow specks that caught the light like a butterfly's winged beauty. His olive skin—smooth and clear, and his face handsomely defined by a square jaw and high cheekbones—his face took on an attractive appearance that I had not noticed before this moment. I felt a strange, puzzling warmness run through me as I stared at him.

I knew he accepted the challenge when he walked away with my arrow tucked securely under his arm. His shoulders were broader now, and his belly and legs began to fill in more. He had learned to hunt and defend himself, and the exercises we all practiced had rapidly increased and shaped his muscle mass.

My archery skills improved greatly with time—complementing my hunting efforts; food became more plentiful as Alisia and Brosh successfully joined in the gathering and finding of new food sources. Nevertheless, food remained a priority due to all the calories we burned during our daily endeavors.

Our family grew stronger as we bonded together thanks to mother's guidance and wisdom. Lusine's time with mother increased the teen's cooking and sewing abilities. Mother's medical knowledge proved to be most valuable despite our limited resources. Lusine shadowed her throughout the day like a Guardian Angel and slept beside her at night. Mother became her guiding light, and Lusine blossomed before our eyes.

We continued to move our band through different terrain: rocky gorges, verdant valleys, mountainous ridges, forested hillsides, and high-desert plateaus. We knew the risks were greater in populated areas, so we skirted towns and villages unless we needed something desperately. In such cases, two or three of us would disguise ourselves and move in and out quickly and surreptitiously—wearing local shirts, long skirts, and peasant trappings—faces partially covered with scarves or hats.

However, we could not cover our eyes. There is something special about Armenian eyes that defies description. Some say such eyes are the windows of the soul, but I believe they are the translucent portals of the body of a ship that God has allowed us the free will to control. Someday, I hope to prove myself worthy of such a holy trust.

Chapter 18

THE ORIGIN OF PARADISE LOST ~

Long ago, it was was written that if the Bible's scriptures are truthfully interpreted, ancient Armenia rightfully claims to be the origin of Paradise—Armenia, a country known for its steadfast perseverance since the beginning of original sin. Armenia, who stayed faithful after the loss of perfection. Armenia, who found in its soil the happiness of human life created from dust and ready to embrace it once again. It was in Armenia that the God-given seas first receded, and Noah stepped out onto the wooden deck of the blessed ark. Within his hands, he gently held the symbolic bird of peace that finally rested its weary wings on the newly discovered soil of Mt. Ararat. Sweet, sweet, bittersweet Armenia....

Time's winged chariot knows no obstacles or delays; it never slows for anyone. So, while we may not be able to make Time stand still; we can always make it run. Thus, mankind moved forward, but not necessarily upward, for evolution offers only petty advances in the face of immortality. Yet, even promised immortality cannot stand up to the mysterious power of love. So, Adam lovingly chose to grow old with Eve—choosing mortality over everlasting life, and—Paradise was lost. Yet even with the loss of Paradise itself—when Adam relinquished immortality and embraced mortal love; yes, his love for Eve soared over Mt. Ararat like a love-struck shooting star seeking its singular place in the starry heavens above. Understanding the love in Adam's eyes, God allowed Eve's sin to turn into ephemeral ashes—for man remains incomplete without woman to balance and temper him.

Armenia's woebegone existence from powerful kingdom to land-locked entity with fierce borders remains peopled by individuals who espouse a resiliency bred deep within the hearts of its descendants. Armenia's independence was clearly jeopardized, but its significance remains forever reverent. Amen.

⁊⥩

Author's note: **The reader can find an impressive painted rendition (by William Blake) of God creating Eve from Adam's rib.**

Search the internet for William Blake paintings: Adam and Eve.

Chapter 19

DEFYING DEATH ~ A PHOENIX APPEARS

Brosh awoke to the early sounds of morning's first harbingers of light. The tiny wrens and sparrows flittered back and forth in the branches above his head. His half- opened eyes surveyed the grey sky as clouds reflected the shifting hues of dawn.

Rolling over onto his stomach, he pushed his body away from the warm bedroll and kneeled alongside it as he rolled it into a neat bundle, tightened its rope around the circumference, and placed it off to one side. Next, he splashed a bit of cold water onto his face to wash away sleep's salty remnants and returned the small container to its place under a shade tree by the edge of camp. The moist air cleared his nostrils as he breathed in the morning's dampness made sweet terra firma, loam, and ferns.

Brosh's stomach growled and churned reminding him of its emptiness. He ignored this hunger, for he was eager to try out his archery skills (and newly made arrows) on some unsuspecting animal—maybe a squirrel or rabbit or even larger game, so armed with arrows and optimism, he shifted into hunter mode and left the camp. He knew Diana was a much better hunter, but she still could use help providing the growing clan with food. Thus, the young man left the quiet camp—determined to prove his worth.

He headed west after whispering his intentions into Lusine's ear as she was just beginning to rise and face the new day. Keeping the rising sun at his back, Brosh ventured into the wilderness. He remained alert and cautious—for he had been trained by his "new family" that danger lurked behind every rock and bush. To remain invisible was the goal—to see, but not be seen was an artful practice that must be learned and then honored.

After the sun had rose higher in the trees, Brosh heard a muffled sound—like a baby moaning perhaps. Taking short, careful steps, he noticed a break in the leaves. As he crept closer, loose dirt revealed several dark spots. Drops of blood led to a cherry-stained path.

Looking just beyond the shrubbery, Brosh discerned a bare foot. His eyes traveled up its leg as he parted the branches. Long black hair knotted and grimy fell over the face of what appeared to be a young woman or girl who was curled up into a ball. She had managed to hide in a shaded place between some rock outcroppings. The gruesome sight followed by a fetid breeze knocked him backward as if hit by an invisible barrier. He wrinkled his nose, held his breath, and slowly moved forward again to study the form. Crouching low, he took another tentative step forward and squinted at the twisted, naked form lying motionless. The feet were ringed black and bleeding as were the legs and arms. As he quietly moved around the body, he saw her weathered face partially covered by matted hair. The small body remained deathly still. Was she dead or just sleeping? He leaned forward—did her bony chest rise? As he peered at her mouth, both eyes snapped open!

Brosh jumped back so quickly he forgot his feet and fell backwards onto his ass and hands. The sudden action left him sitting on the dirt trail with eyes wide open. Lickety-split, he scrambled back on to his now working feet as he broke into a frenetic run back to the group's makeshift camp.

Diana describes what happened next.

After listening to Brosh's exhortations, mother and I followed him double-time back to the source of his fright.

The half-dead woman could be heard moaning and crying before we even saw her. As we approached, mother spoke soothingly.

"It's okay now my little one; we are here to help you."

Mother (ignoring the fetid stench of the girl's body) covered her skinny body with a long shirt as she took the wary girl into her arms and placed her on her lap—rocking her and stroking her forehead—erasing smudges of dirt and blood. Her age remained a mystery for a while as her physical state had been compromised to such a degree of degradation we could only guess.

After Mother examined her, Alisia and I gently washed her body from head to toes. Once clean and dressed, she seemed to be mid-twenties or older as she sipped her soup holding her bowl carefully, not spilling a drop. Her age was hard to distinguish, and Alisia secretly pointed out her rib cage that protruded out just above her absent stomach. Her skin seemed to barely cover her bones, so we knew she had been starved.

Eventually, we discovered the source of her shame, her nightmares, her grievous guilt—indelible—haunting—forever.

~~~

Days passed before, the near-dead young woman gained back enough strength to speak. On this day, she drank tea and ate bread, yogurt, and berries. Afterwards, she began to explain what happened as the Armenians arrived at a rectangular trench— the size of a long street but more narrow and about six or more feet deep. The few hundred or so Armenians who survived the march thus far were driven forward into the furrow. The hole already had rotting bodies in it—possibly the Armenians who were forced to dig it. If anyone did not jump into the cavity, they were bayoneted, stabbed, or shot. Swords flashed as loud, angry voices shouted at the crowd of Armenians.

The young woman looked down at the dirt as she shared what happened next. She spoke slowly as she recounted the painful memories. Her words described how the Armenians struggled against being thrown into the pit. Despite their efforts, the Turks stabbed, bayoneted, clubbed and beat them as they were forced toward the edge of the long trench. Soon, hundreds of bodies were savagely thrown in as others were pushed, shoved, and kicked forward. Once down in the hole, the shooting began. Hundreds of women, children, teens, elders were falling and screaming, trying to escape as bullets rained down on them. Bodies writhed and twisted in pain until they collapsed and lay still—one atop of the other. She was knocked down by several flailing bodies that had been shot—her body soon coated in hot blood, she could barely breathe, but before she passed out—the shooting stopped.

Next, amid the moans, she heard a Turkish officer yell down to the bloody bodies. "Okay, enough—you that are still alive have suffered enough! Come climb out, and I swear on all the holy Muslim prophets that you will be allowed to leave unharmed."

She heard more moaning but did not move—soon some Armenians began to climb toward the saving officer's voice. She tried to move as well, but could not budge the many bodies piled on top of her. BANG, BOOM!...the explosions began again and those who tried to climb out were ripped apart by bullets—more screaming, more weight fell down upon her. The screams, the pressure, she could not breathe—darkness set in and she passed out.

When she woke, she could not see, but the fetid stench almost overwhelmed her. Dried blood crusted over her face and eyes…her throat and mouth—dry as sand. Her breath came in shallow gasps as she felt a crushing weight above her. Disoriented at first, she suddenly remembered where she was, and her skin crawled as reality set in— she'd been buried alive—covered with dead bodies! Desiccated—no tears would come.

She continued to tell how she tried to move, but the bodies were too heavy and she too weak from her recent ordeal—no food or water for days. She resigned herself to death's arrival—welcomed it as one would a guarantee of peace and serenity. A reward for one's undying Faith.

At least those were her thoughts as she lie in the throes of despair and death.

⌒⫯⌒

Yet, sometimes life stubbornly refuses to dim its light….Sometimes, we human animals are not granted our wishes. The vicissitudes of life can easily trump our desires, wants, druthers, and sincere pleas for mercy. So be it—so it was….

Suddenly, as the sun moved higher in the sky, a slivered ray of sunlight shined from the heavens and momentarily caught her left eye. How it filtered through all the bodies piled above her, she did not know, but the light delivered hope (like the Armenian Solar Symbol from centuries ago), and in that moment, she grew a bit stronger, managing to slightly move her head, her shoulder, and finally wedge an arm into a moveable position.

Armenian Solar Symbol

Sleep must have worked its therapeutic and restorative magic; strength returned to her arms. Yet, her mind screamed for water, food, air—the bodies were beginning to decay from the inside—putrid olfactory sensory overload—*must get out,* she thought—*but how?*

Moving her head toward the thin ray of light, her lips brushed against the smooth upper arm of what appeared to be a child—its cold skin sent a shiver through her body, but in another part of her, it ignited a flame of self-preservation—tears she could not afford to lose slipped from her eyes as she opened her mouth, chin jutting forward, teeth asking her powerful jaw to do its bidding—she bit down—hard! When she woke, clarity presented itself anew. Her blood rushed through her veins with a renewed vigor; her throat was slacked, and she drew a strong, deep breath as she tested the strength in her legs—all parts seemed functional. She began to climb and tried not to focus on the body parts she stepped on as she crawled little by little toward the light—hours resulted in inches—and as she moved upward the pressure lightened. By

nightfall, she lay drained of energy. Still, any progress sparked hope—
she rested— night fell—she slept.

She repeated her grisly actions the next day... and the next...and the
light grew brighter. Finally, she emerged like Lazarus and did not look
back....

"Sofi — my name is Sofi." She closed her eyes and bowed her head
as she curled up into a fetal position. "I am sorry... so ashamed...."

"Shhhhh.... Shhhhh...." Mother held her...Christ forgave her.

Mother also made her sip water and drink tea until Sofi drifted into
an exhaustive slumber. The group looked at one another in stunned
silence.

Finally, Lusine spoke.... "Only now, do I understand what my
parents were talking about when they said that oft used phrase—God
works in mysterious ways."

Chapter 20

WHO ARE WE? WE ARE OUR PARENTS' HOPE ~

Diana rose at dawn's first light—a sip of water, a wipe of her face with a moist cloth, and a silent prayer offered in memory of her father. She moved quietly about the camp making a small fire to boil water for tea—awakened by the slight movement, her mother soon joined her.

"Mother, why are we not moving more quickly? Shouldn't we try to make it to the coast as soon as possible?"

Mother stared at the fire as she held the steaming tea in both hands close to her lips. "The coast will be there. Remember, danger is afoot—they who run too fast often stumble. We must be sure-footed and vigilant. We are not in a race—another sunrise, another day, a way to survive to tell our story to the world."

"But what will the world do? Isn't it too late? We've lost so much." Her head bowed as her last words trailed off. Regretting her pessimistic words as soon as they left her mouth, Diana turned on her heels and pushed aside the early morning dew-laden branches screening out the morning sun. In a moment, the forest embraced her in its protective arms.

Mother thought to herself.... *Yes, my daughter, we suffer, but we struggle on not just for ourselves. We carry on for the souls who look to us to make their sacrifice be not in vain. We live not for ourselves, but for our next generation...and the ones after.... We will never be defeated because we never lose sight of the power within us. Faith in God, faith in ourselves, and devotion to those who gave of themselves. For these reasons, we can and must move forward. That is who we are...and why we will succeed.*

The aging matriarch looked lovingly at her youngest daughter as Diana returned to add wood to the struggling fire. Isgouhi hummed into her tea nodding her head in solemn thought, and as the morning light warmed her daughter's body, she noticed the girl's figure had changed. Despite the layers of clothing, Mother noticed her daughter's physical maturation. Not only was she taller, stronger, and more coordinated—her body language had changed. She moved like a goddess on earth—fluid, precise, and graceful—no wasted movement. Her transformative physique more womanly—her mind more serious. Just then—at that divinely timed moment, her raised cheekbones and smooth skin captured the golden bright rays of the rising son and painted a blindingly beautiful image of her daughter that Isgouhi would always treasure and remember—a visual moment that would provide this mother everlasting comfort to her grave and beyond.

There are moments parents experience that defy a child's understanding. Moments that remain ineffable and inspirational—ones that peel away all the layers of an imperfect youth only to leave a raw, pure love—a love that reveals a spiritual sense of immortality in a mortal world. A love so strong and resilient—it can only exist in the all-knowing heart...of a parent.

Chapter 21

TOO HARD TO LOVE ~ TO EASY TO HATE

Sofi's recovery continued with each family member offering encouragement embroidered with the miraculous power of love. In a little more than two weeks, she was helping around the camp, foraging for firewood and berries. She told Alisia that she turned 21 years of age just before her family was forced from their home. Sofi knew how to cook, sew, start a fire, heal a wound, nurse a cold, hunt game, and ride horses; she knew how to do many things that were most helpful—<u>and</u>...her advanced schooling helped as well.

That night, Sofi continued to share. Her confessional tone seemed to help her as if she was purging herself of the corrosive poison eating away at her soul.

She spoke slowly and deliberately as she sat by the flickering fire—her face a contoured canvas of marbled firelight and shadows.

"I remember the crying of women and children being driven out of their homes and into the streets—forced to pull wagons filled with axes, hatchets, hoes, swords, machetes, and other weapons of death and dismemberment as well as heavy wagons weighed down with lime. The Turks had a plan; it was <u>not</u> deportation to another village.

I can still hear the primal screams of horror and pain as Turkish police, soldiers, and even the Turkish townspeople preyed upon the helpless victims—showing no mercy, instead—relishing in the act of murdering women and children with a cold-blooded zeal I could not comprehend or even imagine. Such a heinous crime against humanity—I would not have believed it possible had I not seen it with my own eyes.

The bodies were continually hacked at and dismembered by unhinged men and even some women… until sunset… when the townspeople were tired and hungry; reluctantly, they headed back to town. However, before they left, they stripped the bloody bodies of shoes, shirts—all clothing or items worth any value. Only then did the exhausted cutthroats return triumphantly to town. Some of these human butchers unrepentantly wore their blood-stained confiscated items back to town jostling one another as they staggered down the street gleefully celebrating their ill-gotten goods.

Later that night, I hid in the rocks as the hyenas and other scavengers waited restlessly on the edge of the forest for the tired Turks to leave. As darkness set in, the hungry beasts crept forward. Their hideous feast would continue throughout the growling night."

Unknown to Sofi and the others, such night-dwellers followed all the marches, for they had learned that their patience would be rewarded with plenty of meat for their voracious appetites.

Sofi also did not know that there were sympathetic Turks who refused to join in the slaughter. These good souls would later share how the townspeople (mostly young men) would continue on throughout the night bragging about the perverse deeds of torture and death they had inflicted upon the Armenians. Telling others of the great numbers they killed by hand. Pridefully retelling of their deadly deeds and how they had served Allah and insured their place in the afterlife surrounded by beautiful virgins.

As the night wore on, Sofi stopped her telling abruptly; it was as if she hit a wall. Perhaps she did—the human psyche still remains a mystery.

She sat straight up and announced, "That is all I want to say right now." She bowed her head, then turned and stretched out on the ground—her head rested on her bed roll—her eyes searched the stars....

Sofi's mind wondered about those stars whose light traveled millions of miles just to assure her of a place in a world too hard to love and too easy to hate.

Silence settled in as the fire crackled and popped angrily. Just when the mood could not have been more morose, Alisia spoke.

"Let us remember Sofi's story. It will make our arrows fly straight through the black hearts of our enemies."

Mother looked up, "Yes, my child. Vengeance is your right, but remember, hate is too injurious to carry for very long. We must learn to let it go. Let love be our salvation, our saving grace, our spiritual goal." Mother placed her arm over Alisia's shoulder as the others' thoughts remained private—perhaps contradicting the pervasive anger in their hearts.

As Diana stood up to roll out her blanket, a shooting star high-tailed it across the sky and hid behind the towering trees. It reminded her of her childhood. She smiled inwardly.

That night, Diana dreamed of a sky filled with shooting stars, and she was one of them. They lit up the dark sky and offered a guiding light in the darkness. *From now on, whenever I see a shooting star, it will remind me to focus on the light... not the darkness, on hope...not despair.*

Unknown to the Armenians at the time, Turkish leaders employed spies (and sadly...some were Armenian traitors) to identify the most prominent Armenian leaders throughout Armenia and Turkey. Such surreptitious chicanery helped the Turkish police and soldiers find

and arrest the best and brightest of the Armenians. Thus, Armenian politicians, writers, businessmen, craftsmen, priests, artists, teachers, professors, engineers, architects, doctors, lawyers, high-ranking soldiers, government officials, and others were arrested, cajoled, tricked, or forced into captivity. In every case, these Armenian men were slain and their bodies often displayed for ridicule.

One way the Turks did this was public hangings—another...decapitation. The heads were later displayed publicly. Anyone helping or hiding an Armenian was to be sentenced to death.

Despite these threats, there were many good Turks who helped their Armenian neighbors. Some hid the Armenian children and raised them as their own children. These children would later be referred to as the "Hidden Armenians".

Illustration: Nancy Doud-Badrigian

Chapter 22

SEDA'S STREAM OF LIFE ~

About a week later, while Sofi searched for food along a tiny stream, she reflected upon her current state of being: *I feel strong, healthy once again. My mind remains clouded with hate, yet my newly found family holds the heavenly antidote to dispel such negativity. My family now gone... I feel you in my heart...my innermost being; I will live my life in memory of you, may it be long and fruitful.*

Two sharp slaps on water—SMACK! SPLAT! pulled her from her reverie as she quickly moved into a defensive crouch which Alisia had shown her during family practice sessions. Sofi's skin tingled as she turned to her right and hid under the cover of a nearby bush. As she peeked through its branches she spotted the source of the splashing. A small body—face down in the stream—struggling. Sofi stood upright for a moment, surveyed the scene, and then with a mighty move leaped over the bush and sprinted to the child. She grabbed the child's hair and lifted. It was a girl—she grunted when Sofi yanked her head out of the water. Once on the edge of the stream, Sofi inspected the girl's battered body. Her forehead was split open from hairline to mid-forehead. The gash was deep enough to leave a scar, but not deep enough for arterial bleeding. However, plenty of blood had trickled down over her face and chest. Her shirt was soaked in crimson.

After she caught her breath, Sofi asked the girl her name.

"My name is Seda. My family—all dead." She began to shake and cry.

"You are safe now…I will take care of you. Can you walk? Come with me."

The two of them approached the camp with Sofi chirping out the safety signal which was returned by Lusine standing watch. Seda sat down on a rock by the fire as the others circled around her.

Mother looked at Sofi for answers. "I found her by the stream. She is hurt and in need of first-aid. Mother made a simple gesture and Sofi was handed the canvas bag that held some medicines, bandages, and oils.

After some bread and tea, She told Sofi and the others her story in child-like fashion, and Sofi interpreted it as follows.

"She was one of the survivors of the death march like me, and she is only twelve years old. She remembers being knocked unconscious by a vicious blow that hewed a deep cut above her forehead and covered her face and chest in blood. When she awoke, the smart young girl had pretended to be dead and later crawled to safety among a small outcropping of rocks. She wedged herself into a crevasse and hid until nightfall. She witnessed the departing Turks, and later, hesitantly peeked at the descending animals as they began their sickening work. Somehow, she had made her way to a nearby stream, and that is where I found her. I heard her mewling and sobbing—tucked into a fetal position, shivering and almost naked. When I spotted her in the running water, I ran to her. It looked as if she was drowning as she drank the stream's water down in urgent gulps."

Diana adds the following description.

When Sofi brought the girl to our camp, she was mere skin and bones—sunken black eyes peering out from a traumatized face. Eyes that stared blankly as they peered through us and into a realm only victims can see. Her oily hair (much of it gone) matted flat against her face and head. From the neck down, she had been bitten by bugs and had scratched the swollen areas raw leaving an open invitation to more parasites. Her fingernails were black, jagged, broken and bleeding. When Sofi examined the girl, she recognized the look on her face—the desperation—the I-am-ready-to-die look on her face. Still looking at the girl, she pulled a piece of dried fruit from her pouch. She held it up, and lightly tossed it to the girl now sitting on a rock in long grass; it landed at her bare feet. The girl's eyes locked with Sofi's only for a moment, and she quickly reached down and plucked the fruit from the grass. She smelled it briefly and bit into it cautiously. She closed her eyes and began to chew voraciously."

When she met the family, they learned her name was Seda (See-dah). She embodied the spirit of the forest which provided her sanctuary. Seda became the newest member of the growing clan.

The group continued to work on the camp quickly and efficiently while Seda recovered with careful nourishment slowly introduced until she ate normal portions with the rest of us. When she was ready to talk some more, she told the rapt group she had returned to the bodies the next morning looking for her twin sister and her mother only to find them dead and lying beside one another. Their bodies were barely recognizable due to lacerations and fatal puncture wounds. Body parts had been chewed and gnawed off by animals. After viewing her family members, Seda's stomach turned sick; she crawled away—too weak to even walk.

Her withered body wasted away in the woods for a week or longer taking on a cadaverous appearance. In spite of that, Seda knew she needed water. Thus, defying Death's early call, she wormed her way down toward the sound of running water.

That is how Sofi found her—by the gentle stream—the stream of life.

Chapter 23

/|/|

FAMILIES WHO FIGHT TOGETHER ~

Diana describes how regular training saved their lives.

Days, weeks, months of secrecy and disguise led us slowly toward our goal. We knew we were not alone as we found signs revealing other Armenian bands were moving under the radar of those who sought desperately to eliminate all Armenians. Knowing that we were not alone gave us even more hope. Thus, we carried on with our purpose— to survive, to find a new home, to preserve our lineage,

Despite our clandestine existence and harsh living circumstances, our "family" members grew stronger, healthier, and mentally sharper than ever. Yes, we were all damaged products of a fate we did not deserve, but we knew we had to temporarily put aside our grief if we were to survive our journey. We also knew we were only as strong as the one next to us; thus, the loving bond between us became sacred as we swore to protect each other from the dangers that lie ahead.

Often, week after week, we began our day with a family meeting to plan out the day's goals. Some days it was as simple as hunt for food, rest, look for a new camp or practice our survival skills and emergency routines. Each of us had our own skill-set to add to the group's overall efficiency and survival. We were encouraged to help one another learn each other's strengths and to always lift up another's spirit with positive words of hope and trust. We repeatedly drilled and practiced routines for escape, separation, and surprise attacks. Our response times became quicker—our skills sharper—our reactions automatic.

As our skills overlapped, we became stronger, more confident, and much wiser. We practiced for hours because we often could not move safely for certain periods of time. I served as scout, but soon trained the others to sharpen their eyes to a degree akin to another sense—a sixth sense. We proceeded cautiously.

This morning's meeting was to be short as were almost all of our regular meetings, for during this time, we posted no guards due to the meetings' sacred status. Otherwise, we always posted a lookout—a role of the utmost importance to our survival.

Mother began our meeting with a simple question. What do you need? Search your heart and share with us what it is you need the most at this time.

After a long silence, mother looked to her left and as her eyes rested on mine, she nodded, so I began.

"I need to bridle my anger to prevent it from clouding my judgment. I want to be in control of my emotions, so I can control my body."

Alisia continued—"I just want us to find peace at the end of our journey. I need for us to stay together. I love my extended family."

Sofi followed—"I died and was reborn thanks to all of you. My life is now yours, and all I want is to be worthy of your kindness—I need this to repay my debt."

Brosh—"I was lost, but now I am found. My life belongs to each of you." He bowed his head and fell silent. "Yet, I need to find justice; it may be the antidote to my deep anger."

Lusine—"I need to believe my family is in heaven. Diana remains my bright angel, my savior, my sister who baptized me with her own blood. I owe her my life, my devotion."

Seda—"Th...th..thank you...I..." Tears drowned her words as she sobbed into her sleeve. I could see down the wordless avenue of her heart—we all could.

Mother spoke last— "Each of you must realize your purpose in life. Your survival is proof; you are here for a reason. Our Maker has plans for each one of us, and to bring those plans to fruition, we follow the belief that we are His servants—and if He sometimes takes us into troubled waters, we know that our pain is only temporary and God's plan is eternal." The sun filtered through the distant trees and a gentle breeze stirred the smoke from the unattended fire. Mother continued....

"Finally, when you become lonely, remember this—we have no friends here in this country—only family (again her piercing eyes met ours). Lean only on one another, protect one another, for as we go forth to our destinies with our heads held high and our bodies ready to fight for our right to life, we shall overcome all obstacles!"

As if on cue, our heads turned without delay to the the ground-breaking sounds of hoofbeats coming over the ridge. With the rising sun at their backs, five Chetes on horseback suddenly stopped their horses at the top of the ridge. Mother's inspiring edict suddenly rang true—her timing beyond compare—enemies were upon us!

When the motley crew of men spied our small circle, they were also surprised, but only for a moment—just long enough to realize the small band below must be more Armenian runaways and easy targets to be exploited. Loosening their reins, they leaned toward our campsite as knees gripped saddles tightly urging the small, stocky horses forward as sharp heels dug into firm horse flanks. Screaming in delight, they headed down the hill and traversed the terrain in what seemed less than a minute.

Little did they know those precious seconds were all the time this atypical family needed....

Diana continues her eyewitness account of the following bloody encounter.

Unbeknownst to these raiders (used to killing helpless Armenian women and children), our small brood regularly practiced such a scenario, for we knew the possibility of attack was not an "if" but a "when".

Out of the corner of my eye, I caught a glimpse of Brosh scurrying toward our bows and quivers which were always on the ready and nearby. My bow (leaning against a rock behind me) jumped into my hand as I slung its quiver of arrows over my shoulder. Each of us carried a hunting knife in our belt for protection from wild animals such as wolves, hyenas, mountain lions and worse—which we now faced in the bright clear air of morning with dew still on the ground and tea brewing on the fire.

Mother's strong arm was around Seda's shoulders as they scrambled behind some bushes with Lusine protectively close behind. Eyes wide and alert—their right hands already moving to their belted sheaths.

Alisia caught my eye, and pointed to the Chete on the left and quickly indexed her own chest. Our hours of drilling and practice made our motions automatic as I returned Alisia's gesture—automatically signaling the screaming Chete on the right as my target.

My hands shook for a moment, but once my favorite arrow was notched in its place, an eery calm washed over me. I looked straight into the eyes of this bearded man (less than ten yards from me and closing fast). Upon his face a painted picture of excited delight—a young helpless girl before him unable to ward off his evil advances. *Not this time!* I thought to myself as I waited for the right moment, bow ready...arrow aimed at his heart.

As soon as the taught string sprang off my lip, the righteous arrow left its beloved bow with a twang that sent a shiver up my spine.

On the receiving end, the doubting Chete's murderous smile turned to disbelief just a split-second before my arrow pierced his upper left chest with a sickening thud. I had aimed for the center of his chest to insure my best chance of a solid hit as man and horse bounced erratically in front of me.

To avoid the barrel-chested horse (now in a panic as its master tumbled over its right side—right foot trapped in the stirrup), my leg muscles kicked into action. As I dived left, I caught a glimpse of fear spread over my target's face—arrow deeply embedded in his heart. I rolled once and landed firmly on my feet in a crouch with one knee lightly touching the ground as the string of my bow quickly found the nock of another arrow.

Alisia's arrow had flown higher than mine; it caught her culprit in the throat and tore all the way through the frayed sinews with a pulsing red spray shooting from where the feathers of her arrow sliced like a needle sewing together a wound—conversely, rather than stitching together, this needle opened the skin to let loose the foul blood of its owner.

The other three Chetes' momentum carried them into the fray as the first two riderless horses careened into them. The third Chete managed to pull up his horse and aim his rifle. As he braced his rifle, he fired a shot at me, but the bullet flew wide and ricocheted off a boulder to my right. Arrow at the ready, I took a stance against a well-rooted tree to steady myself, and as soon as the tight string kissed my upper lip, I released it in the direction of my attacker. Once again, my arrow found its moving target. As it pierced the Chete's shoulder, he shuddered for a moment, but then reached up and snapped the arrow angrily as he glared at me. Suddenly, Lusine burst from the bushes and sank her knife deep into the man's leg. The horse, spooked by Lusine's sudden appearance, turned suddenly and broadsided the young girl. She tried to break her fall by rolling forward but stumbled over the rocks by the fire landing hard on her back.

A loud bellow sounded from the wounded man as he pulled back hard on the reins to try and regain his balance and control, but as he did, man and horse reared backwards with the Chete falling to the ground on his back. Lusine jumped to her feet, but stumbled to the ground not ten feet from the wounded attacker.

The Chete twisted sideways trying to assume an upright position as he struggled to get to his feet. A knife appeared in his hand as he stepped toward Lusine. Before I could find another arrow, mother appeared and sank her bright blade into the back of the Chete's neck. He fell forward in a writhing heap grasping at his neck.

Surprised, shocked, and unsure of the changing situation, the fourth Chete violently pulled on his horse's reins in an effort to turn around and aim his rifle. However, when he found himself looking at Alisia already in a formal standing position and ready to let loose another lethal arrow, he lost his courage and turned tail to make a run for the woods.

Now, my arrow was also cocked and ready, and with twin-sister timing, we both unloosed our messengers of death. Both arrows hit their target. In response to the surprised invasion, the rider's body jerked backward twisting violently in the air and descended awkwardly to the earth. The twice-pierced rider landed on his head and shoulder. After coming to rest, his body lie still—frozen in death's cold embrace.

Suddenly, out of the corner of my eye, I noticed movement heading toward Alisia. The last Chete pulled his sword from his belt; the frightening, yet familiar, scimitar sword used by many Chetes to decapitate and amputate women and babies screaming for mercy. Lacking the time to pull another arrow, I screamed a warning at my sister who was also unarmed for the moment of impact. Alisia pirouetted skillfully, but the

Chete's horse brushed her aside, and as she spun out of control; her body landed abruptly and inelegantly on to our small woodpile.

The Chete's arm moved threateningly high overhead as he lifted himself out of the saddle ready to deliver a deadly blow on Alisia's fallen body—shhwisshhh! An arrow out of nowhere struck him under his arm and rendered his blow askew. He lost his stirrups, his balance, and his breath when he hit the ground. He struggled awkwardly to his feet, and with labored breathing, moved desperately toward his scimitar sword partially covered with leaves and dirt on the ground beside him.

I positioned another arrow, but before I could take proper aim, a figure leaped out of the bushes and onto the man's back as he struggled to stand upright. A blurred flurry of stabbing from this new assailant punctured the back of the villain's neck as he stumbled forward a couple of steps before falling face-first onto the useless sword. Rivulets of blood ran slowly down the Chete's outstretched arm and onto his out-of-reach sword—only stopping when they reached the dirty handle.

Standing up slowly, still astride the now still body, covered in purple-red blood and breathing recklessly—stood Sofi. Her tears mixed with the ruddy rivulets running down her cheek and sparkling in the sun like the morning dew earlier.

Brosh strode forward and turned over the Chete and pulled the familiar hand-made red and white feathered arrow from the murderer's body. For a moment, we just stared down at the broken body.

Suddenly, Alisia ran forward and crying passionately embraced her little brother, "Thank you Brosh, thank you for my life!" She smothered him with kisses knocking them both embarrassingly to the ground.

Brosh's measure had been taken—a young man, a gentle soul, a warrior when he needed to be. He pointed to Alisia's leg which had been punctured by a sharp piece of wood when the riderless horse charged into her and sent her flying. In all the excitement, she hadn't even felt it.

However, when I looked at the wound, a red fleshy orifice bleeding steadily, my eyes warily followed its stream down her leg. A black reddish pool formed around Alisia's foot. My stomach flipped over as I rushed to her side.

"Down, lay her down! Elevate her leg! Quickly!" Everyone now moving together—mother held Alisia's head in her lap as Sofi applied direct pressure using her scarf.

"Sofi, what should we do?" Sofi's medical knowledge helped us many times in the past; still, this wound looked intimidating even to her. She paused, thought...looked at the fire and pulled out her knife. She looked directly at me and in a calm, clear voice, made her decision known. "Diana, take my knife and place the blade in the fire until it is red hot."

I understood immediately, but tried desperately to think of another way. I knocked the tea kettle off its hook as I slid the blade into the red hot coals. More wood for the fire to add heat, and I knew it would be ready in minutes.

Mother talked softly into Alisia's ear and held her head. Lusine offered a small, green branch from a nearby tree and told Alisia to bite down on it. In a few minutes, I brought the glowing, red-tipped knife to Sofi.

Sofi looked at the others, "Hold her tight! I need her to be completely still." We took our positions—hands squeezing tightly around Alisia's appendages. I watched as she slid the knife deep into the puncture wound cauterizing the now sizzling arteries with a series of light pressure and well-timed touches. Acrid smoke from the burning flesh violated our olfactory senses, but we held on fiercely—our fingertips pressed deep into our sister's soft, smooth flesh as Alisia's screams pierced our ears and made our skin crawl. Finally, the last pressure was applied melting capillaries together. Sofi carefully pulled out the blackened blade and checked the bleeding; it had stopped.

Alisia's reverberating screams had scared the birds away and seared my own heart as her pain became mine. Alisia's shirt dripped with sweat and tears as she buried her face into our mother's breasts. Soon, Sofi was applying alcohol—dabbing gently at the hole and all around it. By the concerned look on Sofi's face, I knew Alisia's fate still hung in the balance.

Chapter 24

WHAT WAS STOLEN ~ SHALL BE RETURNED

Diana describes how the family's fortune suddenly changes.

Our small band slowly came together as the forest grew quiet once again, and the tiny birds began to return. We surveyed the bloody battleground that was once our peaceful camp. Still in shock, we hugged one another—touching, feeling, checking each other for wounds.

Sofi sat by Alisia with her small canvas bag and continued to apply antiseptics and medicine for Alisia's wound. She watched my sister closely and told me to check her forehead repeatedly during the next twenty-four hours. A sudden increase in temperature would signal an infection that could prove to be fatal without the proper medical supplies. We were all thankful for Sofi and Mother's nursing skills, and for their foresight— had they not made it a priority early on to collect and purchase simple medicines, disease and sickness would have visited us more often and stayed much longer.

Meanwhile, Brosh collected the horses from afar as the others searched the dead bodies. One Chete had been dragged half a mile— twisted foot still stuck in the stirrup and inert body attached to the exhausted animal. After disengaging the dead soldier from the horse, Brosh used a rope and looped one end around the two feet of the stiffening body and the other end to the horn of the saddle. Brosh spoke soothingly into the horse's ear as they dragged the body back to camp.

As we cleaned the area and tried to hide signs of a skirmish, Lusine bent over the leader's body and while rifling through his belongings, she found a small, yet heavily-laden cloth bag. She untied the rawhide string and opened the bag. Unexpectedly, we heard her gasp and sit back on her haunches in amazement.

"Come!" she yelled. "Come quickly!"

When we circled around her, she slowly opened the bag and dramatically dumped its contents onto the bare earth— gold! Gold coins— handfuls! More gold than any of us had ever seen! We rejoiced knowing this meant we could purchase essential items we needed such as medicine, essential items, clothing, and yes—food.

"Stolen Armenian gold back in the hands of Armenians—thank you Jesus, Mary, and Joseph—God has smiled down upon us! He rewards all of us for our courage in the face of adversity!" Mother followed her words with a blessing as she looked skyward. The rest of us allowed the bright yellow coins to slip slowly through our fingers as we felt their weight and texture, smelled their imagined rich scent, and even tasted the bright coins in celebratory delight as we laughed at our own silliness.

After a bit, Mother brought us back to our senses. "There remains work to do, bodies to move, evidence to hide. Let us proceed; there may be other murderers nearby."

We did as we were asked, yet I could not stop imagining what the gold meant to us. I thought about where we began and how far we had come. An Armenian saying came to me from the recesses of my brain.

A river cuts through rock not by using its power; rather, it cuts through the hardest rock by using its persistence.

Our family worked efficiently and cooperatively as we dragged the bodies to a common site.

Mother bowed her head and whispered, "Lord above, thank you for having opened our eyes and for letting us see our glorious future. We thank you for our fortune and for our health, strength, keen minds, and ability to forgive as we forgive these here we lay before You—have mercy on their souls. Amen."

God, however, remained silent.

Chapter 25

PURITY OF HEART ~
CLARITY OF MIND

Sofi and Lusine covered the bodies with leaves and branches, and Brosh found a grazing spot for the horses and watched over them—a responsible shepherd. It was decided to sell the horses at the next village for they would need feeding and be difficult to hide quickly in an emergency. However, Diana suggested the family might keep one horse for a while longer, for Alisia needed to rest her leg to allow the wound to close and heal properly. Mother suggested the family move to a safer place, so plans were made to leave the desecrated camp as soon as possible. The family still needed provisions besides the ones they were able to salvage from the dead Chetes. Regardless, the group did strip them of knives, swords, rifles, leather bags, and other items they could use, sell, or trade.

The horses increased the family's pace and soon several miles were covered as the sun began to sink slowly into the distant western hills.

That night, the family prayed to God to forgive their sins and to ask for His help to heal Alisia. They prayed to Mother Mary and her blessed Son, Jesus Christ. Before dark, Diana walked to the small opening where grass and wild weeds grew. Brosh was there overseeing the horses while they grazed.

"You would have made a fine shepherd because of your caring soul and watchful eyes."

The young man smiled shyly when he heard his sister's compliment. "My heart feels what my brain can't understand when it comes to horses; I am even more amazed by what they allow us to do to them. My mother told me God made horses from the breath of the wind, the richness of the earth, and the spirit of a guardian angel. I wish we could keep them; I would be at peace serving as their shepherd."

Diana smiled and sat down beside the young man.

"My father once told me that being a shepherd was a noble act. He explained that on a symbolic level God is our Shepherd, and we…his sheep. He then taught me about the dangers of twisted religious interpretations. For example, do you know what a shepherd carries with him when he tends his sheep? Yes, of course, he carries a rod. This rod is in the shape of a long pole with a hook at the end of it that looks a bit like a question mark. Yes, I knew you would be familiar with it. Well, father said that at one point in the Bible it says, 'Spare the rod, and you spoil the child.' He explained how some Christians interpreted this saying to mean a parent must beat his child if he does wrong; otherwise, the child will become spoiled. Having said that, Father shed light on a different interpretation.

Many of us Christians see the quote in a more compassionate and tolerant light. Think for a moment about the rod used by the watchful shepherd. Does the shepherd use the rod to beat his sheep who stray from the path, or does he use the rod to guide the stray back to the flock? Also, the end of the rod with the half loop—like a question mark— what is its use? Is it used to punish the sheep who goes awry, or is it used to tuck under the sheep's chin to rescue it from danger by pulling it out of a crevasse by the neck and head?

Father told me to remember one final thought—Religions are only as righteous as the people who interpret their basic tenets with purity of heart and clarity of mind." So be it then…so be it now.

Brosh stood up and stretched. As he did, he leaned over and kissed Diana's cheek. "Your father taught you well. Now (he smiled), he teaches me as well."

Diana and Brosh walked back toward camp as the last light gave way to night.

He's smart, kind, and handsome; yet he remains a mystery to me—yes, a precious presence in my life. Diana slept better than she had in a long time.

Chapter 26

WORDLESS AVENUES OF THE HEART ~

April 18, 1915—Alisia's body temperature continued to rise; a dry mouth, constant sweating, and red eyes followed. Sofi scrutinized her carefully as she administered soup, water, tea, and whatever food Alisia's fevered body could keep down. She sipped the tea that her mother sweetened with honey, and smiled weakly before closing her eyes.

Off in the distance, Brosh spied dark vultures riding the updrafts of a southernly wind not far from the family's previous camp. *The vultures are cleaning the bones we left behind*, he thought. *They will leave no trace of what happened there.* He turned his back to the rising sun and continued to hunt for food for the family.

Diana recalls her thoughts as she shares the following scene.

"Some see with their eyes, others with their hearts—I dreamed of a new life where fear no longer visited my heart nor stole my peace.

True freedom—is freedom from fear.

Cloudy skies but no rain this month. The dry weather limited game and challenged our best hunting efforts. Brosh seemed to be the most successful—bringing back a rabbit or a squirrel—even an occasional snake.

We ate a breakfast of unleavened bread, a bit of cheese, and water. Our camp included a fire pit, a shaded area where one could meditate, pray, or take a nap on a clean, hand-woven carpet, and a tented area for shelter. The weather permitted light clothing during the day and another layer at night. The stars blinked out beautiful stories of hope as the moon moved gracefully across the horizon. An occasional night Lark skittered across the knighted filigree accompanied by a few hungry bats sporadically devouring their weight in bugs every few hours. The next night, Alisia's fever broke. She remained weak as a baby, but her improved color revealed her growing strength. Our prayers had been heard.

Sitting around a small fire after dinner, mother told us of something else she heard in one of the villages. First, she produced a map of the area she had purchased from an old woman in a curio shop. The map was well-worn and repeatedly folded, so it had faded some, but it clearly showed an area from Yerevan to Musa Dagh on the shores of the Mediterranean Sea. She pointed to the areas in question that aligned with the story she heard."

Isgouhi pointed to a town named Urfa. "Twenty years ago, 3500 Armenians were massacred at the Great Gregorian Church at Urfa—1500 of them slaughtered in the Church where they had taken refuge. It remains dangerous for us. The area is also near the Der Zor Desert where many Armenians are forced to walk only to die painful, torturous deaths. We must be most vigilant as we near these areas." All agreed.

Chapter 27

SOMEWHERE ~ FAR FROM HERE

As the days turned into weeks, Alisia's strength returned. The wound on her leg healed unevenly—leaving behind an indented and discolored scar—a noble battle scar reminder for the rest of her life.

Meanwhile, members of the group became most adept at disguising themselves. Such artifice became one of their strongest chameleon-like powers. Often, two or three would enter a village or town under one pretense or another. Using subterfuge, different accents, dress, and ingenuity, they were able to secure items of necessity. Without tarrying, they would return to the forest—their most safe and secure haven.

Mother and Lusine entered the next village. They were dressed simply as mother and daughter meeting Turkish relatives in town. After surveying the town's layout, they stopped at a market to purchase fruit and Isgouhi thought she heard an elderly woman speaking Armenian to a similar elderly women. The woman's fruit stand seemed inviting, so Isgouhi and Lusine stopped; Isgouhi bought several pieces, and she and Lusine sat down to eat some of their fruit and listened.

One women, slightly older than the others, pushed her greying hair behind her ears, blinked her eyes rapidly and looked closely at Isgouhi. Mother lowered her scarf and walked up to the woman; Armenian eyes met and Isgouhi spoke, "Bari luys" (thank you) she whispered in Armenian. The old woman smiled knowingly and placed her index finger upon her lips. She made a simple gesture, and we sat down.

"My name is Yana and this is my sister Karina. We do not speak Armenian when others are near, but my intuition told me you were Armenian, so I took a chance. Where are you headed?"

Isgouhi shared a bit of the family's past as the old ladies nodded sympathetically. "Thank God you don't look like what you've been through. We also suffered the horrors you speak of, but we are protected here as long as we stay quiet." The grey-haired woman looked both ways and then began her tale. "After the males were taken from our village, the girls and women were next. Fortunately, we grew up wth Turkish friends who saved us by hiding us in their home. They took us in seventy carriages, and we traveled about an hour and a half. We stopped by a bridge. When we looked behind us, there were a mob of Turks following us. We were herded to an area under the bridge where the police and soldiers joined the mob in our slaughter. These were defenseless women, girls, babies—cut down with bill-hooked knives, swords, hatchets, shovels, pitchforks, and axes. I fell off to the side and watched as arms, legs, ears, noses, were hacked off by the bloodthirsty mob. Fingers and hands and arms were cleaved off while trying to ward off the deadly blows. They ripped babies from their mothers and dashed their heads against the rocks as the mothers screamed for their children. All the while, the Turks screamed even louder, 'Allah, Allah!' "

The old ladies adjusted the fruit laden baskets as the one continued.

"The men became drunk with perverse power over the young women and girls, and forced them to do unspeakable acts. Sword handles were stuck deep in the ground leaving the sharp blades pointing upward. The Armenian women and girls were told to sit on the swords or the swords would be shoved up into them. The poor girls were forced to perform this sadistic feat as the men laughed and cheered. Many of the girls collapsed on the pointed blades and were fatally pierced while others refused and were tortured without mercy. We watched horror-stricken as the barbarity continued. We wanted to scream and inter-cede, but there was nothing we could do. Our friends tried to turn us away from the abomination outside; we wept in each other's arms but still we looked. We heard one of the Turks yell, 'So, you want to be like your Jesus Christ! Well then— you can die like the Jewish dog died— crucified! Strip these girls! Nail them to their crosses! Do it now!

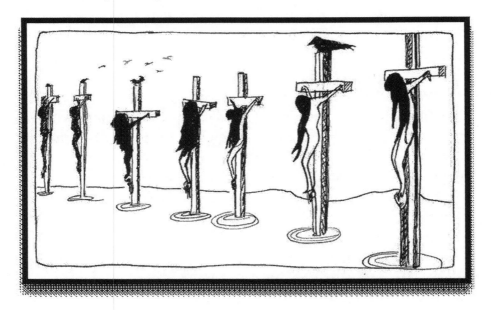

Author's note: *The above illustration is a creative interpretation of the above description by artist Nancy Doud-Badrigian.*

The story of the crucified girls is from a first-hand account from one of the Armenian survivors of the Genocide.

With unquenchable vileness, the men seized seven girls, teenagers or younger, and nailed them to huge wooden crosses—Christ-like. Their abused, bare bodies, white as snow, were spread and nailed to roughly hewn crosses. The girls' hands were spread east and west and feet overlapped as long spikes were hammered through flesh and bone...heads bowed—dying a slow death. The crosses were then raised up and sunk into deeply dug holes which were quickly filled in with dirt. The girls' long black hair blew softly in the wind momentarily covering their budding breasts and blackened eyes. The horrific moment burned through my eyes and into my brain. The last thing I remember before turning away were the crows that began to land on the crosses."

The old lady closed her eyes for a moment. When she opened them, she stared at Isgouhi. "Keep your children as safe as you can, but know this—we Armenians left are now God's witnesses."

Isgouhi touched Lusine on her shoulder; it was time to go. Mother walked over to the women and dropped a few coins into one of the baskets.

The old lady took the satchel from Lusine and filled it with more fruit.

Lusine smiled and one of the old ladies smiled back.

Mother was already walking away, for they had miles to go before they would sleep...miles to go before they were safe. As they walked out of town, Lusine peeked at Mother's face—the blood had drained out of her complexion, and her hands twisted in on one another. Lusine knew that Mother was imagining her own daughters on those crosses; she softly placed her hand over Mother's.

As the afternoon grew cool encouraged by a bracing breeze, Mother and Alisia returned to the new camp with much needed provisions. That night, the family listened to Lusine retell the haunting stories told by the old ladies. When she finished, Mother continued....

"I heard many things in the village," said Mother at the next family meeting. "No one knows for sure, but Armenian survivors are saying that entire Armenian cities have been wiped out. They tell a similar story where Turkish gendarmes, police, soldiers come and force people to move out with little notice or preparation. Next, these uprooted Armenians are told they are being deported to a safer city where they will meet up with their husbands and sons. However, it is all a cruel ruse. Once the Armenian population is marched out of town or crowded into cattle cars on trains, the real purpose behind the deportation is learned—merciless mayhem, torture, rape, murder, execution!"

Mother shook her head as Diana and Alisia tried to console her. The sad news settled in like a dark cloud over the small family, and they knew what they had feared had come true—they had no home to return to and must carry on to make new lives somewhere else— somewhere safe, somewhere new, somewhere...far away from here.

Chapter 28

IN THE FOREST ~ IN THE NIGHT ~ AN OZANIAN LION ROAMS

As the family sat around the crackling fire, the orange sun slowly set behind them. Mother spoke softly. "There roams a lion in the forests of ancient Armenia. No Turk can track this king of beasts for he changes forms in the wind and moves through the trees like fog-laden mist. His human form has a name, and that name is General Andranik Ozanian ** . He leads a brave group of Armenian Freedom Fighters against unfair odds. Still, these free spirits fight the good fight for all our ancestors. They show no fear, they know no home, they live to protect the unprotected and provoke the interlopers.

"Where is he mother? Is he real? Are the Turks going to kill him?

"No one knows where he will be from one day to the next. His reality dwells in surprise and mystery. One cannot kill what one cannot see. However, I see the hope he brings to the remaining Armenians. Hope and our Faith—two of our strongest arrows in a quiver filled with possibilities."

Diana poked the fire angrily with a stick. "Why does God answer some of our prayers and not others? He healed Alisia, but he let our father be killed."

Mother sat across from the fire from Diana and the others, and when she spoke, her words cut through the smoke like lightning through the darkest clouds. "God <u>always</u> answers our prayers—but sometimes, in His infinite wisdom…the answer is <u>no</u>."

The silence was deafening as yellow/orange flames licked away the darkness. Mother looked at her daughters and continued, "Words are only fragile cobwebs not always capable of capturing one's innermost feelings. Fortunately, there are wordless avenues of the heart where one can communicate with grace and understanding when one believes in another—as I believe in each of you."

Mother's eyes glistened as she looked at each member of her extended family before bowing her head. The greying streaks of hair glistened silver and black—more silver now, less black.

**Author's note: Andranik Ozanian led one of the first Armenian Volunteer Battalions of Fedayi (irregular soldiers) and heroically battled the Ottoman Army. He stood up to the Young Turks and the Ottoman Empire and defended many Armenian cities with only a small battalion of loyal Armenian volunteers. Despite being vastly outnumbered, his Freedom Fighters continued to protect the Armenian people. He became known as The Braveheart of the Caucasus.

He lived the last years of his life in Fresno, CA.**

Author's note: *More information on Andranik and his long fight against injustice toward Armenians may be found online.*

Chapter 29

MEETING TWO LIONS
~ AND A SON ~

April 22, 1915—The family's progress toward the Mediterranean Coast slowed considerably as the territory became more hostile. Despite this, the family members had to acquire food, scout the area surrounding their camp, and garner certain dwindling supplies. On one of these explorations, Brosh, Lusine, and Seda accompanied Diana while Sofi and Alisia stayed behind with Mother to protect their well-camouflaged camp and tend to their daily chores.

Seda was still young, but at thirteen, she wanted to learn more skills, so the small cluster allowed her to follow. Her job was to protect the group's rear exposure—look forward but also behind.

Once again, Diana shares her perspective while the group forges ahead.

"On this afternoon, we trekked east by southeast and saw little game. When we were about ready to turn around, we saw a flock of birds suddenly take flight from beyond an opening in a glade bordered by rock outcroppings. Following the rock line, we carefully crept forward until we heard shouting and fierce snarling sounds. We sprinted toward the source of the uproar. Twenty yards from us, a young man who looked to be in his twenties tried to lift his bloody leg out of the reach of an angry mountain lion that seemed determined to tear him asunder. The lion's head shook as he ferociously displayed long bright-white fangs dripping with saliva that sprayed the surrounding brush when he roared frothily in vexed frustration.

The man bravely held off the lion with a bone-handle dagger and loud desperate shouts, but the lion's claws repeatedly raked at the ground near the man's leg which extended slightly beyond the crevasse that offered protection. Again, the lion clawed at the man's leg trying to find the best angle to sink in his prominent fangs. The young man wedged himself deeper between the two rocks as he fiercely gestured his knife toward the animal. His fist appeared bloody as he protected himself from the probing claws.

It did not look promising for the trapped man, so I nodded to Brosh who stepped forward and leaned the long untested rifle on a rock as he took careful aim at the beast. As the loud shot rang out, Brosh was knocked backward from the unexpected recoil. The bullet struck a boulder wide of its target, but the resounding explosion of gunpowder reverberated loudly, and with the combination of the careening bullet ricocheting off the rocks and the unexpected fiery explosion from the flintlock rifle, the lion pulled back—quickly crouching into a defensive stance; instinctively, he recoiled back on his haunches and scanned the area for the source of the explosion.

At that moment, I jumped up and started shouting and waving my arms as I ran toward the surprised figures—both lion and its victim. Lusine, and Seda were close behind, and Brosh jumped to his feet and joined the wild fray.

Reluctantly, the tawny beast slowly retreated until he disappeared into the woods. His disgruntled growling form could still be heard as he made his slow-moving exit.

As we approached the young man, my arrow and bow remained at the ready (for who knew which animal was more dangerous to us). I looked carefully at his aquiline profile, olive skin, and clear eyes—*he is an Armenian! I am sure of it.*"

⌒⑅⌒

Diana approached the young man warily. She noted, surprisingly, that he was not malnourished; rather, he appeared healthy, lean, wiry, and his muscles rippled through his torn clothing. When he finally stood with one hand on the nearby rock, Diana was surprised at his height, for he stood a head above her despite her own tall stature.

Surprised by these four young figures who appeared out of nowhere, he stared in wonder. After scrutinizing the four youths, he spoke.

"Who are you that roam the forests as if you own it?"

"We are like you—Armenian survivors." Diana took a step closer as the others stood behind her.

Diana looked him over and relates what happened next.

Lusine produced a satchel and brought out bandages to stop the bleeding. His name was Aram, and he belonged to a group of Freedom Fighters. He stated his camp was about two miles away. Assessing his wounds, I thought it best if we accompany him. Aram tried to walk on his bloody leg, but it began to cramp and caused him pain, so I offered my shoulder for him to lean on as a crutch.

His grip was strong, but his hands were gentle. He smiled at me as he thanked me for my kindness. My whole body flushed with a warm sensation. His body felt good against mine, the warmth spread between us—he stumbled, I caught him and lifted him up as our bodies met chest-to-chest in an awkward hug. I heard the others softly giggling at my awkward embrace, but as I looked up into his eyes; they were kind, searching, inquisitive—I quickly looked straight ahead as I slowly pushed him away.

With him once again braced on my shoulder, we moved forward. What _are_ these puzzling feelings? I tried to concentrate on the directions he provided, and only answered a few of his questions as we walked.

"Do you often confront angry lions by screaming and running at them like a wild-woman out of her mind?"

"Maybe wild animals only fear other wild animals. It seemed to me your strategy only made the beast more hungry for your blood. Do you often provoke such dangerous adversaries during your nature walks?"

Aram raised his eyebrows. Who was this young woman who seemed so confident and comfortable verbally jousting with him right after she saved his life? He longed to learn more about her, but she ignored most of his questions and focused on his directions to the nearby camp.

Seda carried a leather bag that belonged to Aram, and Lusine carried the long spear that he had dropped in his struggles.

In a flash, two well-armed men appeared suddenly from behind some trees. I stepped back and held up a closed fist. My brother and sisters stopped in their tracks as they read my body language. Their hands readied their weapons. Brosh had already loaded his flintlock rifle, so he pointed it toward one of the men. All was quiet for a moment.

Aram quickly held out his hands as he stepped between us and ended the standoff. He began to shout commands to the men. "Stand down! These are our friends, our lost family. They rescued me —saved my life. We are honored by their presence."

The tone changed as the men smiled nodding their heads. "They are Hye." I heard one whisper. We were escorted into the camp—not as invaders, but as heroes.

As we entered the center of the camp, many eyes were upon us. Some belonged to well camouflaged sentries posted at the outskirts. Others stood outside a small shelter. In a few moments, an older man with salt and pepper hair thick upon his head stepped out of a make-shift tent. Aram limped over to the man, and kissed him on the cheek. The greybeard surveyed the situation as he listened to Aram who bent down a bit to whisper in his ear. The older man nodded his head approvingly and hugged his son warmly noticing his wounds that had been tended to with proper care and skill.

He stepped forward and turned toward Diana. "I thank you for saving my son's life. I am in your debt. These men you see around you are friends and family who freely join me in fighting for our freedom and defending the remaining Armenians; we fight for our dead family members, and we fight for all Armenians seeking life and liberty. My name is Andranik Ozanian. Who are you?"

Diana took a step forward (Brosh, Lusine, and Seda looked on... taken aback by the announcement). At first, she was speechless; *were they truly in the presence of the legendary "Lion of the Forest"?* The four were in awe; the rumors were true.

Diana moved a strand of hair from the corner of her mouth, "My name is Diana, and we are Armenians as well. We also seek life and liberty. My mother told us of you and your men, but we thought... I thought... you were a myth."

Andranik laughed loud and deep as his entire body shook. Then his face grew serious. "Perhaps, it is as it should be; it will be harder for the Turks to kill a myth."

Diana describes the rest of the encounter....

As time passed, we were given meat and rice, tea, yogurt, and bread. "We have heard of your presence. 'Archers of Death' they call you youngsters, and tell tall tales of how you fight for freedom, but we were not sure. Now, we rejoice in your actual presence. May your future bring you what your heart desires."

The old Lion smiled and continued, "We also fight for our heritage. We owe that to our ancestors. Others join us almost daily—the survivors. We train them, build them into warriors ready and able to fight back against those who wish us harm, and when they are nourished and skilled, they become one of us. You are welcome to join us if you wish."

I told him of our experiences and our plans and respectfully rejected his generous offer. He listened quietly and added, "Your youthful courage honors all Armenians—especially your father. Your deeds will continue to make him proud, and he will guide your footsteps from above. My wish is that we meet again in happier times."

I stepped toward him to shake his hand, but as he stood, he ignored my hand and hugged me like my father—a big, bold, hearty hug that enthusiastically squeezed the remaining breath out of my lungs.

As my lungs filled once again, I spoke, "Regretfully, we must leave. Our family will be worried for us. If we go now, we can make it back to our camp by nightfall."

"I understand. We will provide an escort for you to insure your safety. Is there anything you need?"

I shook my head no, but Brosh spoke up. "We only have a few balls left for this rifle, and the gunpowder is almost gone as well. Do you have any?"

Andranik smiled at the young boy. "My men will give you powder and balls as a small gift. However, let me see your rifle." General Ozanian flipped the rifle easily as he inspected it from front to back. "As I thought, look here…he pointed to a point above the trigger—your flint is almost gone and the smooth barrel needs to be cleaned. Do you get tired of carrying this heavy old rifle?

Brosh shyly nodded.

I thought so. Here, take my pistol instead. The Old Lion set the rifle aside carefully and stood up as he pulled a shiny horse pistol with a wooden grip from his belt. Brosh's eyes grew wide. "Oh, no sir—that's your pistol; you may need it in battle."

"Yes, it is handy in battle, and that is why I want you to have it. It will be easier to handle for someone your size and much easier to use in battle. You can move like the Praying Mantis; I can tell." As if to demonstrate his point, Andranik tossed the pistol up into the air in front of him and easily caught the barrel end. He offered the handle-grip to the mesmerized boy.

Brosh blushed proudly, shuffled his feet a bit... and with a slight bow—he accepted the prized pistol.

Brosh thanked the general as he grasped the horse pistol and marveled at its artistic craftsmanship. One of the Freedom Fighters stepped forward and began showing Brosh how to load the pistol.

Andranik turned his attention back to Diana.

He stepped toward the young woman, placed a heavy hand on her shoulder and spoke softly into her ear.... "Remember Diana—the Almighty seeks justice through you; I remain in your debt. Someday, I hope our paths will cross again, so I can repay you for your courage and goodwill in bringing my son back to me. The Old Lion placed his other hand on her remaining shoulder. He lifted his head hand and looked deeply into her eyes and soul. What he glimpsed made his heart soar—an Armenian princess! The Old Lion stepped back and loudly voiced his heart-felt announcement. "Here within our humble camp walks an Armenian princess! May she and her friends be blessed by the God who watches over us all, and may she continue to be a protector of our people." The camp exploded with shouts of joy and acclaim as the small family were slapped on their backs, hugged, and jostled with affection.

"Sir, you are most kind. We are not used to such accolades, but gladly accept your blessing. Please know that our small band is trying to reach Aleppo with our lives. From there, the Mediterranean Sea, and hopefully, we will gain passage on a boat to a friendly country where we may live in peace."

"You are wise beyond your years, my dear one. If I were young, I might even join you—but I am old now, and my blood is destined to be spilled here where my ancestors were born and died."

Diana bowed in respect to the Old Lion, and turned to go. Aram stood in her way and spoke, "I would be honored to go with you to your camp to insure safe passage."

Diana smiled and nodded her head.

Aram gestured to his right and Diana led the way. Soon they were walking side-by-side. The two of them were followed by Lusine who matched their long strides. Aram's cramp abated and his leg had stopped bleeding; he quickened his pace bent on hearing every word Diana uttered.

"As I said, we are trying to make it to Aleppo where we will find passage to another country—perhaps America. I heard America is a young country welcoming immigrants from all over the world. My family dreams of a land of peace and freedom."

"You would leave your homeland for a foreign country where you do not even speak the language—are you sure you were not horse-kicked in the head as an infant?"

Both laughed—however, in a moment, Diana grew serious, "My father is dead—a victim of twisted religious interpretations and fanatical ultimatums. In America, there is freedom of religion. People seek out this young country, so they can be free of religious tyranny. I love my country, but it carries the burden of hatred and intolerance; I will not raise a family here and risk the same outcome as my parents—I will not!"

She stopped walking and faced the young man. Trying to read his mind, she softened her tone. "Do you think less of me now?" She did not wait long....and strode forward once again.

Aram thought about what she said and realized that he had never met anyone like this woman. Her youth belied her intellect, and every time she spoke, he lost a bit of his heart to hers. Yes, the more she allowed him to see into her head, heart, and soul—the more he wanted to know. He watched her move gracefully along the path—almost animalistic at times, and other times...her feet barely touched the ground. She walked softly, left no trace, and seemed to be one with nature. Her inner beauty manifested itself in her outer body, and he felt himself being drawn to her.

Finally, he spoke haltingly, "I think... your words ring true... and wise, but my place is here with my father. My mother died long ago, but my father—he needs me."

Diana paused... looked at Aram again, "Your father is a legend, and will be remembered forever. Perhaps, it is time for you to shape your own destiny." She glanced back at him over her shoulder as she picked up her pace, and he hurried to catch up with her not wanting to be left behind.

"Do you wish to remain here where hatred has made its home? Does revenge slack the thirst of the victim? I think not, for my arrows were guided by the winds of revenge and spilled the blood that spilled my people's blood. Still, I feel empty inside. Forgiveness is my goal, for hatred is too heavy a burden for me to carry forever. If not for my sister and my adopted brother and sisters, I could not bear the heartache of such a senseless loss." She was thinking how much Aram's father reminded her of her own father. Diana wiped her eyes and nose but looked straight ahead.

Aram knew she was right, but her ideas were too new and would take time to ferment in his brain. He knew one thing for sure; he did not want to leave her side. He wanted to comfort her—to tell her he also felt loneliness and loss, but his words scared him and would not come out right, so he bit his tongue to keep it still.

Brosh walked with Seda for a long ways until she looked at him and said, "Your new pistol must be easier to carry; do you think it will shoot straight?"

Brosh thought about it and replied, "It is much newer than my old rifle, and I like how it fits into my belt, so I can keep my hands free. I still want to learn to use the bow better though. I can see how _you_ improve every day." He watched her face redden with pride. He laughed and punched her shoulder lightly, knocking her a bit off balance.

Seda smiled back thinking that was the first time she ever saw Brosh smile. "Do you think you would like to go to America? I heard Diana talking about it to Aram."

"I have no family; I have no ties here. You and the others are my family now, and I am honored to be with you. If there is room for me, I would go and follow my family. How about you?"

"Well, I want to be a better family member. You heard me tell of my guilt—the result of my selfishness. Maybe now, I have a second chance to prove myself good enough to be part of this family."

Brosh threw an arm around her shoulder and squeezed, "Don't you know you already proved yourself by agreeing to be my little sister? It is _I_ who owe you. Besides, someday, you may be the one to save my life." He nudged her with his elbow.

Seda blushed, laughed, and pushed him away. "Awww, you are just saying that—Do you really think I could someday? I am improving my archery skills with Diana's help.

Brosh laughed as they walked on. "See, I told you. I can see the future, and so can you." He draped an arm over her shoulder and squeezed her neck. She threw an arm around his waist.

⌒⌒⌒

As the sun disappeared, the group approached the camp. Coded bird calls sounded and were returned—all was clear. Sofi ran out from the camp to greet the group. Introductions were followed by hugs and words of thanks echoed throughout the small circle.

After a few minutes, "We must head back soon. The moon is rising and it will offer us enough light to find our way." Aram began to step away.

Diana gestured toward the camp, "Won't you take tea with us for a bit while the moon rises and offers you more light? Sofi and Alisia will want to hear to hear what happened, and you _must_ meet my sisters and mother."

Aram shrugged, he didn't need to be asked twice.

Sofi fell into step with Lusine as they neared the camp. Soon they made their way around a small grove of trees. Sofi soon appeared from the trees and as she did, Lusine began to tell her about Aram and the conversation concerning America.

Sofi softly asked Lusine if she thought they would find passage to America.

Lusine flashed a glance at Sofi, "So far, God's guidance steered me to you and the others; can I be more blessed? If we find passage, I will go and embrace a new life. Will you do the same?"

Sofi's eyes traveled upward towards the sunset-touched clouds. "I should be dead, for I was buried alive; yet, like Lazarus, Jesus' hand rescued me. I am no longer my own person; God wanted me here for a purpose. Perhaps it is to be part of this family, or it could be that my earthly work is not done; whatever it is, I am ready to devote my life to His glory, for he showed me the light when darkness surrounded me."

The group arrived at the camp at sunset, Mother's face relaxed, and a long sigh of relief escaped her lips. Mother met Aram and immediately liked the demeanor of the the young man. Although, the looks exchanged between Diana and Aram were not lost on this mother's intuition. Tea boiled, food passed from hand to hand, and the group chatted away until it was time to go. Aram rose to his feet and thanked the group. Mother took his cup of tea and smiled approvingly of his polite gestures.

Diana walked him to the edge of camp and as she looked back over her shoulder, she sensed someone watching her; however, the Freedom Fighters left the trail just before the group reached camp.

"You sense someone out there, and you are right. They are my father's men, and they would never leave his son alone in the forest at night even though I dismissed them."

Before they left, Aram pulled Diana aside, "My father's wisdom is fathomless, so my words may seem simple, but I want you to know that I shall not forget you, nor will I forget your dream of finding a new country where peace is king and violence only a memory. May God protect you and may your dreams come true."

That night, dreams of Aram ran repeatedly through Diana's subconscious as she wrestled with her curious feelings toward this remarkable young man.

Will I ever see him again?

⌒⌒⌒

The next day, Brosh left camp early on a mission to sell the horses that had already touched heart. Fortunately, he was able to sell them all to a farmer who needed such animals to work his fields where he grew hay, wheat, and rye. In return, the farmer gave him cheese, bread, milk, leather, and a few bullets. He thanked Brosh profusely, "I never thought I could afford such fine horses...thank you my son."

It was not easy for Brosh to let the horses go. His bond with them had already been established. Nevertheless, it had to be done, and the family agreed. Besides, the old man seemed kind and needed them more than Brosh. However, in his head and heart, Brosh knew that someday he would bond with his own horses, and with that thought, he found peace.

Chapter 30

LOOK WITH YOUR HEART ~ NOT YOUR EYES

A tiny hummingbird with blurred wings flitted from one flower to the next. Diana looked upon it as the humming whirr of its arial efforts penetrated her inner ear. Nature often took her breath away in wonder and surprise. *God's manifestation*....she thought.

Diana began to ponder how the egg of the hummingbird is the smallest egg of all the birds. Conversely, the Ostrich's egg is the largest. So it is—the wide physical range between birds and the extensive range between people's beliefs, biases, prejudices, and attitudes. Her thoughts were interrupted by a cry of delight.

"Look!" Alisia pointed toward Brosh returning to camp with a small deer over his shoulder. His pride could be seen clearly in his springy step despite his best attempts to conceal it. Venison would bring much needed protein to the young bodies.

Diana tells of the preparation process....

After a prayer of thanks, the deer was prepared (with many busy hands participating in the process), I smiled knowingly that every part of its body would be used wisely. The hide tanned for moccasins, the small hooves into drinking cups, the bones into arrowheads, and even the sinews to form a thread so strong it would not break.

I watched as the group propped the carcass against a rock— belly-up with the head higher than the body. Sofi took a 4-inch razor-sharp blade and carefully angled the edge toward the sky as she sliced a two-inch deep opening from the deer's anus all the way up to the bottom of the rib-cage. The others rolled the body onto its side and gravity did its job pulling the organs down and out. Sofi made a few more clean cuts on connective tissue and sat back on her haunches—her bloody hands holding the knife as she took a deep breath.

After a moment, she leaned forward and carved out the diaphragm, the muscle situated below the heart and lungs and above the intestines. Next, she reached in and with a strong grip grabbed the esophagus moving it out of the way. With that, the rest of the organs were ready to harvest.

Later, we would cook the heart and liver for dinner. Some also ate the kidneys, but they were a bit too husky for me.

The life-giving animal was then suspended in the shade with head above for a few days to cure. We carefully disposed of the waste to lower the threat of other animals coming into camp drawn by the smell of a fresh kill.

After a few days, we cleaned the animal. Again, Sofi did the cutting with a skillful hand as the children watched and learned. She cut carefully all the way around the deer's neckline until the cut intersected with the earlier cut to splay the deer open. Next, she began peeling away the hide from the body—her knife flashing in the sun as she delicately perform the process with the deftness of a surgeon.

She then sat back and rested for a moment as she switched knives— selecting a longer, heavier blade. She took hold of one of the forelegs and cut it off just above the knee joint.

She stopped, paused, looked at the others carefully watching her every move. She held out her crimson hand with the long blade and gestured for Lusine to take it from her."

"You should learn this; I will help you. Cut just above the other knee." Sofi offered her the razor-sharp knife.

Lusine hesitantly took the knife from Sofi; her hand remained steady. She positioned herself close to the animal, and with Sofi whispering directions in her ear, she performed a clean cut and amputated the other foreleg. Sofi congratulated her, and together they cut off the hind legs right above the glands.

The rest of the hide was stripped off to be used for other purposes.

Mother made stew that night with chunks of meat and other scraps that were left over from the cleaning process. We ate heartily, and thanked God for our profound providence. I took the first watch, and afterwards, slept through to morning.

Sitting around the campfire that night, I remember us sharing stories—our only entertainment besides chess, our repeated drills, and archery practice. Brosh taught each of us how to fire his new pistol. 'In case of an emergency', he stated with furrowed brow. I smiled when he wasn't looking. My respect for him grew every day, and even though he was only in his mid-teens, his body was now lean, wiry, and strong. He defied his age and could easily pass for one much older.

Sofi began her story by breathing in the vapor of her tea held in both hands below her nose. Her gleaming profile reflected the firelight making her look mysteriously striking in a regal way. She was early-twenties, slender, loose-limbed, and nimble.

Sofi began to speak, "My father told me what his father told him, and now I tell you. In 301 AD, under St. Gregory the Illuminator, the Armenian King found it in his heart to accept Christianity and founded the National Apostolic Church of Armenia. This all occurred years before Constantine saw the airborne cross.

During this time, old Armenia stretched from the Caspian sea, almost to the southern border of the Black Sea, and all the way to almost the eastern edge of the Mediterranean Sea—vast valleys, wide open plains, huge lakes and mountains of wonder. My mother, her name was Vartiter (which means Rose), shared her history as well. She described how the Armenians were the first country in the world to accept Christianity as their state religion. They paid dearly for their faith in battles fought to preserve Christianity.

The Persian fire worshippers were the first to come. Then in 1774, the Moslem Arabs would appear, initiating the oppression and massacres which would henceforth be the fate of the Armenians."

"Sofi, tell us again of the girl who was pursued by the Turkish youth," whispered Seda making the saddest face of appeal she could possibly muster.

"It is not a happy story little one, but for you, I will share it." She touched Seda slightly on her shoulder.

"When the Turks marched us out of our village, one Turkish youth who was following the caravan of women and girls to be slaughtered took a liking to one of the beautiful young Armenian virgins. The more he stared, the more he became attracted to not just her beauty, but her noble composure, posture, and presence despite the chaos surrounding her. His eyes were glued to her as she carried herself indignantly, yet gracefully toward her doom. Her head remained high on her graceful neck and her posture erect and unbowed. She was like a bright, blooming flower among many other flowers that were trampled upon and broken.

Finally, he could no longer contain his feelings. He approached her and professed his love.

'Come with me and I will save you from certain death. Marry me, and become a good Muslim. I want to save you.'

The Armenian girl looked at him solemnly and said, 'If you love me, save me by taking me away and becoming a good Armenian. Only then will I marry you.'

The love-struck Turk tried again to convince this beauty of mind and body, but she would not budge; she would not betray her religion, her family, her values. The man sadly gave up and walked away. As soon as he did, the Turkish butchers who witnessed the exchange threw her to the ground and viciously slammed her face into the dirt. Taking umbrage at her rejection of the young man, they proceeded to jump on her back with their knees crushing her chest and rib cage. Next, they took to various forms of torture and abuses before they finally cut off her head. They couldn't satisfy their vengefulness enough for she had disrespected a Turk and rejected their religion. Several Armenians who loved her tried to intervene, but these women and old men were also killed without mercy. The others could only watch in despair.

The macabre scene finally ended with the possessed men cutting her dead body into pieces and scattering the parts asunder.

Strangely enough, that night, there came a bright meteor shower that rained down fire on the sleeping Turks. While the fireballs rained down death and destruction upon the Turks, the parts of the young Armenian beauty miraculously joined back together seamlessly as her radiant body absorbed the heaven sent stardust, and the young virgin ascended into the heavens. Her name was Carina, and as she left Earth behind she smiled at the upturned Armenian faces who looked up to her saying, 'Don't be surprised, Angels always come to you disguised, so look with your heart ~ not your eyes.'"

Chapter 31

THE BACKBONE OF THE TURKISH EMPIRE ~

Diana describes one of the family's repeated practices.

"The next day we practiced our emergency responses, drills, and skills. We tried to imagine different scenarios: what if we were: surprised by Turkish police while we visited a village, captured by an enemy while we were out hunting, hurt while scouting the area surrounding our camp, and always—sudden invasion of our camp at night or by day? We imagined what we would do if we were separated during a skirmish, or if we were forced to flee for our lives in different directions, or if, God forbid, one or more of us were killed unexpectedly. We talked about where we would go, how we would contact one another, possible rendezvous points, and what we should do to achieve these goals."

Later that evening, Mother responded to Seda who asked, "Why did the Turks kill my family? Why do they wish us harm?"

"Her simple questions (she was now 13 years old and her smooth olive skin shined copper-bright in the firelight) reminded me of the questions I had asked my father when I was close to her age. 'I will give you a shiny coin if you can ask me a question that I can not answer' he would say when he tucked us in for the night. I would always fall asleep trying to think of difficult questions—such a strain on my brain always made me tired...."

Mother smiled, hugged little Seda tight and kissed the top of her head. She then turned the young girl around and placed Seda's back against her chest. Seda sat between mother's legs as mother's hands began to knead through the young girl's knotted hair strand by strand readying the black tresses to be transformed into gorgeous plaits and long braids. She performed her magic on each of us girls at different times, so we knew what was coming—a story told with hands and mouth.

As her fingers wove in and out, Isgouhi began to speak of Armenian history—how the Armenian people were industrious tradesmen, thoughtful artists, clever merchants, judicious bankers, creative and imaginative architects, and renowned craftsmen—they were (she paused to move the hair out of her own eyes) the backbone of the growing Turkish empire for five centuries. However, whenever a Turk killed an Armenian (and these killings occurred off and on throughout the centuries), a bit more of that backbone cracked leaving a weak, teetering vertebrae that lacked the internal sturdiness to prop up an unwise, unjust, and selfish nation that grew half-witted, pea-brained, and moronic from a lack of education and an apathetic indifference toward leaders who manipulated its national conscience and led its people down a path paved with jealousy, xenophobia, and twisted entitlement.

Such indoctrination set the scene for a genocidal attempt never before heard of or even imagined in the modern world.

Chapter 32

~ SOFI'S STORY ~

April 28, 1915 Sofi and Lusine returned from an early morning hunt with surprising news. At one point, they crossed the main road and came upon an old woman leading a donkey pulling a small cart filled with milk cans. Sofi asked the woman her destination. She told her how she regularly made this short sojourn to the neighboring town to sell her cows' milk.

The young women continued the conversation with the old woman.

"Good morning dear lady. We are traveling to a relative's house and wondered if you could help us with some directions?"

The lady freely entered into conversation and seemed to welcome the company of the two young women. So, the three traveled on together sharing stories and an occasional laugh.

They rested together for a while, and the woman offered them a drink of fresh milk. In return, Lusine offered the woman a leather pouch she had sewn by hand. The woman was quite impressed and moved by her generosity, so she babbled on about one thing or another until an hour had expired.

Lusine stood up and said they should leave, but clearly the elderly woman's loneliness led to her earnest attempt to keep the two young

women engaged—or perhaps, she suspected they were Armenians....
because she soon told of a group of Armenians being marched past her
village and how she witnessed a grey-haired woman yelling wildly at the
straight-faced gendarmes and the Turkish police.

"You will be cursed forever! Taking away innocent people and
murdering them—shame! Shame on you! Kadir ne' use o olur (your
fate is sealed). Because of you (she gestured wildy at the Turkish
officers), our enemies will come and do the same to us—you taint
our future and jeopardize our children and grandchildren's future
happiness!"

She turned her back on the officers, and spread her arms in the direction of the bedraggled Armenians. "And _you_—my poor Armenian
children, may your God welcome your poor souls and take you into his
merciful arms forever." With that, the old woman hung her head and
sat down heavily on her stoop—exhausted.

After the refugees had passed, a middle-aged lady (perhaps the older
lady's daughter) approached a Turkish captain bringing up the rear and
urging on the stragglers in the back. She walked a short way with the
captain, so she could ask him a question.

"How do you sleep at night after slaughtering thousands of innocent
Armenian girls?"

The captain stoically endured the presence of this assertive woman,
until she asked her question. At that point, he stopped abruptly, and
holding his head high, replied without hesitation. "I sleep very well. I
am a soldier following the orders of his king. I kneel on my prayer rug
after every cleansing and pray to Allah to thank him for helping me do
his work." He then sharply turned on his heel, and left the woman and
her questions alone in the dust.

The milk lady looked at the two youths with genuine concern as
tears ran down her wrinkled cheeks filling each sagging fold of skin
with the wetness of sincere compassion.

Sofi leaned down as she passed the old woman. "Thank you for your kindness," she whispered, "I know you to be true and bless you for your encouragement."

As the two continued to follow the bumpy path, Sofi told Lusine that she knew of such villages where the Muslim sectarians still practiced ancient Christian customs. These Muslims never liked the Turks for they were good people who believed in peace and respect for others. They practiced tolerance and patience and judged people by their actions—not their religious beliefs.

Sofi continued to talk as if she were talking to herself and began a narrative of her own experiences with the Turks. The Turks often used the word *cleanse* when referring to the Armenian Genocide—a euphemistic term that softened the brutality of attempted genocide.

"Our village stood amidst the white-capped mountains and verdant, vibrant valleys. Its beauty was second to none, but when the Turks came…. Well, most of our family homes had to be left behind in a hurry. My family watched as smiling Turkish officials moved in their own families and claimed instant ownership. My parents' hard work and fastidious care of our home and land—all for naught. I cried as I was led away.

The young Armenian children were spared deportation; instead, they were ripped out of their mother's or grandmother's arms and separated. Later, they were forced to denounce Christianity and become Muslims with new Turkish names. Such conversion also included painful circumcision (normally performed at birth) on the young boys as required by Islamic custom. They learned quickly that their lives would not know love—just servitude. These stolen youths aged quickly under the yoke of heavy burdens and meager rations. My little brother, Anastas, was only seven and my baby sister, Khatun, just four years of age. My heart still breaks when I remember the look of despair and grief on their confused and frightened faces as they were dragged away."

Sofi paused to take a sip of water and wipe her moist eyes which were busy trying to hold back a sea of tears.

"Individual caravans consisting of thousands of deported Armenians joined us as my mother and I were escorted away by the Turkish gendarmes under the pretext of being taken to another town. The officials in charge of the march would accept bribes for small favors, but once they were out in the wilderness away from prying eyes, everything changed. Every woman and child would be stripped and ridiculed, and every coin, trinket, or medallion would be taken from them. I was forced to stand naked in front of smirking men who ordered me to turn around, bend over, spread my legs, as they poked and probed my defenseless body. I tried not to cry as they laughed and made rude comments."

Lusine wanted to comfort Sofi—to hug and hold her, but she sensed Sofi needed to tell her story—a cathartic confession she had held in too long. She watched her "sister" regain her composure and continue.

"Later, the guards allowed roving government bands of hardened criminals known as the "Special Organization" to attack us —such "brave" men beating and raping defenseless women and children. The guards also allowed Kurdish bandits to raid the caravans and steal anything they could find. We had nothing left, so they took my innocence. Some of the more attractive women were kidnapped for a life of involuntary servitude. Others scarred themselves—or worse.

At one point, we were approaching a small city where we hoped for a bit of bread and some water. As we drew closer, I could not believe my eyes. There were nine crucifixes set alongside the road as we approached the city. Nailed to these hand-made wooden crosses were teenage Armenian girls. Their bodies completely naked except for their long black hair blowing in the wind. Their bodies were chalk white except for the bruises and cuts. They stared down at us with unseeing eyes. I tried not to look, but when I stared at the ground, I walked upon their shadows and my tears wet the ground with silent drops. We shivered with fear as we glanced up at these desecrated girls clothed only in their black/ brown tresses that would never be braided with loving hands again. As we walked by, the long metal spikes pounded through their feet and hands glistened red/black in the sunlight, and I began to pray silently for their souls.

We cried and lamented thinking this would also be our fate. Yet, we continued forward; it was not to be—our torture would continue on for much longer."

Lusine stared at Sofi in wonder. *This was the second time she had heard the description of crucified teen girls? There could be no doubt; the stories were true.*

"The marches, we called them death marches, covered hundreds of miles and lasted months. Out of a thousand people, only a couple hundred survived to the end. Bodies were scattered across the deserts, plains, and mountains. Children were taken and bayoneted for not keeping up, and mothers who carried their fathers or mothers or children who somehow escaped being separated, collapsed from exhaustion and were left to die. Our food that we brought was soon gone, and the guards gave us no other food or water. Such suffering overwhelmed even the strongest of us. Death became a merciful friend—patiently waiting." Sofi glanced in Lusine's direction. They stopped walking for a moment. "I am sorry; I should not burden you with my painful past."

Lusine placed a gentle hand on the back of Sofi's neck and pulled her in close to her face. Sofi could feel Lusine's warm breath as she said, "Sofi, I want you to tell me everything. I want to share your pain. You are my sister; I love you." Sofi kissed Lusine on the cheek and the two continued to walk as Sofi once again began to speak.

"One day, a woman with whom I walked many miles began to stray from the line. I watched her with concern because a few days before she was forced to leave her son and daughter behind— toddlers who could not keep up and were suffering terribly. She laid the little bodies down on the path—covered them carefully with a blanket; she knew they were close to death. 'Go to sleep my little children—rest your heavy heads—Mother loves you.' They were so exhausted, sleep took them immediately. A Turkish officer prodded the weeping mother with a bayonet.

'Move... or stay and die with your mongrels! Move!'

"I watched as she staggered onward as did other mothers who suffered the same experience. Some mothers stayed behind to starve with their children while others were killed for not leaving their children upon the orders of the officer in charge. This distraught mother walked several miles until we passed a deep gorge. She calmly walked toward the edge of the cliff, and before I realized what she was doing, she jumped to her death." Sofi shuddered at the memory.

"Heads down, we walked on...."

Sofi sat down on a log and unwrapped her long scarf. She rolled up her shawl and tied both items into a neat roll she could easily carry on her back. She looked ahead at the winding path and sighed heavily before she stood and adjusted her belongings. Sipping water from a leather bag, Lusine waited patiently. Soon, Sofi set the pace and continued her story.

"Eventually, shoes wore out, clothes in tatters, some walked naked and burned in the scorching sun. Exhaustion and dehydration brought the strongest of us to our knees—at night, moaning and crying filled the starry skies. I did not know it them, but we were only a short distance from the trench where Brosh found me."

Chapter 33

TO TAKE AWAY THE SINS OF THE WORLD ~ A SISTER

Sofi continued her narration after the two broke bread and rested. She told Lusine how she prayed for her family and for little Anastas and baby Khatun whom she hoped to see again some day.

"I remember being overjoyed when some of the brave young Armenian boys would escape into the forests and hide in the caves. When the Turks pursued them, these young dauntless children would ambush and kill the heathen savages with their bare hands and take their weapons for their own. An animalistic sense of survival helped these supposed renegade boys live off the land while their minds remained bent on revenge for their lost families and loved ones. I never thought that someday I would actually become part of one of these extraordinary bands who formed their own families with their own rules of survival."

Sofi wiped her mouth on her sleeve and drank a bit more water to wet her throat.

"Some of these youthful clans would descend upon small Turkish villages they encountered and force the residents to give them provisions. The Turkish officials became enraged, but since they could not catch the elusive Armenian youths and were too fearful of pursuing them into the forest, the frustrated Turks would severely punish the poor villagers who had no choice and thus had to suffer doubly. The Turks justified these punishments by slandering the villagers—telling others the villagers were punished for helping the enemy."

"Sofi, how did you learn so much? I mean—you knew how to fix Alisia's puncture wound, cure her fever, and help her recover quickly. You've taught me more than I can repay—how can I ever thank you?"

"Lusine, you can thank me by being my sister—the sister I lost still haunts me, but you...you've brought me hope—a sister whom I can love and who loves me."

She stopped walking, placed her hands gently on Lusine's shoulders and looked affectionately into her eyes. She smiled down at the shorter girl as she smiled adoringly at her older "sister"— "The kind of sister I can reveal my heart to and unburden my overwrought head with the nightmares I must get out of my mind to find peace in my heart. You listen to my stories, nod your head without judging me, and share my grief; you, my little sister, take away the sins of the world—much like Christ did for all of mankind. Such warm-hearted devotion means everything to me, and I would do anything for you. I am sure you agree that we would do the same for our new family—our family—the family who saved us and gave us a new life."

The two sisters walked on quietly as Sofi's words descended from Lusine's brain and into her redoubtable beating heart.

Chapter 34

A VISIT WITH THE DEVIL ~

The young women maintained a steady pace until they came upon an isolated farm. Always cautious, they spied on its occupants for a while to see if they appeared friendly before going closer. Before long, an older man was spotted gathering eggs from a wooden chicken coop. He stood up, bent over, stood up, and bent over again placing egg after egg into a woven basket under his arm. The time-bent figure moved slowly in geriatric fashion and rested often as he looked over his property. It seemed like he had forgotten to do something. No one else seemed to be present. Two horses were in a corral built off the side of the barn that seemed to be leaning to the left. A large oak tree spread its gnarled branches offering a bit of shade for the standing horses. The garden fence stood fairly high to keep out deer and appeared to be cross-hatched below to discourage other critters. A well-worn Lilliputian-like porch framed the entrance way with a chair on one side of the door and a pair of wooden clogs on the other.

After several minutes had gone by, the two felt it was safe to approach.

"I will knock on the door; you be the lookout. Stay hidden just in case something goes wrong. Hopefully, the old man will sell us some eggs and vegetables." Sofi strode out from the bushes and quietly walked up to the front door.

A dog barked—and before Sofi's knuckles could knock, the door swung open and the old man shouted, "Get off my porch! Who are you?" He pointed a double-barreled shotgun at her chest.

Sofi almost fell backwards holding her hands up in a defensive gesture.

"Please, I mean you no harm. I am a simple peasant woman on my way to the next town. I just wanted to buy some eggs and vegetables. I have money. I mean no harm."

Lusine's heart raced wildly while she watched the old man threaten Sofi. She had her bow and her dagger, but her bow would be no help if the old man fired the shotgun. Slowly, the old man lowered the heavy gun a bit.

"How do I know you are not one of those damned starving Armenian refugees?" he snarled.

Sofi cringed inside but collected herself and answered, "You don't, except, do I look like I am starving? If you do not have enough food, I will gladly be on my way, but if you are a _kind_ man, you will help a single woman on her way to join her husband after visiting her sister whom she tended to while she was sick."

The old man hesitated.

"Well, show me your money, and I will decide. I live here alone and can't be too careful of strangers."

Sir, I would feel more comfortable if you would lower your gun; I am no criminal."

The grizzled man leaned the gun against the door, still within reach. He loosened one of the buttons on his tattered flannel shirt as long grey chest hairs fought their way over the top of the garment. He watched Sofi carefully. Slowly, she unfolded the top of her long skirt. A folded, sewn-in pouch held a few coins which she fingered lightly and cupped three into her palm. She looked up at the suspicious man—his face covered with an almost all white beard and narrow, beady eyes framed with crow's-feet wrinkles on both sides. Sofi took a step forward and extended her hand displaying a few coins.

Suddenly, the man's grizzled face turned vicious; he speedily snatched up his shotgun.

"What keeps me from blowing off your damn head and burying you out in the back field? If I let _you_ go, who knows how many others you will tell. I can't trust you!"

The old man's hands began to shake.

"Please, don't hurt me." Sofi stepped back. She could see the craziness in the old man's eyes now. His demented brain only knew fear, mistrust, and hatred.

"You are a devil. Now, you must die!"

"Stop!" shouted a voice from the side of the porch. Less than 10 feet away appeared Lusine, her bowstring strained in its pulled-back position. A feathered arrow pointed at the surprised old man. During his confusion, Sofi leaped forward lickety-split and with one vigorous pull, yanked the gun from the old man's hands. The force of the action jerked the crazy one forward, and he fell to his knees.

"Noooo, oh, no! I knew you were the devil!" he screamed with spittle spraying from his toothless mouth.

"You crazy old loon!" shouted Sofi. "If you weren't such a senile excuse for a man, we would have paid you and left in peace, but instead you choose to kill. _You_ are the devil who deserves to die. Look into your own heart!"

"Wait!" shouted Lusine whose arrow remain cocked and aimed at the cowering figure. "We will spare your life if you give us food. She is right; you deserve to die, but we can also see your mind left you some time ago. We are sorry for you, but we truly meant you no harm. Now get up and gather us some food!"

The old man wobbled back to his feet and opened the door as the women followed him into the dark house. Inside, the smell of dog mixed with musky mold told a story of neglect and dementia. The threadbare furniture showed stains of different colors, and the girls' feet scratched gratingly on the floor as they entered the room. A dog growled from one corner, but looked as if he could not move off of the rags which served as its bed. Cautiously, Sofi carried the shotgun and kept it pointed at the snarling canine.

Defeated and despondent, the old man sat down at the small kitchen table and stared at the empty chair opposite him.

"Where is your wife?" asked Sofi while Lusine searched the cupboards and storage bins.

The man raised his arm reluctantly and pointed out the window. A dirt mound with a stone marker appeared in the shadows of a large tree.

"Not much here, but I found a few things and a bag of rice." She glanced at Sofi and looked out the front door for any other visitors. "We should go."

Sofi pointed the shotgun at the old man. "If you tell anyone of our visit, we will come back and make you pay." She unloaded the gun and dropped it loudly it on the table. "This weapon is for your protection from wild animals, not peaceful women offering to pay you for your trouble."

The two women walked out the front door. Lusine glanced back to see the old man's head buried in his arms as his shoulders shook uncontrollably.

Sofi strode briskly and disappeared into the forest. Lusine ran to catch up. The sun had disappeared behind the clouds; it would be dark soon—just enough time to make it back to camp... with a bag of rice and a story to tell.

Leaving camp is easy…making it back to camp without incident—well, danger lurked behind every bush, trouble just around the corner, and surprise was no stranger. Still, the two girls covered ground rapidly, silently, intently, until…they were almost at their camp.

Chapter 35

FIGHT OR FLEE ~ ON A WET, DARK NIGHT

As the two women approached their camp, an owl silently dropped from a branch on high—its silent wings spread suddenly to give it lift as it glided effortlessly on wings lined perfectly with feathers designed by its Maker to offer no sound to even the most wary prey. When it passed close to Sofi's head, only the air it moved over the back of her neck made her cast an askew glance to her left. Sofi's epiphany entered her mind as swiftly as the snowy owl in flight—an omen. Instead of following the owl's flight down the path, she stared intently into the semi-darkness where the owl had suddenly taken flight. There it was, the source of the owl's discomfort—a human shift in the shadows... and another.

Hmmm...the shape seemed too large to be one of our family members; plus, our family members would be spread out around the camp. They would not be so close to one another, nor would they move so clumsily, she thought to herself. Sofi froze and held her left hand at a right angle and made a fist. Lusine recognized the sign and walked on cat's paws to Sofi's spot just off the road between a bush and several small trees.

Lusine's hand touched Sofi's heaving chest—her heart pounded in anticipation. After a few moments, Sofi spoke softly. "The owl warned us; we are invisible to them; however, they are hunting someone, and I fear it is our family. Let's let them pass, and we will circle behind them to see what they are planning."

The shadowy figures moved as quietly as possible as they sneakily approached the quiet camp. The glow of the small fire could just barely be seen for it was tiny and partly concealed to protect it from the rain.

Shee-Chee, Shee-Chee echoed from the woods and Sofi and Lusine recognized mother's bird call. She must have been just beginning her watch after dinner. They knew their furtive efforts had paid off. Hiding behind some boulders, the girls looked down into the meadow. A wagon and two horses were waiting below. They spied at least one person watching and guarding the wagon.

As the two young woman moved closer, something shiny glistened in the rain—brass buttons—*police! Turkish police were after our family.*

Like her namesake, Lusine moved lightly through the woods— _she_ was the light. Sofi maneuvered herself into a position of higher ground and returned her own bird call.

The police soldiers aimed their rifles at the camp, but the camp was deserted. The fire spit and popped a bit as the raindrops grew larger, but something eerie was about to happen.

Suddenly, a mustachioed man stood straight up and shouted, "We are the Turkish Police and order you to lower your weapons and come out, so we can see you. We will not hurt you if you come out now."

He waited…after a few moments, he disgustedly shouted, "Okay, you Armenians are now under arrest and will be taken dead or alive. You have been warned!"

The captain gestured to his right and then to his left. A few men moved in both directions. He planned to surround and divide these women and children. Clearly, these men had performed this routine of capture and kill many times.

Lusine's first soldier walked right in front of her— in a crouched position with his rifle pointed straight ahead. Lusine picked up a heavy stone the size of a soccer ball. As the man dropped to one knee and adjusted his aim, the rock dropped with such force that the back of his head cracked open. He dropped with a thud.

One of the young policeman paused in mid-step. "Are you okay? Did you fall? We are coming!" With bayoneted rifles pointing the way, the second policeman ran toward the last sound—Lusine was waiting.

The young woman's arrow—at such close range—hit with the speed of a lightning bolt as it ripped through the first man's Adam's apple and stuck out the other side of his neck. Blood started squirting out of both gaping holes as the man dropped to the ground and rolled onto his back pulling frantically at the bloody arrow. The frightened officer fired his rifle immediately in the direction where he thought he saw movement, but only empty bushes were there.

The other policemen encountered Sofi in the dark. Her first officer stood up straight when he heard the rifle shot. Sofi ran by him like a deer except for the deadly sharp dagger in her right hand that shot out in a flash as she whizzed by leaving behind a fatal red-line-wound on the young man's neck just to the right of and below his jaw. He didn't feel but a knick, but when his hand shakily touched the spot—blood was everywhere and the bottom of his stomach dropped in panic. The bright red geyser continued its arterial spurts perfectly in time with his racing heart.

The falling man fired off one rifle shot as the bloody throat gurgled out a weak cry for help. Diana and Alisia had already picked out their targets and quickly dispatched the desperate men with the precise accuracy of many practiced hours of archery.

Next, the chilling sound of two more bodies hitting the ground, some cries for help, but no one answered them here in the dark forest where Nature lives by Her own rules.

Only the captain remained standing. He pointed his gun to and fro in all directions, but no one moved.

Mother finally stepped forward, "Put your gun down; we want to talk to you."

'How do I know you won't kill me?" He was shaking as he took a few steps back.

"You do not know, but you have no choice if you wish to live a bit longer."

He looked warily at the figures surrounding him and reluctantly placed the pistol on the ground.

"More Police will come after me; you should surrender."

However, after the officer closely surveyed the fierce faces surrounding him, he knew in his heart that surrender was not an option for these individuals.

Next, he begged for mercy. "I have a family; spare me for my children's sake! he cried.

Mother stepped forward. "Children? How many of our children have you killed?

The officer looked at Mother with a confused expression.

How many Armenians have you personally killed?

When the man hesitated, Mother spoke again—louder.

"Hundreds, thousands? What mercy did you show them? What mercy did you show our children? **How many!"**

Mother's shout startled the officer.

Diana looked at her mother's face and did not recognize it—a face she had never seen before.

Mother continued, "On your knees. How many other police or soldiers are close by? Where are you taking my people? Who can be saved? Tell us, and we will kill you quickly." Mother waited.

"N…No…No one is nearby. We were just wandering, looking for food."

"He is lying!" said Lusine. "Sofi and I saw a wagon below and at least one other police soldier. They probably planned to take our dead bodies and display them in public as they did our brothers and fathers!"

While on his knees, the shaken man kissed the ground… desperately praying to his god. When he was done, Mother walked up behind him, knocked off his hat, and grasping his hair tightly, held her dagger to his throat. Her hand shook for a moment as she pressed the sharp edge against his sweaty neck. A wet spot began to appear around his groin area. Moments passed….before a heaving sigh left Mother's shaking body—-she let him go and turned her back in disgust. All was silent.…

As most of the family members' eyes shifted to mother, the officer seized the moment and jumped to his feet in an effort to flee toward the trees.…

BOOM! The force of the unexpected noise almost knocked the group off their feet.

With a sudden jerk, the captain's body slumped forward as he fell to his knees once again, paused awkwardly while a look of bewilderment spread across his face. His eyes rolled up into his head as his chest and head fell forward into the wet dirt.

Everyone turned to the source of the explosion. There stood Brosh— standing still…no expression on his face…a solitary statue—with his smoking horse pistol pointed at the fallen form.

Chapter 36

HOME IS WHERE YOU ARE LOVED ~

"**B**e invisible my daughters and return unharmed." Mother made the sign of the cross and kissed each one's forehead.

The three women armed themselves with their bows, but at the last moment, Sofi set her bow aside and walked over to Brosh as he sat by himself methodically reloading the pistol. Sofi held out her hand—their eyes met for a moment, and Brosh understood; he looked at the pistol. "Here, it is a good weapon." He offered it to her with both hands.

"Thank you, my brother. You have taught me well. I will shoot straight."

Sofi took the horse pistol and began to turn away when Brosh quickly sprang to her side and hugged her tightly. Their embrace lasted just long enough for the clouds to part and allow the crescent moon to light the way.

Alisia noted the moon's position amid the scattered clouds. The semi-darkness may help them during their deadly endeavor. She caught Sofi's eye and nodded her head toward the forest; it was time.

Meanwhile, Diana placed her hand gently on Brosh's shoulder; as she led him away, she nodded in the direction of an old oak whose burly roots had formed a makeshift bench. The two walked over and sat down on the ancient roots. Diana looked up—Sofi and Lusine were disappearing into the forest to locate the wagon and the threat the last policeman posed if he escaped and alerted others to their presence. She would join them in a bit, but Brosh required her counsel first.

"Let me tell you something my father told me before he died. Once upon a time, there were approximately five million Armenians who had settled for thousands of years between the Mediterranean Sea and the Caucasus Mountains. These mountains were considered spiritual—much like Mount Ararat. They prominently divided Russia, Armenia, Turkey, Georgia, and Azerbaijan. The range of these mountains were bounded by the Black Sea on the west and the Caspian Sea on the east. The reason for the mountains' spiritual influence date back over twenty million years when they were first formed. That was when the Arabian tectonic plate met head-on with the Eurasian plate and God lifted their massive peaks heavenward as if they were on a celestial rope being pulled up through the clouds. Using His thunderous arms, God lifted up its highest peak to an astonishing 18,510 feet from sea level.

Today this peak is called Mount Elbrus and is considered the highest point in Europe. Because of the great diversity of peoples living near these mountains, fighting broke out regularly between different warring factions. Despite these calamities, the Armenians survived and became one of the most respected races in the area. Sagacious and patient, the Armenians also led by example in architecture, music, chess, crafts, money matters, and education (including girls and women).

These devoted people helped Armenia become the first nation state to accept Christianity—even before the time when the Romans were distributed among three nations: Russia, Persia, and the Ottoman

Empire. After Germany and Russia went to war against one another beginning in 1914, Turkey joined the central powers around Germany and Austria-Hungary, and despite their most forceful efforts, could not convince the Armenians to enthusiastically join them. Thus, our people were trapped between the Russian anvil and the Turkish/German hammer.

At first, the Russians decided to destroy the Armenians, but their best efforts failed as the Armenians would not be subdued. Exercising wisdom, Russia then offered its hand in friendship—the Armenians accepted and steadfastly refused to help the Turks and the Nazis fight the Russians.

Not only was their defiance perceived as traitorous, their religion offended the Turks' beliefs and made the Armenians infidels and enemies of Allah. Retribution by the Turks, Kurds, and other Muslims guaranteed that Armenians would suffer more than one would think humanly possible.

You and I must embrace a different destiny—one that holds hope in continuance and continuity. We are survivors with a purpose, and that purpose is to find a new home. One that will allow us to prosper and procreate as we ground ourselves once again in faith and renewal. The soldier you shot back there…he meant your family harm. You responded protectively; you did nothing wrong. Do you understand what I am saying? Listen, during the time of Jesus, one of his first disciples was Brosh—also known as Bart or Bartholomew. He was Jesus' rock… as you…are mine."

Brosh closed his eyes, and when he opened them, the moonlight painted tiny diamonds in the moist wetness of his eyes. "I do understand…my parents taught me how to love, not to kill. So, I hope God will understand my sinful actions. Yet, my heart remains filled with empty anger that threatens to erupt when I least expect it. But…I feel myself changing…with your help. When my new family rescued me, I learned it does not matter where home is located, for home is where you are loved."

Diana's eyes brimmed over blinking black eyelashes—Brosh hugged her. She knew she loved this young boy as she would her own brother. She always thought about a brother and felt amiss without one, but now she realized that when one has no brother, or no sister, or no mother or father—one need not despair. God will provide one in a way only He can. We are meant to bond with others, and blood is not the only adhesive element available—placing one's life in another's hands will also provide the glue of brotherhood. The more love one gives, the more love one receives. Is there anything else that increases the more you give it away? The yin and the yang, the balance and the design, the holding and the letting go—just as the bow loves the arrow but knows it must let it go, just as the thoughtful parent releases the child, and the fragile body releases the infinite soul—truly, the child is the father of the man.

Chapter 37

A LEGEND ~ AN INSPIRATION

By moonlight, Mother, Seda, Lusine, and Brosh began to pack up their few belongings. Hiding the bodies presented a dilemma—leave them for the animals to pick clean or bury them. The first may attract attention to the family's existence and place them all at risk. Unfortunately, the second choice would hide the evidence for a while, but time and energy remained an issue. The family decided it best to move as soon as possible.

Therefore, a concerted action began— strip the bodies to make it easy for the animals and birds to complete their work and prevent recognition of the men. After a few days, anyone finding the bodies would think they were just more slaughtered Armenians. The uniforms and other raiment would be buried at a different site.

As Seda helped mother, she looked up and asked, "Are you worried for them—in the dark?"

Mother paused only for a moment and returned to her packing. "When we fled the Turks, they were but girls—now, they are women-warriors much like Hayk Nahapet".

"Who was Hayk Nahapet? I never heard of him."

Mother turned and looked directly at Seda. She spoke gently but firmly, "If you can't work and talk at the same time, don't talk."

"Yes, mother."

Mother soon softened and replied, "According to Armenian lore, Hayk fought fiercely for his people and founded our culture. His legend lives on—he was a mighty archer and fearless warrior who led his people to Mount Ararat where they prospered for many centuries."

Author's note: ***Pictures and details of Hayk Nahapet can be found on the internet.***

Author's note:

According to a wide variety of sources, it is most often agreed that Christianity was first adopted in the Roman Empire (specifically in Armenia).

When Jesus told the disciples to go into all the world, they literally followed his holy order and spread the Word. Bartholomew and Thaddeus wound up in Armenia. The evangelization of Armenia climaxed in A.D. 301 when St. Gregory the Illuminator converted king Tiridates III (A.D. 238-314) who then proclaimed Christianity the state religion of Armenia. Tiridates was the first ruler to officially Christianize his people; his conversion predated the conventional date of Constantine the Great's personal acceptance of Christianity on behalf of the Eastern Roman Empire.

Throughout their entire history, Armenian Christians have been under almost constant persecution: first by Persians, then Arabs, and then Turks. When Armenia came under the Soviet Union, they were persecuted by the Communists until Mikhail Sergeyevich Gorbachev came into power.

Gorbachev was a former Soviet statesman and the eighth and last leader of the Soviet Union. Gorbachev served as General Secretary of the Communist Party of the Soviet Union from 1985 until 1991 when the party was dissolved. He also initiated the term *glasnost* which was the policy or practice of more open consultative government and wider dissemination of information. The term came to represent a new openness representing Gorbachev's style of politics.

"Jesus was the first socialist, the first to seek a better life for mankind."
General Secretary Gorbachev

Today, Armenians remain very proud to be the first Christian nation in the world.

See next page for a map of Greater Armenia circa 95—55 A.D.

The Kingdom of Armenia at its greatest extent under Tigranes the Great (95–55 BC)

I, Aivazovsky, the copyright holder of the above work, hereby publishes it under the following licenses:

Chapter 38

HUNTER BECOMES PREY ~

Sofi led the way followed by Alisia. The horse pistol felt smooth and reassuring in her hands. No one spoke as they moved carefully and quietly. Their leather footing made hardly any noise as their light feet padded softly on the ground. Before they located the wagon, the two stopped for a moment at the edge of an opening glade. The moonlight bathed the opening with light as their eyes scanned the area.

"Shireee...Shireee", a familiar bird call echoed through the trees nearby; it was Diana. She caught up to them after seeing to Brosh. Her rapid pace left her panting as she approached her sisters. "Have you spotted the wagon?"

Following Sofi's hand signals, the wagon could barely be seen through the branches of the forest and the tall brush on the other side of the glade. As the triad made their way stealthily along the edge of the trees, they peered into the light of a lantern which silhouetted the wagon's exterior edges; the shape of one man standing by the wagon could be seen. As the three crept closer, they could read his body language. His head swiveled nervously as he remained alert to any negligible sound.

The recent screaming and shooting heightened his awareness. His eyes squinted…his brow frowned, but he could not see or hear anything to any degree of certainty. Still, he rubbernecked this way and that… looking deep into the dark forest. *Why is it taking so long for the others to return?* His mind was on fire; his body tense— his finger on the trigger of his rifle.

The three young woman had already devised on a plan.

Diana veered off toward the back of the wagon while Alisia crawled forward toward its side where the light emanated outward. Sofi made her way to a knoll where she could set the horse pistol's barrel on a steady stand of wood or rock.

Meanwhile, Diana had made it all the way around to the other side of the wagon; in doing so, the triad surrounded the police officer.

Alisia tied a length of vine she acquired to a low hanging branch and crawled to a safe spot nearby. The three waited patiently for Sofi's bird call.

When it came, it pierced the still night, and the soldier jumped off the wagon and took a defensive stance.

"Who's there!?

The young man wiped his forehead, brow, eyes, and nose; his hand came away wet. *My men? Is it them? What could take so long? Just a few starving Armenians—not much of a fight.*

Just then, Alisia worked the branch vigorously.

"Hey, show yourself!" shouted the strained voice of the uniformed man as he aimed his rifle at the tree. It was dark, hard to see—he exercised great restraint not to fire his weapon. *It may be just some animal looking for a meal.* Instinctively, he moved closer to the four horses for protection.

The three women had hoped the man might panic and fire his weapon and expose himself enough for Sofi to take a high percentage shot, but he did not commit. Still, the two sisters were not done, and a back-up plan was already in place.

Alisia abandoned the rope and crawled to her left. She was still too far away for an accurate arrow shot, and the man's rifle's range would easily outmatch hers.

Diana moved in closer, but could not secure a position for a good shot with her bow.

Sofi crawled closer, took aim, yet decided to hold off because the man was partly hidden by the horses.

On the other side of the wagon, crawling on her hands and knees, Diana slithered within range, selected an arrow, and proceeded to snap off the very sharp point of its head by pressing it at angle against a solid grey rock. With its point dulled, Diana moved in slow motion as she notched her arrow and took careful aim. Her arrow flew silently through the cool night air and straight into the rear flank of one of the lead horses. Springing to life, a loud screaming whinnying sound emerged from the thunderstruck horse as it bolted forward startling and pulling the other now-spooked horses forward with erratic leaps into the darkness.

The wagon lurched forward leaving the man open and exposed.

Stunned by the sudden cacophony of events, the young man desperately pursued the panic-stricken beasts over the uneven ground.

As the man moved within range, Sofi breathed slowly and waited for the right moment. She knew a moving target in the near-dark is not easy to hit. Still, he came closer with each misstep.

Meanwhile, Diana and Alisia's fleet feet closed the gap between themselves and the preoccupied man as both sisters shortened the proximity between each other.

When the running man crossed into Sofi's range, the sudden report of the pistol rang out through the night air. However, the stumbling officer luckily evaded the deadly lead ball; still, the explosion caused the man's knees to buckle—his whole body hit the dirt. He frantically checked his parts; he was not hit. He hurriedly searched the dirt for his rifle.

When the man fell, Diana and Alisia were close behind and took aim at the horizontal body, but they could not see the partially hidden figure clearly through the grass and sparse illumination. The moon played hide and seek with the clouds, so the sisters approached cautiously—silence once again.

Meanwhile, little-by-little, Sofi lifted her head to see if her bullet hit its target. In doing so, she became a target!

The man lie prone in the grass breathing heavily as the horse-pulled wagon veered off in the distance. Swallowing hard, he slowly took aim where the muzzle flash occurred. There it was—he could just make out a human head lifting up steadily. Trying to calm his heart, he sighted the target and squeezed the trigger.

The shot rang out as the silence amplified the explosion and the recoil bit into his shoulder. He slowly rose to his knees peering ahead; in doing so, he became the final target for the two arrows skillfully sent on their deadly way.

The policeman's bullet sped straight at Sofi's head, and although her lightning fast reflexes served her well in the past, this time, even those reflexes could not move her head fast enough to avoid the well-aimed deadly projectile speeding her way.

Sofi's wide eyes keenly sighted the flash of the rifle before she heard the sound; light travels faster than sound. She immediately collapsed her arms and hoped that gravity would work faster than a speeding bullet—it did not.

The lead ball made contact with the ducking head, but because of Sofia's quick action, it was not solid contact; rather, the bullet ripped through the skin on her side forehead above her right ear and glanced off course when it made contact with her bony skull. Her head jerked to one side like she'd been kicked in the head by an angry mule. She lost consciousness on her way to the ground where her head landed solidly against the base of the rock she used for cover.

Diana and Alisia closed in on the stretched out man. They retrieved their arrows and headed toward Sofi's position. They signaled her, but received no answer. They quickened their pace. In a few moments, they discovered her body in the rocks. Blood ran down the side of her head, filled up her ear and overflowed down her neck. Diana ripped a strip of cloth from her shirt as Alisia pressed down hard on the wound to stop the flow of blood. A piece of cloth was placed on her gash, and a long strip wrapped her head tightly.

"What happened?" Sofi asked blinking her eyes. "Owww, why does my head hurt so much?"

Diana held her head and looked into the dazed girl's eyes. "You were shot, but your head is filled with rocks, so the bullet just bounced off. You are going to be fine." Alisia knew Diana's words belied her feelings of concern for Sofi. Diana's heart raced and sweat ran down her face. Alisia placed her hand on her sister's back....

"Easy Diana, easy...she is going to be okay. The bleeding has already stopped. You did a fine job. Let us carry her back to camp where we can clean and sanitize her cut."

Diana took a deep breath. The girls picked up Sofi, but before they could carry her, she cried out. "Let me go, all I need is a shoulder; I can walk. I just have a headache. I am fine, really, I am."

With a sister of each side, they headed back to camp. Alisia looked across at her sister. Diana's eyes made contact with Alisia's. Their silent thanks spread over their faces.

"Let us rest here for a moment," stated Sofi. "I feel a bit dizzy." The girls sat while Sofi caught her breath and regained her senses. "I guess I missed my shot."

Diana and Alisia laughed. "We just want to thank God for making that officer miss his his shot as well," remarked Diana. "Can you walk or do you want me to carry you?"

"Just be my crutch, I am feeling stronger already."

As they entered the camp, the others ran out to greet them. Sofi tried to fend off Mother and Lusine, but her efforts were of no avail. They immediately began redressing the wound. When the impromptu bandage was peeled off, Seda gasped, "Oh my dear God, what a bump she has on her head!"

It was true, the site of the wound had swollen to the size of a plum. Cold compresses were applied and Sofi was made as comfortable as possible.

Mother took Lusine, Diana, and Alisia aside. "Do not let her fall asleep for a while; her head injury may be more serious than it looks. Talk to her, sing to her, but don't let her go to sleep for a few hours."

The girls did as they were told. Brosh and Seda straightened out the camp. Brosh would go and find the horses and bring them back in the morning and feed them. Lusine was dispatched with Alisia to hide the body of the soldier who shot Sofi. They would leave this place the next day and take their chances on the roadway.

Chapter 39

SEPARATED BY BLOOD ~ JOINED TOGETHER BY LOVE

*May 1, 1915*At daybreak, Brosh set out to find the horses. Seda and Lusine accompanied him. The distraught beasts were tangled up in broken branches with loose reins around their legs. Brosh calmed the horses, gave them a few carrots, and adjusted their harness. Soon, they were trotting back to camp with the three youngsters calmly sitting high in the wagon.

Once the campsite was swept clean of incriminating evidence, the family piled into the purloined wagon. The horses were strong and allowed the group to cover ground quickly and put more distance between themselves and their discovered camp.

Nevertheless, such a luxury must be sold or left behind soon, for true safety could not be found on even the rural roads. For now, wheels and hooves helped the family flee the scene quickly and put distance between themselves and the dead police.

Seda and Brosh wanted to know what happened with the soldier who guarded the wagon. Seda asked the questions, but Brosh hung on every word.

"Tell us, please," Seda begged as she looked imploringly from one face to the next.

Diana finally spoke. "Look, we knew if the last police soldier was left alive, he would immediately go and tell his superiors. Many soldiers would then be sent to find the Armenian murderers— hundreds of soldiers—like the ones that were sent to other places where resistance occurred. We would be hunted down and killed." She took a sip of water and wiped her mouth. "We would never needlessly kill anyone; it is a sin. However, the policeman's bullet almost killed Sofi. So, the soldier at the wagon is dead as are his brothers who came to harm us. We will no longer be helpless victims."

Many hands patted Diana's back in agreement.

"We can only pray God will understand and forgive us for the blood on our hands." Brosh nodded his head.

Mother spoke next. "Let us go farther west; we must cover as much ground as possible and be on the lookout for a place to sell or lose these horses and wagon. Nightfall will come quickly."

The dirt road only allowed for a slow to medium pace which was fine, for one of the horse's flanks still bled a bit from Diana's blunted arrow earlier. Fortunately, due to its shallow penetration, the minor wound would heal quickly with the help of Sofi's herbs and salves.

At mid-day, the group stopped for food. A blanket was laid out and legs were stretched. The horses drank and each ate an apple and some old carrots. We talked as we ate and counted our blessings. However, an unwelcome surprise approached us as soon as the wagon's wheels touched the road.

A small band of criminals dressed in mismatched coverings could be seen in the distance. They approached the small family menacingly and positioned their horses right in front of the family's horses and cart. From their motley raiment, Mother could tell these men wore the stolen garments of Armenian refugees.

"What is your business in these parts?" asked the well-armed leader of the group.

"We are going to visit my sister as she is ill. This is my family," replied mother.

The grizzled leader gestured angrily at Isghoui. "The Sultan has ordered us to round up all Armenians, and you look Armenian to me. Show me your papers!"

Mother opened her hands, "We have no papers; we lost all our things when we were attacked and robbed on the road."

The leader shook his head and tightened his lips, "Then you will come with us," he blurted casting a lewd look at the young girls.

The small family of Armenians had discussed this kind of situation—one of fight or flee. The group agreed mother should make the call, and Diana would be second in command.

Diana glanced at mother while her hand slowly moved toward her belt and the dagger within.

"We will follow you, so lead the way," said mother matter-of- factly.

"No!" shouted the leader. "We will take the horses and wagon first. You all should follow us on foot."

Mother gave the signal (a slight nod) as two smirking men climbed down from their horses and walked over to the horses leading the wagon. Brosh had already secured his bow, but the pistol remained covered in the wagon. Releasing the wagon was not an option, for a search would reveal the gun and other items that would immediately put all lives in jeopardy. Heartbeats began to race (adrenaline multiplied on the inside—only calm showed on the outside) as the two men in charge stepped forward.

Diana and Alisia moved slowly toward the wagon with Sofi close behind. Diana looked at her mother's eyes and read the message within her visage. Lusine flanked the opposite side of the wagon as non-verbal signs spread from one family member to the next.

There would be no retreat—no running this time.

Seda sat on the wagon's bench with mother. She followed Mother's example and climbed down from the bench seat. Brosh brought up the rear, his bow and arrows just inside the back of the wagon.

"What do you have covered in the back of this wagon?" asked the first Turk as he approached Diana. He feared little from this young woman and her adolescent cohorts.

"Nothing much," replied Diana calmly, "let me pull back the tarps for you."

Diana deliberately stepped in front of the larger man stopping his progress toward the wagon as she positioned herself for what was to come next. After making eye contact with Alisia, Diana firmly yanked back the first tarp.

"What the hell is this!" shouted the officer angrily as he spied the horse pistol, bows, and arrows.

Before he could move again, Diana leaned over the wagon-side and swiftly grabbed the loaded pistol, and in one fluid motion, threw it in the air as nonchalantly as if she was playing a simple game of keep-away. It seemed to float above everyone's head, and the first Turk watched the pistol float over his head as if in slow motion—its business end pointing toward Heaven above before landing softly in Alisia's outstretched hands.

Too shocked to stop the toss, the first Turk's hands thrust out forcefully reaching for Diana's throat just as Sofi stepped up from behind her and intervened. Sofi forcefully plunged her dagger into his chest where his heart should have been, twisted it once, and pulled it out quickly. His facial expression changed from anger to surprise to outright fear as he tried to cover the now gaping hole in his chest. Blood squirted rhythmically through his tightly clenched fingers as he staggered backwards looking frantically to his comrades for help.

The second Turk quickly brandished a pistol, but before it could be raised to accurately aim at Sofi, an arrow flew by Diana's head at a downward angle and landed squarely between the Turk's chin and breastbone. A squishy noise was followed by a wet gasp as the wounded officer dropped his pistol and grabbed at the embedded arrow. Diana looked behind her to see Brosh standing in the back of the wagon notching another arrow from his quiver.

Soon the other men dismounted and ran toward the group as everyone scrambled for their weapons. The men brandished swords, knives, and a rifle and charged the small family from both sides. These men moved quickly as they strategically separated in an effort to divide these suddenly violent youngsters.

On one side, Alisia leaned against the back wagon wheel as she aimed the pistol carefully and waited for her chance. Diana placed one foot on the wagon wheel and leaped into the wagon to retrieved her bow. She kneeled behind the seat. Sofi and mother sought cover behind the wagon as mother pushed Seda under the wagon's belly.

The startled men could not understand how helpless women could put up a such a fierce fight. *They are just women—not warriors; they are just stupid mongrels who should be easy to kill.* Shouting, cursing, and firing, the men continued to advance on the small family.

One bullet struck the side of the wagon—splintered wood flew in all directions. The women steeled themselves and waited for the right moment. When the men stepped within the group's range, Diana gave a shout and the well-versed response was orchestrated close to perfection. Family members picked their targets and fired almost simultaneously.

Alisia's pistol detonated loudly as the gun's recoil threw her arm straight up toward the sky. The bullet grazed the head of the assailant closing in on her, but it did not knock him off his feet as he stumbled but continued his charge raising his sword threateningly—crimson blood running down alongside one eye. Alisia dropped the heavy pistol and pulled out her dagger and poised herself for a defensive move. The wounded Turk brought down his sword with fury and conviction as he attempted to cleave Alisia's head from her shoulders; alas, she was no longer there having rolled forward and almost right into his knees. As he turned to thrust again, Diana sent her second arrow through his broad back dropping him to his knees.

At almost the same time, Alisia thrust her dagger upwards into the groin area of the wounded man. She placed her other hand on the falling criminal and pushed the gasping body out of her way—she sprang to her feet, and in an instant began running to help the others.

Brosh and Diana were both standing behind the seat of the wagon. The four horses stutter-stepped nervously and the wagon rocked back and forth. Diana's first arrow sailed just over the shoulder of an advancing attacker while Brosh jumped from the wagon and quickly notched another arrow. He braced himself by dropping to one knee as he let the hand-crafted projectile fly just under the horse's neck; it pierced the advancing threat dead-center just below the stomach. With a cry, the wounded assailant hit the ground as his head slammed into the horses' hooves. As the man rolled onto his back, he tried to pull out the arrow, but Brosh jumped on him with both knees, held his greasy hair in one strong left hand, and cut his throat deep and decisively.

At the same time, Sofi's target had stopped his charge and took cover while he steadied his aim by leaning against a tree. His rifle pointed right at her as she aimed her bow at him. Realizing she did not have a clear shot, she defensively dove to the dirt. The rifle's bullet slammed into the wagon right where Sofi had been standing. A quick push-up and she was on her feet running at the man as he tried to reload for another shot. Having witnessed the exchange, Alisia followed Sofi's footsteps toward the occupied man.

Glancing at this crazed woman holding a bow at shoulder level and running like the wind towards him with a savage expression framing her face—it was too much to comprehend while trying to steady his shaking hand to load another bullet. The lead ball could not be manipulated properly with trembling fingers, and it fell aimlessly on the ground; the gunman's heart sank with it.

In a moment, Sofi was within an arm's length. Despite that, she ran right by him as he pressed against the tree for protection; suddenly, at the last moment before sprinting past the fearful figure, Sofi deftly angled her bow so its tip slapped him in the face cutting his lip open. His surprise pulled him away from the tree as she slid to a stop, turned, aimed and let loose her arrow at his cowering figure. As soon as Sofi's arrow found a home in the man's upper chest, another pierced his side. Sofi looked across the field and there kneeling on one knee... less than a stone's throw away—Alisia. Her bow now empty and sweat shining on her high brow.

The skittish horses jumped, pulled, and whinnied excitedly as Brosh alertly grabbed the reins. He leaped upon the top of the front wheel of the wagon and catapulted into the seat while holding firmly to the reins. Brosh called out and the seven ran toward the now moving wagon. With horses pulling anxiously at the reins, Brosh manipulated the reins until the excited stallions' staccato steps coordinated with each other into a gallop.

Diana gazed back at the battle scene and the scattered bodies dead or dying near the road. The battle-shocked family held on for dear life while Brosh drove the sweat-lathered horses to near exhaustion before slowing down their frantic pace and allowing them to breathe as they slowed to a walk; the group covered many miles of dirt road before finding a place to pull off and hide the wagon.

When the breathless horses came to a complete halt, each member stepped shakily from the wagon and inspected and hugged one another. They gathered together at mother's signal—sitting, drinking water, and slowing down their heart rates. Mother spoke briefly and the group made a decision. After stripping the sweaty horses, Mother, Lusine, Seda, Alisia, and Brosh would go one way and look for a new campsite at the base of a distant rock precipice that mother pointed out. Diana and Sofi would each ride one horse and tow the other two horses behind them. Eventually, in case they were followed by more enemies, the two would let the horses loose leaving a false trail for others to follow. Diana and Sofi would find their way back to camp on foot using a compass mother had given Diana for this purpose. The plan would lead any possible trackers astray—sending them after the horses. However, this would only work if the two on foot erased all footprints from the scene.

Diana and Sofi grabbed their sleeping rolls, knowing they would probably need two days before they would find their way back to the family's new camp.

"Do you see that cliffside? The one that looks like a woman's profile." Diana pointed out the rocks that jutted straight up against a blue sky. "We will meet you there the day after tomorrow when the sun reaches its apex. Meet us at its base as we face it now." Alisia nodded her head. The two sisters hugged, Diana secured her bow and quiver to the saddle, and Sofi and she rode off with the other two horses in tow.

Once again, the group knew their existence depended on their ability to become invisible. Still, there seemed to be increasing impediments the closer they came to the coast.

After covering the wagon in branches and brush, the five of them walked on for hours, leaving no traces of their presence—progress was slow as they brushed away any footprints or signs of their existence— but eventually, they spotted an opening beside a small stream running off the same mountain Diana had pointed out earlier. The ground was mostly level—a perfect place for a camp and close enough for the scheduled rendezvous in a couple of days.

The family made camp, bathed and washed their clothes in the stream, and proceeded to hunt this new area. Lying on her back, Alisia gazed up at the rock precipice that served as a marker for her absent sister. *I wonder where she is right now…what danger she may face…I should have gone with her.*

Splaaattt!, a brown mess of mud and pebbles splattered against her flat, bare stomach. She bolted upright trying to cover her nakedness and at the same time reach for her nearby bow. Looking up toward the source of the attack, there stood Brosh dripping wet and smiling—more brown muddy ammunition in his hands.

"Brossshhh! You are going to pay for that!" Fast as a lean fox, Brosh sprinted across the stream with Alisia in hot pursuit. Mother sat in the shade of a Willow watching the two splash and wrestle on the muddy banks of the life-giving water. She smiled contentedly, a *brother and sister...separated by blood—brought together by circumstance—joined together by love.*

Photo by Stephen Van R. Trowbridge

HAJI AGHA, A KINDLY NEIGHBOR AND A MOST LOYAL FRIEND TO THE AMERICAN HOSPITAL IN AINTAB

In the massacre of 1895 he posted himself at the hospital entrance and prevented the mob from entering. He represents the better type of Moslem, who are not responsible for the Armenian massacres.

Chapter 40

A CHILD'S GUILT ~ A MOTHER'S FORGIVENESS ~

Family meeting. The small-flame fire gave off no smoke as it heated the tea while the morning sun met evaporating dew to form a smoking presence around the five individuals. Brosh patrolled the outer ring of the campsite as he completed the end of his watch.

Mother spoke first, "I am proud of each of you and your remarkable abilities—your growth, stamina, and perseverance. Now, I cautiously ask you to be hopeful. Together, we've traveled hundreds of miles, added to our family, and spilled blood and tears during our sojourn to this point. We are now drawing closer to our destination—the historic city of Aleppo." She sipped her tea with both hands.

"Once there, we will try to find passage to another country—one willing to open its doors and treat us fairly. The future for us remains uncertain, but one thing is clear. Each of you has earned the right to make your own decisions. You are young, but those individuals who have been tested in battle—as you've been—know neither age nor limitations; you can do anything, go anywhere, be anyone. For 3,000 years, your ancestors lived in Paradise's Garden with the mighty Mount Ararat feeding fresh mountain spring water to its people. Now, you must find a new life to raise your own families and begin your own legacies. I know you can accomplish such a dream, and.... I know I may not be there with you." Mother glanced from one to another as she paused.... "Be that as it may, I want you to know that your presence—your love— has made me whole and mended my broken heart. No one could ask for more." Mother's head bowed and she dropped to her knees, "Thanks be to God for my blessed children."

The forest remained quiet as her words sunk into each individual's mind and trickled down warmly into each large heart. Rare were the thoughts about such a future when day-to-day survival remained paramount. Now, thinking about a real future, a new country, a new language—seemed unnerving and exciting at the same time.

Seda surprised everyone when she started to speak. Her eyes brimmed with tears as she looked up at the group. "I am so ashamed. I must confess. I don't deserve to be with you. When my family was forced to walk more miles than possible, my mother bribed an official who let us use our donkey. My mother put my sister and I in the saddle and led the way. After many days, mother asked my sister and I to get down so she could ride a bit and rest her swollen feet. We cried in protest complaining that our feet hurt, too. My selfishness led to more suffering for my poor mother who loved us too much to refuse our childish complaints. You see—I am not worthy of your presence. I am not worthy of being loved!" She sobbed uncontrollably for a moment and then threw her tea down and sprang up like a cat and sprinted headlong into the forest.

Mother reached for her, but she flew past her. Lusine leaned forward grasping mother's hand, "Let me go to her. I will bring her back."

Brosh saw Seda running from camp, but when he called out to her, she waved him off and ignored his questioning look as she continued on erratically. Lusine soon followed and gestured that she would go after her. Brosh simply nodded.

Chapter 41

UNEXPECTED
CIRCUMSTANCES ~

When Lusine finally found Seda, she was rolled up into a fetal position under the ledge of a rock. Her face smudged with dirt wet from her tears.

Lusine sat down beside her. "When Diana rescued me, I was naked, scared, and about to be raped by two awful men. She offered me a choice. Take her hand and trust her, or stay and die. I decided to trust Diana; I decided to live. Nightmares haunt me, and my survivor's guilt still visits regularly, but I am not giving up. Instead, I am standing up. I am standing up for my mother, for my family, for my right to be alive." She moved closer to Seda's shaking body and touched her back. "You have a right to be alive. Your mother understands your youthful mistakes; we all do. We understand and still love you as part of our family because we all make mistakes; we are only human. We need you as much as you need us, but you must stand up. So, you have a choice. Are you going to lie there and cry, or are you going to stand up and be part of our family?" Lusine stood up and waited. When Seda did not move, Lusine started to walk away.

"Wait! Wait! I do love you, Lusine. I love you more than ever!" Seda ran to the taller girl. Lusine dropped to one knee and opened her arms." The two hugged, cried, and soon laughed their way back to camp.

～7Ⅳ～

The rendezvous occurred at high noon as planned just below the mountain rock's female profile. Diana and Sofi appeared just after the sun passed its zenith. Alisia ran to greet them as the triad hugged each other happily. "Oh, you are so thin; you must be hungry! Come eat." Alisia led the way.

When they returned to camp, stories were told and laughs shared. Later, Mother asked Diana and Lusine if they would accompany her in the morning to a small village to see about supplies. Some essentials were necessary to replace despite the overall risk.

～7Ⅳ～

Lusine and Diana rose early and Mother joined them soon after as they tended the fire and stirred the soup that would serve as breakfast. The birds sang out their happiness before the sun broke through the trees. Dew-kissed leaves shivered and shook reflecting their vibrant colors off the morning light. All life stirred eagerly looking forward to the new day.

Mother, Diana, and Lusine made ready by disguising themselves as Kurdish women visiting relatives. At least, that was the plan....

～7Ⅳ～

As the changelings had done before, they entered the village and tried to blend seamlessly into its daily activities. Unfortunately, small villages tend to be places where everyone knows everyone else. Nevertheless, the three disguised women carefully proceeded to a small shop to buy some thread and new needles.

The shopkeeper looked the strange triad up and down suspiciously, but then her expression changed and she came from behind the counter and asked seemingly innocuous questions.

"Good morning. Are you travelers? I haven't seen you around here before. May I get you some water?"

"Yes, please—you are most kind. We are just visiting my cousin who lives nearby, and we thought we would visit your charming village to buy a few things to bring them." Diana and Lusine pretended to be interested in a few items along the wall.

The suspicious shopkeeper narrowed her eyes, "What is your cousin's name? Maybe I know him."

"Oh, I don't think so, for he and his wife live outside of town; they are new to this area and have not lived here very long." Mother moved away a bit hoping to avoid further questions. After ferreting through some wicker baskets, she found some thread and selected several needles of varying sizes.

The shopkeeper returned with the water. When she handed the small cup to mother, she did not release it right away. This subtle move caused fingertip contact between the two women forcing mother to look up into the old lady's searching grey eyes. The two stared at each other for a long moment.

"You are right. Even though I have lived here my entire life, I probably do not know everyone." She smiled wryly and slowly released the cup.

Mother carefully placed the items on the counter, and sipped the water while watching the older woman carefully finger the items. Mother's sixth sense sent cautionary vibrations to her brain—warning her that this shopkeeper presented a clear danger. The monetary exchange took only a few moments, and the three exited gracefully onto the street. As

Diana looked back, she saw the old lady talking to a young man who nodded his head and left swiftly in the opposite direction.

Diana touched her mother's elbow, "I don't like that shopkeeper; she just sent a boy on an errand. Are we safe here?"

"I sense danger as well." Mother slowly walked over to Lusine and touched her arm lightly. Lusine could see the concern in Mother's eyes.

"Let's head back the way we came." The three women picked up their pace as they headed out along the dusty road following the same steps they made earlier.

When Mother heard the quickly approaching hoofbeats, her heart fluttered. Before the triad even reached the edge of town, they were stopped by men on horseback who circled around the three refugees and blocked their path. A Turkish officer who appeared to be in charge signaled the other three horsemen mounted close behind him.

The moustachioed man inched his horse forward until the nervous beast was directly in front of Mother. "Ma'am, we'd like you to come with us—you girls as well."

Mother remained calm. "Is something wrong, sir. We did nothing wrong."

The officer grinned complacently, "No need for alarm, Ma'am—we just have our orders. I am sure we can clear this up in no time."

The other gendarmes smiled at each other as they shifted the weight of their rifles in the direction of all three but not right at them—not yet. Mother looked again at the brightly buttoned man sitting high above her on his horse as a dark cloud passed over head and blocked out the sun.

A sign—this man is a messenger of Death—dangerous and deadly; I can feel it, thought Mother. She considered her limited options.

Mother knew if the three followed the officer, he would ask for their identification papers—they had none. A small group of peasants began to congregate including the old shopkeeper. Diana and Lusine's hands were ready to grasp their daggers and die protecting their mother, but they did not have their bows; it was mother's decision—they waited.

The officer nudged his horse closer to mother. "Are these your daughters? They should come along as well. My men are stationed up the street."

Mother remained calm and carefully walked between the girls and the soldiers as she continued the tenuous conversation. "Why are soldiers here in this small village? Is there trouble nearby?

"We are on our way to Aleppo; we stopped here to rest and feed our horses. Now, come along." The officer's tone began to take on a hint of impatience.

Mother sensed the shift and noted the officer's change in body language. With demurred grace, she nodded her head and turned back toward the town. Diana and Lusine followed in her footsteps. When the three women approached the rest of the troops, the other men stood up to better view the young women more clearly. There were at least a dozen men stationed outside a large barn preparing food, rolling out bedrolls, starting a fire, and making themselves comfortable. As Isgouhi and her daughters drew closer, all took notice and heads turned—all activity stopped as the soldiers stared unabashedly.

"Are they Armenians?" The men began talking and asking questions amongst themselves. The commanding officer stepped down off his horse and handed the reins to a waiting young soldier who walked the horse over to the barn. With a pointing gesture, the officer directed the three women toward a table by the barn. He sat down behind the table as the three females stood side-by-side, straight and stiff. The three motionless women could hear the soldiers whispering to each other. In a not-so-covert manner, a surreptitious circling of soldiers now stood behind them blocking any exit. On the table, he held out his hand toward mother.

"Your papers please—and then you are free to go." Hand extended—the dead-pan face stared in mock innocence.

Mother stared back at the acting officer as the charade continued, "We are simple Kurdish women. We have no papers on us. We are traveling to visit my cousin. He will vouch for us."

The officer just looked at her for a long time—no kindness in his eyes now. His men looked on as he clasped his hands together.

"Well, that is most unfortunate. You see, we are on strict orders to arrest all Armenians, and you look like you could be Armenian, so this is what we will do. You will leave your daughters here, and two of my men will escort you to your cousin's house where he can vouch for you. I am sure he will be able to produce proper papers."

The surrounding soldiers nodded enthusiastically in agreement looking lustfully at the youthful girls.

"No, I can not leave my daughters alone. I will send one of my daughters with your men, and she can show them the way. They will be back well before dark."

The officer looked thoughtfully at the daughters and then back to the mother. He was almost positive there would be no papers, but he felt satisfied by the fact that the mother and daughter would both be held in town thus insuring the capture of all three women. He confidently nodded his approval.

"Very well." The officer signaled to one of his men, and two men saddled up and produced a horse for Diana. Lusine stayed behind with Mother.

Mother held her head high and looked straight ahead. Diana and Lusine did the same, yet inside, they both were trembling. Their hearts' arrhythmic beating brought fresh blood to their faces as they considered their precarious situation.

Lusine heard one of the men say, "I hope they are Armenian. We will enjoy them tonight and make them scream." The soldiers laughed while moving closer and openly leering at Lusine.

"Enough! Back to work I say! The Officer shot the man a severe look. He knew these men were used to having their way sexually with Armenian girls. Such sexual conquests strategically crippled Armenian survivors and insured the Turkification of future offspring. Rape served as an effective weapon against one's enemy, and the officer acquiesced to his young charges' lust-filled atrocities. Yet, he had to be sure, so he asserted his authority over the excited men. There would be no rapes—at least, not yet.

Mother and Lusine sat stone-faced on the ground—backs pressed firmly against the weather-beaten wood of the barn.

The men continued to cast side glances in their direction—mumbling threats under their bated breath.

Chapter 42

~ DIANA'S DARING PLAN ~

The soldiers followed behind Diana and let her lead the way. Their eyes watching her body slightly move up and down as she rode in front of them. While the soldiers trotted their horses side-by-side, they made their own plans.

"Why don't we take a break and have some fun with this one—I like the way she moves." The soldier made an obscene gesture and laughed out loud.

The older soldier shook his head, "We will not act until we know for sure. In a little while, we will know if she is lying, and if she is—we will make her ours on the way back. Save your energies for then—you will need them to keep up with me." Laughter rang out again.

Diana ignored the laughing boors behind her, for she was in deep thought making her _own_ plans.

The young family leader calmly led the soldiers along the same path in which the three had traveled earlier. She thought about trying to overpower the two soldiers, but it would be risky, and mother and sister would still be in captivity. She longed for her bow, but reassuringly felt some comfort knowing she still had her concealed dagger if these men tried to hurt her once they were out of town. She tried to come up with a better plan, yet when none came, she knew what she had to do. Desperate and out of choices, she led the soldiers into the forest from which she had come earlier. It was not long before they approached her family's camp. As Diana knew there would be, someone was on lookout—it was Alisia. Although Diana could not see her yet, she could feel her presence, sense her sister's eyes upon the wicked men close behind her sister as they approached.

Alisia heard the horses' hooves breaking ground, twigs, and rocks long before they approached the camp's boundary. She climbed to a nearby knoll for a better vantage point. Once atop the knoll, she could clearly see the slowly approaching figures on horseback. Her heart began to beat rapidly when she recognized Diana in front with two well-armed Turks riding directly behind her. Alisia ran to the edge of camp and sounded the alarm signal—the emergency whistle alerted the group. Sofi and Seda took immediate action; however, Brosh had already left early that morning to hunt for food and had not yet returned.

Diana slowed down deliberately, as she led the soldiers alongside their small camp. She knew the soldiers would be suspicious once they saw a smoking campfire. As Diana led the soldiers through the trees and into the small opening, she suddenly kicked her horse and veered it off sharply to the right.

The soldiers thought she was trying to escape, so they pursued her right into the camp. The two men were surprised to see a small fire burning and soon realized they were being led into a trap—alas, it was too late.

As Diana rode by the fire, she saw her bow and arrows right where she had left them. She pulled her horse up, threw one leg over the saddle, aligned both legs, and adroitly slid down her horse's side landing evenly on her two feet. She sprinted swiftly across the opening—a do-or-die attempt to secure her trusty bow.

Almost as quickly, one of the soldiers now had his sword out as both men leaned forward as they repeatedly dug their heels into their horses' flanks urging the stocky beasts forward. The horses leaped after Diana as the youngest soldier held the reins in one hand and his threatening sword in the other ready to cut Diana down before she could notch an arrow. Also closing fast on Diana, the older soldier drew his pistol in a headlong attempt to make a deadly shot from his moving horse. As he aimed the pistol, he leaned toward Diana just as she reached her bow.

Unbeknownst to the two deadly soldiers, Sofi and Alisia were armed and ready and as the men tried to cut down Diana, the young women's arrows flew straight and true. The two men were hit almost simultaneously. One arrow pierced a shoulder, the other a thigh—now the battle's momentum shifted as the mounted adversaries were confounded by the unexpected turn of events.

Like the wind between the trees, Diana snatched her bow and notched an arrow in one fluid motion. She stopped suddenly...turned toward her pursuers... and let loose her arrow at the closest soldier. However, his advancing horse jerked wildly and the arrow missed its intended target as it whizzed by the soldier's ear. Thus, both men remained on their wide-eyed horses despite the flesh wounds.

The younger soldier, startled by Diana's arrow that nicked his ear, almost dropped his sword as he struggled desperately to manage his horse with one hand and pull out the precarious arrow with the other. The arrow refused to budge, so he looked hurriedly to the bushes where the first arrows had originated. When Alisia's arrow pierced the older soldier's arm, he pulled up his horse, but held on tight to the unfired pistol despite the painful presence of the black-feathered arrow stuck stubbornly in his bicep. Once his horse halted, the man squeezed his knees together for stability and used his free hand to fire an inept shot at Diana, but the bullet harmlessly sunk into the ground beside her.

The pistol shot echoed through the woods, and with the speed of sound, it quickly reached Brosh's ears. His head snapped up, and he turned away from the doe he was hunting. As soon as his mind had finished calculating the direction of the gunshot, his feet were moving toward the sound <u>and</u> the family's camp.

On the opposite side of the disrupted camp, the younger soldier kicked at his horse and charged toward the brush where Alisia and Sofi were standing. Sword held high, he now could see the two just behind a tree surrounded by low hanging branches. Both women stood their ground—trusty bows at the ready—until the man was almost upon them—his attack scream loud in their ears. At the last moment, the arrows were released instantly hitting the rider in the chest and throat. The attacker twisted, lost his stirrups, and fell head-first to the ground. After bouncing a few times, the twisted body came to rest at Alisia's feet. She adroitly stepped over the young soldier's immobile (except for its last twitches and jerks) body.

Sofi turned her attention to Diana who had darted to the soldier's left and ran back toward Sofi and Alisia. Knowing he could not catch the fleet-footed girl, the remaining soldier attempted to trample her beneath his horse.

Sofi immediately notched a second arrow from behind the dead soldier lying prone at her feet and took aim once again. Alisia sprinted toward her sister. Diana saw the two women ready to help and accelerated her last steps before diving to the ground at the edge of camp.

The last soldier's efforts proved futile, so he turned his horse sharply to avoid Sofi and Alisia's imminent attack. As the man attempted to high-tailed it out of camp, two arrows flew through the air, but in the confusion, neither one hit their intended target. The last soldier frantically whipped his horse for more speed—an opening just ahead—a possible escape route.

Brosh stood breathless at the edge of the frenzied scene. He'd run all the the way back to camp and now stood surveying the last moments of the battle. Seeing his family scattered, but still poised to fight— Brosh made his decision and stepped right in the path of the galloping horse—thus blocking the soldier's escape route. Standing with his legs spread and both hands on his loaded pistol, Brosh's breath came in staccato heaves as he steadied his aim. Before the soldier could focus on the young man, Brosh aimed the the pistol at the man's sweaty face. The close-range shot sent the lethal lead ball whistling between the flying horse's forward-facing ears as it crashed solidly into forehead and skull. The blunt force of the lead ball opened the soldier's head with life-ending force. With the dead man's body in free-fall, Brosh dropped his pistol and dove left as the panic-stricken horse's barrel chest fleetingly brushed Brosh's boots.

The family members ran to Brosh's side. By the time they reached him, he was standing brushing off the dirt and walking over to retrieve his pistol.

"Are you okay?" shouted the circling woman—brushing his front and backside and checking him from top to bottom.

"I am good." He looked at each young woman and wondered aloud, "What did I miss? Where did these soldiers come from? Is anyone hurt?"

"No," said Diana, "but I brought the soldiers back to our camp—I had no choice. Mother and Lusine are captured and held by soldiers. The soldiers were supposed to bring me back with proper papers and identification. I am sorry, and thank you all for saving my life."

Sofi looked down at the dead soldier, "How did all this happen?"

The family members looked from the dying man to Diana.

Diana quickly explained, "We were stopped in the village. A small band of soldiers—I counted a dozen plus an officer in charge—they have Lusine and Mother. I was sent to bring back proof that we were not Armenians. Now, we need a plan."

"Are the people in the village friendly? Or are they Turks who hate us?" asked Sofi.

Diana looked at Sofi, "I believe an old shopkeeper turned us in; they are not friendly."

"We must try and save them. They will not be safe for long with those Turkish soldiers. So, how can we overcome so many soldiers <u>and</u> townspeople?" questioned Alisia.

Diana dropped to one knee and with stick in hand mapped out the plan she devised in her head while being escorted by the two soldiers. First, she drew a map of the town. "Mother and Lusine are here. There are thick woods just beyond the barn where the soldiers wait for us."

"How about this idea?" offered Sofi, "instead of entering through town, let us surprise them by coming in through the back way—through the woods."

"Still, even if we surprise them, in daylight, they will overwhelm us with their numbers and weapons." Alisia shook her head.

"If you kneel before God, you can stand up to any man. Yet...there is another way," said Diana. "We ride down the middle of the street, so all will see us, but what they will see are the two soldiers returning with me as expected."

The family considered the bold plan for a few moments....

"Yes!" Sofi shouted—"that is just crazy enough to work. Can you make me look like a soldier? Alisia, will you be my fellow soldier?"

"No, I will be", stated Brosh. "I can look like a soldier."

"Yes, of course you can, Brosh," nodded Diana.

"I like the idea of a surprise attack; they will not expect such a daring plan."

The group swiftly stripped the soldiers of their uniforms while Alisia and Seda made plans to come through the woods behind the barn once the fighting began.

Alisia threw her arm around Seda. "We will use the element of surprise to our advantage and attack from behind once you are discovered and engage the enemy from the front."

Sofi made adjustments to the too large uniform and smeared a bit of mud on her face to darken her features where a beard should be. The plan was exceedingly dangerous, but no other option was feasible. Time was running out; they needed to move fast before the other soldiers became suspicious.

Diana spoke again, "Know this! We will not die! This is our destiny. We were meant to be here, to spend precious time together, to carry on our line. We will stand on our feet and live, and we will save Mother and Lusine. And if at any point, all seems lost to you, do not fear, for when you are tired, beaten, and down to nothing—_God_ is up to something!"

Diana held out her arms and the group came together for a final embrace. The three horses were found and mounted, and Seda and Alisia set out at a jog hoping to be in position behind the barn when the fighting began—all were armed, disguises in place, and prepared to defend or die for each other—and for that level of sacrifice, there is no greater love.

Chapter 43

SOME GO TO HEAVEN~ SOME HELL...

Mother and Lusine were closely watched by the men. The women held their heads up and sat erect while staring up the street where Diana had rode out of town accompanied by the soldiers. Lusine leaned toward Isgouhi and whispered, "What will become of us Mother?

Without taking her eyes from the road, Mother answered, "Diana will lead the soldiers to our camp where the soldiers will be taken by surprise. Our practice, our constant drills will pay life-preserving dividends today. When the soldiers are dead, I do not know what will happen. I hope they run away and save themselves, but I am afraid they will come and try to save us. Therefore, we must be ready to fight, for death in battle will be a blessing compared to what we will experience if we live."

Lusine nodded. "Thank you my adopted mother for your wisdom, for your grace, for your love—thank you."

The corners of Mother's lips slightly turned up as she she looked down the street waiting for the return of her other daughter. Her hand found Lusine's and squeezed.

Hours passed and the sun began to cast long shadows. Lusine pulled her shawl around her neck, but her other hand rested on the butt of her knife hidden in her belt.

"Here they come!" shouted one of the soldiers. The officer came out of the barn. He squinted under a furrowed brow at the three figures returning in the same order as they had left. The sun was low behind the approaching figures, so the soldiers had to shield their eyes as they watched the three riders come closer.

The officer swaggered over to where Mother and Lusine remained sitting.

"Well, lady, I guess your story must be true. Here comes your daughter with the proof you needed."

Mother and Lusine stood up and looked up the road in wonder— *how could this be?* Yet, as the three grew closer, Mother sensed something was amiss...something familiar about the "soldiers".

Just then, the three advancing figures brought their horses to a trot as if they could not wait to get back to the barn. Some of the soldiers stood up and stared—curiosity piqued as the horses picked up speed.

A moment later, the horses were at a gallop and closing fast on the barn area. Soldiers began to move to see why the three were pushing their horses to charge forward at such a frenzied pace. As suspicions grew, some of the more alert men reached for their rifles. Too late—the three galloping figures were now near the barn and suddenly had bows in their hands. Guiding the horses with only their knees, Alisia, Sofi, and Brosh took aim at the scattering men. The soldiers' surprised faces turned desperate—**they were under attack!**

Arrows and bullets flew wildly in the ensuing exchange. One soldier fell with an arrow through his throat—another one tried desperately to pull an arrow out of his upper stomach, and one spun out of control with an arrow in his rib cage.

One arrow pierced the open mouth of a soldier who tried to mount his horse. The force of it broke teeth and the white/red pieces came out the side of his mouth with the point of the arrow. Another soldier's forehead spurted blood when it was hit by a glancing arrow and was soon followed by another which sunk into his back as he fell to the ground writhing in pain.

The stunned soldiers' bullets were rushed sending them zipping over the heads of the galloping marauders, but one off-target lead ball hit Diana's horse dead-center in the animal's heaving chest sending both horse and rider to the ground face first. Only Diana's athleticism saved her as she managed to tuck her head and shoulder at the last minute and roll with the momentum before the horse's body could crush her, but the impact still knocked the breath from her body, and she lay in the middle of the mayhem dazed but still conscious.

A soldier took aim at her as she struggled to her knees, but just as he steadied the aim of his rifle, his head was suddenly snapped backward and his throat cut with a swift stroke. In all the confusion, Mother and Lusine were running toward the fray. After making the fatal cut on the soldier threatening Diana, Lusine turned the bloody soldier's body toward the other soldiers who were now taking aim at her.

Just as two soldiers aimed their rifles at Lusine, mother sprang into action and with a heart-stopping leap managed to push the deadly rifles off target. Mother fell to the ground, but as she quickly regained her feet, her eyes locked on the arresting officer advancing toward her; his eyes narrowed as his pistol pointed menacingly right at her—he did not hesitate. Before her girls could react, the pistol's charge sent its bullet right into Mother's soft, life-giving stomach. Her eyes widened in surprise, yet her body felt no pain, but the blunt force of the bullet buckled her body, and her knees once again hit the dirt—with one hand on the ground, she tried to steady herself, but blood was already seeping through her fingers as she covered the gaping hole in her stomach.

Diana screamed wildly as she ran for her bow and quiver which was splayed on the ground. Shots ricocheted at her feet and flew by her head, but she ran swiftly and scooped up both and rolled to a kneeling position next to Mother. As Diana readied her bow protectively, her hands shook slightly as she tried to think of a way to get her mother to safety.

Mother remained on her knees as she became light-headed, but before she could think of what to do next, Sofi guided her horse beside mother and held out her arm. Mother instinctively grabbed Sofi's arm and felt herself being pulled up beside the horse. Diana dropped her bow and assisted her mother with a strong shove upwards. With great effort, mother threw her leg over the horse—a sharp pain ripped through her mid-section. Sofi lifted with all her strength and pulled the wounded woman onto the back of the jittery horse. Next, she kicked hard behind her stirrups urging the horse up the street and away from the fighting.

With a short sprint and a well-timed leap, Diana sought cover behind the officer's table. The officer had retreated to the barn as his men continued to load and fire their weapons. However, now their numbers were not so great, and the bewildered soldiers realized these Armenians were skilled fighters who did not hesitate to kill any threat in their way. The rumors were true—Archers of Death did exist and were now directing their wrath at them.

Meanwhile, Diana spotted a horse still tied to the post by the barn. She sprinted across the road with her bow over her shoulder and her quiver bouncing along her side. She stopped long enough to send an arrow over the head of a young Turk who stepped out of the barn and aimed his rifle at her. When he ducked back, she pulled the tie from the post and mounted the horse. Her heels immediately sank firmly into horse flesh and directed the frightened beast back to the area between the soldiers and Sofi's retreating horse with Mother barely hanging on with the support of Sofi's one arm. As Diana bolted away from the barn, she spotted Brosh in the middle of the turmoil.

Brosh shot one soldier point blank, but was then pulled down from his horse by another. Soon, he was pinned and the heavy soldier's bayonet thrust at his bare neck, but Brosh squirmed to the side in a nick of time and the blade only scratched him as it pierced the dusty road. The soldier was about to try again when an arrow lodged itself squarely between his shoulder blades. Brosh stared past his wounded attacker to see little Seda staring at him over her now empty bow. A wondrous, worried look furrowed her brow as she reached for another arrow. Alisia soon stood right beside her with armed bow as well. The two were nearly out of breath after their long run to the battle scene, but their timing—a godsend.

Brosh shed the dead weight above him and scrambled to regain an upright position, but another soldier met him head-on—his strong hands squeezing Brosh's throat. As the soldier's firm grasp threatened to crush his Adam's apple, Brosh reached for his knife, and plunged it into the soldier's side. At almost the same time, Seda's second carefully aimed arrow sunk into the man's back followed by Alisia's arrow that wedged itself beside the man's spinal column—the choking lessened slowly as the soldier's body began to wilt.

The townspeople watched the bloody battle with concern and soon began to arm themselves when they saw the soldiers being defeated by this rag-tag group of lethal archers. The men and women of the town began to form a force ready to stand against these invaders. Rifles were aimed from windows—hoes, knives, and pitchforks appeared in the hands of old men and women.

Alisia grabbed one of the saddled horses by its halter and mounted it with one great running sideways leap as she circled the horse and pulled Seda up behind her. However, before Alisia could secure Seda on her horse, the officer who shot mother saw his chance and now ran at Alisia with his pistol ready to fire again, but as he steadied his aim, Diana rode between him and his intended target. Horse and rider slammed into the officer's arm knocking his pistol to the ground and spinning him around in a circle. Diana then circled back on her mother's assailant as he bent down to pick up the pistol.

Before Diana could gain the advantage, the officer now took aim on her as she urged her horse toward him. Brosh, now back on his feet with his bloody dagger still in his right hand, watched the scene unfold and from ten feet away let loose his dagger end-over-end in the direction of the officer. However, this time the target was not not a tree trunk; it was a moving man with death on his mind. The dagger stuck solidly in the officer's lower back, but after the initial shock, the officer steeled himself stoically and once again steadied his aim at Diana.

Yet, before the officer could fire, the swift-footed Brosh leaped onto the officer's back and retrieved his dagger at the same time. The gun fired straight up into the sky as both figures fell to the ground. The officer used his extra weight and height to overpower Brosh and thwart Brosh's efforts to stab him. As the officer's strength began to turn Brosh's knife backwards towards Brosh's face, Diana rode up and threw her dagger into the back of the officer's neck.

The sudden impact of Diana's dagger stopped the forward motion of the officer, and Brosh regained control of his knife which he promptly plunged into the officer's chest. With a firm push from Brosh, the inert body slid off to one side leaving a blood trail across Brosh's chest.

Diana offered her hand to Brosh who used it to leap up onto Diana's horse before the shouting townspeople were upon him. Lusine led interference by using her horse to knock over two peasants trying to over-run Brosh and Diana. The remaining four rode out of town with stones and bullets whizzing by them. One old woman aimed a long rifle out her shop window; as Diana galloped by, she looked right at the woman— the shopkeeper!

The fatigued family found safety in the forest knowing that neither the townspeople nor the remaining few soldiers would follow them into a place where they could be easily ambushed by crazy lunatics with bows and arrows at the ready.

The riders gathered together as they zig-zagged their way deeper into the forest. When Diana rode up behind Sofi and Mother, she noticed a stream of thick blood on Sofi's horse's back flank. She signaled Sofi to stop, and the others followed her example. When they dismounted, Diana sought out the source of the steady stream. She gasped—the blood wasn't from the horse; mother's lower stomach had been pierced by the officer's bullet. It was worse than Diana feared. Mother's pale face reflected the day's dying light in a luminous hue as she slipped in and out of a semi-conscious state.

"Diana looked up at Lusine. "Go…ride back a bit and make sure no one is following us. Brosh and Seda—you two stand guard! Sofi, come and help Mother! I thought she had a flesh wound."

Alisia lifted her mother's feet, and she and Diana carried her to a level spot that offered cover while the others served as lookouts for any trouble.

Mother's eyes opened slowly, blinked a few times and smiled at her daughters. As her memory returned, she looked at Diana and then to Alisia. Realizing her condition, the bone-weary mother spoke slowly, "Don't fret My children…it is my time…let me go to your father. We will always be with you, for no one with children ever really dies."

Soon, the others returned to Mother's prone figure. When they were all present, she raised her right arm and beckoned them closer. The family closed in on her like a fragile flower closing its petals for the night. Each dropped to a knee as she began drawing upon internal strength to speak her final words.

"Come to me, my faithful children, and receive my final covenant.…" They looked at each other for a moment, and Diana nodded to Lusine who then knelt beside the matriarch's body and bowed her head. Mother's right hand disappeared for a moment under her blood-stained garment; her eyes winced as she pushed aside the bandage Sofi had applied. When her hand reappeared, her fingers were dripping in fresh blood. She made a fist and extended her right index finger coated in crimson. "With this fingerprint, I bless each of you with the ancestral blood of ancient Armenia—never forget your origins— never fear your future." She pressed her bloody finger onto Lusine's forehead whispering, "Worry ends, when Faith begins." Lusine stepped back, and Seda followed, then Brosh…and soon each of the children's foreheads displayed a scarlet fingerprint—a rose-like manifestation of Mother's love temporarily imprinted on their foreheads, yet indelibly printed onto their souls for eternity.

Again, mother beckoned them closer as the first star in the sky made its presence known in accordance, and Mother smiled at its presence as she looked past the sad faces. "Kachadoor calls to me; it is my time. Let this be my final blessing with each of you. When you lose heart and your faith begins to fade, (she took a moment to make eye contact with each one of her children as her eyes glazed wet and iridescent), and tragedy lays its misery upon your shoulders…look to Nature, for God is omniscient—connecting each of you to Him—see the signs He offers you by opening your heart wider than your eyes—a hummingbird's pell-mell visit, a rainbow's iconoclastic ring around the sun, a shooting star's flashing brilliance, a mountain stream's bubbling song, a butter-fly's delicate flutter, a hawk's sudden cry, an owl's nocturnal pleas, or… a tree's everlasting patience—_there_ you will find hope, and find it you must—for it offers untold strength, everlasting life, and infinite love."

The exhortation exhausted the failing figure—Mother's voice dropped off to a whisper…so Diana and Alisia put their straining ears by her lips. "You two will always be my daughters, but now… remember… Father and I love you and are with you…forever. I am…so proud… so…proud…."

Mother's hand slowly released its grip from Alisia's hand as her head bowed gently against Diana's heaving breasts.

Dark clouds covered the setting sun until only its last ephemeral rays were visible streaming upward toward heaven while bowed heads below watered the dry soil. Mother was already gone——her soul soaring...free at last.

Chapter 44

HAIL MARY ~ FULL OF GRACE ~ HAVE MERCY...

The tightly-wrapped body of Mother accompanied the family of six to a verdant valley deep in the forest. They buried Mother's body near a meadow flanked by a green glade bordered by yellow and red wildflowers. A circling hawk screeched out a plaintive call before the last heavy stone was laid upon the freshly turned earth. A cairn of smooth stones formed a small pyramid at its head, and a wooden cross stood solidly behind it. Mother's favorite multi-colored scarf with red, blue, and orange highlights adorned the cross as a gentle wind caressed it allowing its hand-woven filigree to point toward the Mediterranean Sea. Each member of the family solemnly visited the mound of dirt and one-by-one laid a stone on Mother's grave.

When all were done, Diana began to speak.

"My mother's loving heart taught me well. Through her example, I learned life's most important lessons. In her name, I hail Mary, Mother of God, to have mercy on her soul and deliver her to our Father high above for her eternal resting place. I ask this in the name of our Lord, Jesus Christ."

"Amen," echoed forth from the small group of bowed heads. They embraced one another, placed flowers on the grave, and began to walk away as the restless horses stirred at their approach.

After several paces, Diana sensed something…stopped and looked back at Alisia who remained…on her knees…at the foot of her mother's grave—head bowed in prayer, tears watering the dying flowers. Diana raised her fist, kissed the thumbnail of her right thumb and made the sign of the cross—first on her forehead, then her lips, and finally… her heart.

Chapter 45

~ARCHERS OF DEATH~

Native Americans often say, "When you were born, you cried and the world rejoiced. Live your life so that when you die... the world cries and _you_ rejoice."

After mother's ceremony, the family rode the horses to near exhaustion, for they knew many more Turkish soldiers would be looking for the family now known as the Archers of Death. As is the course of oral renditions, the tales of the Archers of Death spread from village to village—growing taller and grander with each retelling. They knew it was only a matter of time before thousands of Turks would descend upon the area seeking revenge and determined to eliminate any possible Armenian leaders. The Turkish leaders promised that any uprising by the Armenians will be nipped in the bud and dealt with severely and permanently.

Thus, the six rode toward the coast...toward their destination... toward their destiny.

CooooOOOOO-woo-woo-woo, coo, coooo, wooo, wooo.... The male mourning dove called out its plaintive call hoping to attract female company. Lusine, Sofi, Diana, and Alisia exchanged a few sleepy words of greeting as they rubbed the sleep from their eyes. Brosh, still on watch, had relieved Seda a few hours ago, so she continued to sleep through the early morning rustling of clothes and bedrolls.

Last night, She and Brosh played chess on a small wooden board Brosh always kept in his pack. All of the group enjoyed playing chess (a long-time Armenian custom) to pass the time, but last night it provided a reparative respite from the despairing grief felt by all after Mother's passing.

Diana knew the group looked to her for guidance and leadership, yet she secretly doubted herself and her abilities to protect and lead. Crestfallen and shaken, she pulled herself together while using Mother's own inspiring words—*Failing and falling are but temporary setbacks in life's plan to insure one builds character. See your failures as opportunities to pick yourself up and show your mettle. Be resilient, strong, unyielding in the face of adversity, and at the same time, stop to feel pain, heartbreak, and loss, for they are all part of the human condition—a purposeful condition in God's infinitely wise plan.*

For a moment, she thought how prescient her mother had been to pick up father's bow that fateful morning. Despite her head injury, the madness of the situation, and father's shouts…she still found the inner strength to procure the one item that would be critical to their long-term survival. She already missed her dearly.

Diana called for the morning meeting. Alisia went to relieve Brosh (Diana and her sister would talk later). The group discussed the proximity to Aleppo—the closer they were to the city, the more likely they would find trouble. They shared ideas on how best to investigate possible transport to another country and what it would cost. The gold reserves they recovered from the fallen Kurdish Chetes would cover the cost of transport, but the logistics still were an obstacle they would have to overcome.

Alisia walked the perimeter of the camp while the others talked, ate, and drank tea. She thought about how much she had changed over the course of a few months. Her memories of her parents often occupied her mind as she remembered family outings as a little girl, being read to by her mother or father, lessons, sayings, arguments, and her own shortcomings. If one observed her from a distance, one would see an elegant mid-teen with perfect posture and animal-like grace and swiftness. Her body remained lean and fit with rippling sinews leading to toned appendages that moved her seamlessly through the forest. She walked silently on her hand-sewn moccasins so as not to disturb the birds and other animals she loved to observe in their natural habitats. Still, she remembered her purpose, and kept a keen eye and ear open for any movement or sound that did not belong.

After listening to Diana's discussion points, Sofi spoke first. "My mind is not made up yet. I followed your mother, and now I will follow you, for your mother's spirit clearly resides within you; besides, my life belongs to my new family. However, I still think of my little brother and sister and wonder if they may have somehow survived the tragedy that took our family. I would hate to leave them behind."

"I feel Sofi's dilemma, yet my family is gone for good, so I am committed to my new family now," spoke Lusine. "My new life began with your family, and God willing, it will follow its path to a better world. Hope rings true in your voice, so let us go forth in noble pursuit of a better place."

Brosh and Seda nodded their heads in agreement.

Brosh stood up, "Aleppo belongs to the Turks; spies are everywhere. Armenians are not safe there. We see the signs at every village and city now. Turks are closing any escape routes by taking control of the cities and towns.

"Brosh is right. Nevertheless, someone must go to the city to try to make arrangements for passage on a ship. We must find locations, destinations, and what such a voyage would cost. I think two people should go, and I should be one. Know that this will be even more dangerous than last time."

The group agreed, and all the others quickly volunteered to accompany Diana into Aleppo.

"Our hearts weep in unity tonight, yet mine is lifted a bit by your willingness to walk beside me. I will pray to the Holy Mother that I may prove myself worthy of your trust."

Suddenly, the group heard Alisia's bird call for immediate danger! With high-speed synchronicity, the members took their positions and armed themselves.

A man and woman on horseback approached the camp. They had wandered off the road and were riding slowly through the forest when they came across this clearing. They stopped by the little fire—confused by the scene. In a moment, they were surrounded by young warriors—weapons pointed in their direction.

Sofi and Lusine took hold of the the two horses' halters.

Diana stepped forward, "Who are you? Where are you going?"

"Please, we mean you no harm. We are American Missionaries on our way to Aleppo. We lost the path…and thought this way would be a shortcut. By using our horses to cover the rougher terrain, we hoped to save time."

"Can you speak Armenian? My English is not very good."

The two looked at each other for a moment. The woman looked back at Diana. "My parents were friends of many Armenians; I can speak some of your language," she said slowly and clearly.

"Dismount, we will not hurt you, but we need information."

The two dismounted and sat down by the fire.

"Are you helping the Armenians or the Turks?"

"We are missionaries, so we help those who need our help; however, we have seen great harm come to the Armenians and hope to continue to help them."

Diana looked at the others; they sat expectantly—waiting for her next question.

"Can you tell us what you've seen?" Diana looked again at the others as if trying to anticipate what they wanted to know. "Are there any Armenians left?"

The woman shifted nervously, looked at her husband, and wrung her hands as she shook her head, "Not too many, I am afraid. The Turks and some of the Kurds—awful, unbelievable, we've never...we can't describe it."

"Please, tell us the truth, we also have seen much, but have heard much more. We want to know."

"A minister we trust told us about an Armenian stand-off where a couple of thousand Armenians bravely fought to protect their homes, wives, and children. They held off an entire Turkish regiment for two weeks. They used simple flintlock rifles, bows, and even knives to fend off these troops. However, they only had so many bullets, and the Turks surrounded them, but they would not give in and were ready to fight to the death.

Finally, a the Turkish officer in charge stepped forward. He spoke sincerely to the Armenian leaders and held up his Koran. He then promised the Armenians that if they would surrender, in deference to their courage, he would allow them to go unharmed. He then took an oath on the Koran, the most binding of all oaths to Moslems, and pleaded with them to surrender.

The Armenians did not trust the Turks, but decided to take this chance rather than to see themselves and their families eventually killed.

The two thousand men surrendered their arms. As soon as they did, they were given picks and spades and forced to dig a long trench. Once they completed it, they were directed into it by soldiers with bayonets on their rifles. The trench is still there—filled with human bones and skulls. The Armenian women and children were taken away. We do not know what happened to them."

Diana sat still for a while. "What else do you know?"

"A while ago, my husband and I," she reached out and took his hand for support, "lived about a kilometer from an Armenian camp. Its location was near Diyarbakir not far from the Tigris River. Late one night, we heard screaming that continued into the early morning hours. When it became light, we went to investigate. Circassian soldiers, under orders from the Turks, told us that children were being taken from their mothers—thus the crying and screaming during the night. They explained that the children were being placed in dormitories to continue their education. I know we were told lies because the next morning we set off and had to cross the River. We were shocked. The river was red with blood and...and the heads on the shore... the heads of the children...the beheaded corpses of tiny children... just floating...as if in slow motion... just floating quietly...motionless on the water. The horror...the horror of it, but there was nothing we could do." Overcome with emotion, the distraught missionary began to cry into her husband's shoulder. After a while, he whispered something into her ear. She looked up at him in desperation, bridled her emotions, and then turned to Diana.

"My husband wants you to know all of what we saw. There are two other massacres, yet we tell you reluctantly; they will break your heart."

Straightening her back, she continued. "We spent time in nearby areas and witnessed repeated mass exterminations of Armenians. We reported these atrocities to our superiors, but nothing was done. About a month after the river incident, we traveled to the heart of Mesopotamia and settled near Baghdad where we helped build and staff a new hospital. One day, we were summoned to travel to a remote area and provide help to rural children who were sick from drinking contaminated water. On our way back, we saw soldiers from the Ottoman Army ordering Armenians to gather thorns and thistles and to pile them high near a large cave at the base of some foothills. After the task was completed, the Armenians' hands were all tied together...there must have been a thousand people of all ages...hand to hand..pulled and prodded and eventually marched into the cave at gunpoint. A few older Armenians refused to enter the cave and were shot on the spot. A few others made an attempt to run away, but they were soon killed by Turks on horseback. The rest of the Armenians entered the cave reluctantly in a long organized line. After a long while, only the Turkish guards came out. The tinder-dry material scratched and scraped the the dirt as it was immediately pushed into place and piled high effectively blocking the entrance of the cave. As soon as the last branches were thrown atop the impressive pyramid, it was set afire at various points simultaneously. In moments, the flames roared into the heavens and into the cave as well. The thick smoke filled the cave and choked the entrance. Soon a cacophony of shouts, howls, cries for help, and bellowing screams from inside the cave violated our ears as our hearts broke for the trapped souls inside. Some were burned as they ran into the flames, and others were asphyxiated by the black/grey smoke that filled their lungs."

The weary woman paused. Sweat had formed on her brow; it glistened in the sunlight. She took out a white handkerchief with embroidered edges and dabbed at her forehead.

"May I bother you for some water, just a sip will do."

Seda brought the woman a cup of water and sat by her as she quenched her dry throat. She continued....

"An acquaintance of ours is a minister. He began a church near the Euphrates river. He told us that he came upon a caravan of Armenians, and noticed they were all children. He approached one of the officers and asked about their destination. The officer angrily replied that the children were being taken to an orphanage almost 100 miles away. He noticed the children were in rags, some naked in the hot sun, and others barefoot. When asked how many more days of travel it would take to deliver the children, the man frowned and said in disgust that it would take longer because the children kept crying and falling down. They cried all night and screamed in pain.

He said his men could not sleep well and were becoming frustrated, losing their patience.

After the minister left, he headed north to visit a member of his church who was ill. He spent the night with the family, and after a warm breakfast, he saddled up and headed for home. As he was on horseback, he made much better time than the caravan. He rode along the Euphrates and noticed the water had changed from clear blue to a smoky purple-red color. As he road up the river, he found hundreds of children's bodies thrown into the river. Most were floating as they had been there many hours.

Upon closer inspection, the minister suffered another shock when he saw that the little bodies all had one thing in common. Their tiny hands had been hacked off. The minister fell to his knees and cried at the horrific sight. He prayed to Jesus and the blessed Mother Mary to carry their souls to heaven.

When he climbed back on his horse and headed up the road away from the river, he immediately recognized the bloody clumps along the side of the road. Again, to his great dismay, he soon leaned down to ascertain that the appendages were most certainly the hands of the dead children who were then dragged into the river for quick disposal.

The minister cried when he told us that there is no greater loss than the death of a child.

Later, when I lamented that it was awful to see the minister weep— my husband said to me that the minister cried not because he was weak, but because he had been too strong for too long.

Before the minister left, he told us of his plan to write a letter to the U.S. Ambassador, Henry Morganthau, and describe the acts of inhumanity he witnessed. He believed the ambassador abhorred the actions of the Turks and Kurds. He quoted him as saying something to the effect that practically all of them were atheists, with no more respect for

Mohammedanism than for Christianity, and with them their one motive was cold-blooded, calculating state policy. The minister thought he could somehow convince the United States of America to intercede on behalf of the Armenians. After all, America is a powerful Christian nation. Why wouldn't it come to the aid of other Christians? My husband and I left him soon after, and ended up here. We've been trying to help as many refugees as possible. I hope you understand. We are not your enemies; we are simply God's instruments."

Brosh laid his horse pistol across his lap as he rubbed the barrel with a bit of oil. The other members of the group looked away as well. The truth too intense—the imagery too specific—the memories too fresh. How does one carry such knowledge and still sleep at night? These young souls knew the way to a new life would be difficult, yet they refused to give up hope; still, they sat stupefied at what they heard—what the world will probably never know—or what it prefers not to know.

Alisia shook her head. No one knew what to say, but they all knew the missionaries told the truth.

Diana broke the silence, "Do you know how we can get passage on a ship to another country? We have money."

The woman looked at her husband and asked him a question. He answered her at length.

She turned to Diana to interpret for her husband, "My husband said there is a ship that has been taking Armenian refugees to America. The ship is called the S/S Armenia and is owned by the American Hamburg Line. Many Armenians paid dearly for the passage, and he heard the voyage is long and arduous with crowded and disease-prone conditions. The ship leaves from Musa Dagh. That is all he knows."

Diana nodded, "You have helped us by honestly answering our questions. I must ask you to swear not to tell anyone you met us here. In return, we shall let you go in peace. Godspeed."

"We give you our word, and please know that we only wish we could help you more."

The husband and wife rose stiffly after sitting on the ground for so long. They mounted their horses and without looking back—soon disappeared from sight.

Diana turned to the others, "Let us move our camp deeper into the forest. We are too close to the road here. In the morning, we will decide our next steps."

The group took only minutes to gather their belongings. All paths soon disappeared as they moved through the darkening wilderness. As the sun set behind the treetops, the weary travelers smoothed out a resting place as Mother Earth welcomed their bruised bodies with soft pine needle mattresses and level land.

A grand old owl hooted in the distance, and just as sleep pulled down heavy eyelids—his song was answered from afar. Hope springs eternal in the deep, dark forests where dreams are king and nightmares flee the righteous.

Author's note:

German aspiring writer Armin T. Wegner enrolled as a medic in the winter of 1914–15. He defied censorship by taking hundreds of photographs of Armenians being deported and subsequently starving in northern Syrian camps and in the deserts of Deir-er-Zor. Wegner was part of a German detachment and stationed near the Baghdad Railway in Mesopotamia. He was eventually arrested by the Germans and re-called to Germany. This handsome young medic paid a price for his moral rectitude, and all Armenians will forever be in his debt.

"I venture to claim the right of setting before you these pictures of misery and terror which passed before my eyes during nearly two years, and which will never be obliterated from my mind." Armin T. Wegner

The photos covertly taken by Armin T. Wegner are among the few that capture the bleak struggle to survive facing Armenian deportees. As a second-lieutenant in the German army stationed in the Ottoman empire in April 1915, Wegner took the initiative to investigate reports of Armenian massacres. Disobeying orders intended to stifle news of the massacres, he collected information on the genocide and took hundreds of photographs of Armenian deportation camps—primarily in the Syrian desert.

Wegner was eventually arrested, but not before he had succeeded in channeling a portion of his research material to Germany and the United States through clandestine mail routes. When he was transferred to Constantinople in November 1916, he secretly took with him photographic plates of images he and other German officers recorded.

The above mentioned photographs may be found online:

www.armenian-genocide.org

www.armeniapedia.org

Chapter 46

THE BAGHDAD RAILWAY ~

The forest retained the coolness left over from the evening, but the sun's heat beat down relentlessly upon the bare brown blank areas devoid of visible wildlife with no shade or protection.

Diana thought about the stories she'd been told and what she'd witnessed thus far. The unprotected Armenians being marched through the desert without protection from the sun...without food...without water. Mothers forced to leave their children behind or watch them die of thirst or hunger...or worse. Thousands more forced onto various ships and boats of different sizes and taken out on the Black Sea and thrown into the frigid water to drown. The despair and anguish they must have felt as they took their last breaths before being enveloped by a cold, dark, indifferent sea.

Diana's sudden sadness washed over her in waves of survivor guilt. She tried her best to lock it away in a secretive place—safe from prying eyes, but family knows...family always knows. Such was her one consolation, as she looked at her surrounding family; she was not alone—they shared her suffering, and she shared theirs. *When one shares one's pain, the pain becomes less; it is what makes a family strong—what makes a family resilient.*

Flittering birds woke first and sang out early morning greetings without paying much attention to the humans curled up in their sleep-inducing cocoons. As the animal activity increased and the forest began to open its arms to the morning light, each member began to wake at his/her own pace. One braving the cool morning breeze to empty her bladder nearby while leaning against a young tree to maintain her balance, another rubbing sleep from his eyes, one going off to relieve the night watch, and another stretching with eyes still closed, and all breathing in the fresh, unpretentious earthiness of the early morning—the time had come to move on, to explore and seek, to find passage to a new home.

"No fire this morning. Let us move east and find a new camp. We leave soon, so let us erase our presence here." Diana checked the old reliable compass as she had done hundreds of times. The sun's rays filtered through the treetops—verdant lacework too sophisticated for human hands—God's delicacy and delight.

The family members moved spryly now having shed morning's grogginess. The fire-pit disappeared as did footprints and other tangible evidence—no visible human stain of any kind remained.

The group ate lightly as they walked, and before long, it was midday—time to eat a more substantial meal—dried meat, nuts, a few vegetables, copious amounts of fresh water and cool tea. After they ate, they rested.

Alisia sat beside her sister and placed her hand on her shoulder. "Sister, you have done well by us. Our parents smile down on you."

Diana smiled as she look directly into the kind eyes of her sister, "I worry sometimes, but our new family fills me with hope. They never argue or complain—such strong hearts tempered with tragedy.... And you... my twin, my soulmate, my guiding star—I would be nothing without you."

The sisters hugged as young Seda secretly peeked at them from afar and reflected inwardly on the scene played out before her eyes. *The two of them suffered greatly, yet they still remember to love each other—appreciate each other…every single day. I will learn to love again from them if I am so blessed and can stay alive.*

Sofi returned after scouting the path ahead. "Everything looks clear, we can proceed when ready."

"Thank you Sofi. We should move on—daylight burns as we talk. We will continue traveling southwest toward the city of Urfa. From there, we will head towards Aleppo and finally to Musa Dagh. Of course, all of these plans are subject to change as the winds of destiny may blow us from our course. If so, I cannot think of anyone else I would rather be with than all of you."

The others smiled and laid hands on Diana and her sister—silent prayers floated on updrafts headed for heaven's waiting angels to deliver. With the wind behind them, the nomadic family struck out betwixt the pines and outcroppings.

Placing one foot ahead of the other as thoughts turned into memories and memories morphed into wordless avenues winding through broken hearts, Seda's eagle eyes spotted a thin black line ascending into white clouds.

Diana's eyes squinted as her gaze followed Seda's point of reference, "There is level ground to our left; it is flanked by pines and brush. What do you think?"

"Let's stay near the trees," offered Lusine. The others liked Lusine's idea.

"Okay. We should make camp and then investigate the smoke. Any volunteers?"

Diana looked around.

"I want to go," added Seda quickly. Diana just smiled.

Alisia put a hand on Lusine's shoulder, "Lusine and I could make it there and back before dark if we move swiftly."

The group agreed (Seda frowned), and the two readied themselves.

"We will move unnoticed and bring back information before dark. Don't worry about us." Diana hugged them both.

"I can go as well," offered Sofi.

"Those two move like the wind; they will return before long. You've already done so much for us. Besides, we may need you here for protection. Let's set up camp."

Brosh walked over to Alisia and offered his pistol.

"Thank you my brother, but my bow is much lighter. Besides, our mission is to simply investigate—not to make contact. Keep it here by your side. We don't know if this is a safe haven here. You take the first watch; I will signal our return." Her hand gently stroked his cheek— and she was gone...Lusine right behind her.

The small camp formed quickly and efficiently—simple, effective, transparent. The four family members blended into the woods like camouflage. Seda gathered small pieces of wood, twigs, pine cones, and other dry material for a small keep-me-warm-fire once the sun set. Sofi and Diana set themselves down cross-legged facing one another. Diana repaired a leather moccasin while Sofi stitched a tear in her sleeveless shirt.

"What if we can't find passage right away?" Sofi asked.

Diana pressed the needle hard through the leather and into the metal thimble protecting her thumb. "I know what you mean, but I sense many Christians have already fled before us. The ships will fill their spaces easily, for desperate people will pay—and so will we." She pulled the thick thread the tiny hole.

Sofi shook her head signaling her agreement. "My parents told me America welcomes all immigrants, all religions, but mostly Christians flock to their shores. It is a new country, so there is work for all who are willing. My mother's brother wrote us from America once. He said when he sought out its land of plenty—he thought the streets would be paved with gold. However, when he arrived, he was poked, prodded, and inspected by doctors and nurses looking for diseases. He spoke no English, so he struggled to understand the difficult language. Many travelers died on the ships or arrived sick from the poor provisions and unclean accommodations on overcrowded boats. He went on to say that once he found his footing, the streets were <u>not</u> paved with gold. In fact, they were not paved at all—<u>and</u>, they expected <u>him</u> to pave them. The immigrants worked longer and harder than anyone else for they had something to prove. They worked for less money, and they were treated poorly much of the time by the whites who held all the best jobs. Nevertheless, he was welcomed by other Armenians who had settled before him. They spoke his language, found him work and a place to stay. He believed his future would be better in this young country, so he persevered and prayed often."

Diana listened and found herself encouraged and discouraged by Sofi's story. Still, she knew she wanted a better life for her future family—one free of hatred and intolerance. *I will trust my my heart, my mind, my woman's intuition…. We shall see…we shall see.*

〜〜〜

Alisia and Lusine found the source of the smoke and were astounded by what else they discovered. Peering through the trees, they spied a horizontal clearing of enormous magnitude. Steel parallel rails seemingly touching one another as they disappeared in the far distance. They stared silently at a site neither had ever seen—the building of a railway.

As they crept closer, they could tell that while Germans oversaw the project, other nationalities were amongst the laborers—inching closer, they thought they recognized some of the young men as Armenians, but they could not be sure, for the bedraggled young men seemed broken as they bent over nearly in half toiling away breaking rocks and moving wooden beams.

Unbeknownst to Alisia and Lusine at the time, the two young women were looking at the Baghdad Railway. It would become one of the best known events in economic history in which the Deutsche Bank of Germany participated as financier and operator. Hardly any other railway caused as much excitement before the First World War as this one, which was planned to run from Haydarpasha Station in the Asian part of Istanbul to the Persian Gulf. Britain, France, and others would be watching its progress closely for the political implications of its completion.

At one time, it was supposed to provide a rail line from Badhdad to Constantinople. However, due to war, financial problems, and rugged terrain, a train car would not travel on its rails until 1940—well after the Iraqi Government financed and finally completed the project.

The two scouts carefully crawled backwards away from the preoccupied activity and were soon on their way back to the others with surprising news. Moving quietly between shade and fading light, Lusine and Alisia light-footed their way rapidly over semi-rugged terrain when they suddenly froze simultaneously—a blood-curdling scream halted the teen girls dead in their tracks. Shots rang out so close by the girls ducked for cover—crying and screaming from just over the mound beside them!

As the two unsure girls skirted the hillside to investigate, they located a safe vantage point behind a fallen tree. Their eyes opened wide as they looked down upon a horrible scene. Twenty or so workers from the railroad were being shot one-by-one by five zapitehs who showed no hesitation with their merciless task. The men's hands were tied behind their backs, but in a desperate move, some of the men ran head-first at their attackers and tried to head-butt their cruel killers. It did not work; the last man did get close enough to defiantly spit in the face of his murderer just before he was knocked to the ground and bayoneted in the chest. As the two edged closer, Alisia and Lusine were able to clearly see the victims' faces. The poor men being slain were young Armenian men—workers from the railroad project. Their bodies gaunt, malnourished—ribs poked angrily against paper thin skin.

The two women readied their bows, but they were too late. The last man lay motionless at the foot of the zapiteh who after wiping the Armenian's spit from his lips, bent over the young man's body and spat disgustedly on the young man's still staring face. The zapitehs then inspected the prone bodies, kicking them and turning them over to make sure they were all dead.

The two girls could barely restrain themselves from running down and engaging the murderers, but they managed to bridle their initial impulses. They knew the risk of engagement was too high; nevertheless, youthful bodies and passionate hearts do not always listen to their rational minds. Rather, emotion muddles reason and action carries the day.

Alisia read Lusine's face and understood her feelings immediately. "We are outnumbered and underarmed." Lusine's expression did not change. Alisia felt the same way and resigned herself to the reality. Well then, we better make plan."

Lusine nodded her head in agreement. "We can't just walk away."

As the five zapitehs rifled through the bloody corpses (some corpses with eyes still open and staring blankly at the ones searching their pockets), Lusine took a position with the low-lying sun to her back while Alisia inched forward toward the leader. It was fairly easy for Lusine to sneak up on the distracted policemen bent over their dastardly work.

Shireee! A clear bird call sang out loudly and the zapiteh closest to Lusine stood up as his head swiveled 180 degrees—all seemed normal until an invisible arrow entered his back directly between his shoulder blades. The unexpected blow knocked the breath out of him as he fell to his knees spitting blood from his mouth and wheezing through a punctured lung.

On the other side of the bodies, one of the zapitehs jumped up and pointed his rifle toward his fallen comrade, but his defensive move was interrupted as another arrow pierced his back with silent, deadly force. He fell forward clawing at the earth in pain.

The other three policemen screamed, "Where are they? Look to the trees!" Swinging their rifles to and fro the frightened men could see no one nor hear anything. They grouped together for protection and began to slowly inch their way back toward the train.

Swiiissshhhh, Swiissshhh—two more arrows were sent on their deadly way. One carefully aimed arrow impaled itself just below the retreating man's belt as the wounded zapiteh grabbed his groin only to find an arrow embedded there. He howled as he fell onto his back pulling desperately at the arrow. At about the same time, the other arrow perforated the throat of the leader as blood arterially spurted out in hurried rhythmic pulses.

The last policeman fired his rifle toward the trees, but the only answer was two more arrows—one whizzed by his face and bit into his ear as it whizzed by. The other pointed projectile found his soft shoulder and spun him around like a misaligned top. The two girls charged the fallen man who stared in disbelief at the wiry females now aiming their arrows at the wounded murderers. The last bearded man raised his rifle, but at the close distance his heart was pierced in a split-second. Alisia took down the other wounded man as he struggled to rise. Soon, it was quiet.

The girls were the only ones standing among two dozen men. They looked at each other as they tried to calm their beating hearts. For a moment, time stood still.

As they hurriedly retrieved their arrows, both suddenly turned their heads toward a scurrying sound—a streak of grey zipped across the morose scene.

A squirrel scooted across the ground dodging the bloody bodies as it jumped over a rifle and ran right between the girls. It carried a nut in its mouth and only paused once—at the base of a pine tree. Her bushy tail curled upward as it scanned the area for danger. With an even stare, it looked at the calamity with indifference, and scrambled up the waiting tree to find her warm nest and feed her babies.

"We must go. Let us be quick." They retrieved their last sacred arrows, and took two rifles and ammunition. Their feet flew over the ground—while minds were filled with conflicting thoughts—justice, revenge, guilt, satisfaction, and...fear.

The sun set quickly behind dark, ominous clouds—the kind that threatens regenerative rain, but only spits and sputters. With the light dying, Alisia whistled and called out repeatedly seeking some homing direction from her sister.

Diana and Brosh left camp at sunset to meet the girls on their way back should they need assistance or guidance. Worry weighed heavily on Diana's mind as darkness set in making it nearly impossible to insure safe footing. Just then—whoo-hooo, wooo-hooo, sounded off to her right. She answered the call and set off in the same direction.

In a few minutes the sisters were in each other's arms. Diana breathed a long sigh of relief.

"Much to tell...," Alisia breathed into her sister's ear..."but let us get to camp first." Brosh carried the confiscated rifles. Once in the camp, they sought the warm fire and soon sipped the hot tea while Brosh examined the rifles.

Chapter 47

MOTHERLESS CHILDREN ~ FAR FROM HOME

With the great Euphrates River to their northwest, the six youths decided to move on heading south toward Urfa, Suruch, Birejik, and eventually to Aleppo. While the unknown loomed heavy over their heads and nagged persistently at their hearts, this small family of youthful hearts strode forth undaunted. After all, they knew death quite well—therefore, his tenuous hold over them disappeared like dust in the wind. Due to purity in their hearts, they were granted extensions from the Almighty, so with righteous confidence, they pressed on with sharpened skills and an experiential base that belied their years. Such was the extraordinary nature of this willful young family.

As they approached Urfa, the group's food dwindled down to bits of bread, nuts, and rice. Walking fast and burning calories rapidly, stomachs growled regularly, but these pangs of hunger received no recognition. The family did not want to take time to hunt, but if game presented itself—it was considered providence.

Once near the outskirts of Urfa, they came upon an Armenian school. As was the custom of Armenian villages, there beside the school set an Armenian church. Both places were empty, but a crippled Armenian woman sat outside near the church cemetery as if she were guarding the sacred site. A series of tattoos—dots, symbols, and hieroglyphics not immediately recognizable covered part of the woman's forehead, chin, and cheek. Her right leg was replaced with a wooden prosthetic with a rubber tip on the end—a pair of crutches waited patiently within her reach.

Diana approached the woman and offered her greetings on behalf of the group. The woman touched Diana's hand and nodded. "We are headed to Urfa and then to Aleppo. Can you offer us any advice as we are strangers to these parts?"

The old woman looked confused at first. Slowly her right hand emerged from beneath her shawl. Bony fingers beckoned Diana closer…closer still…closer. The fingers spread and then touched down lightly upon Diana's cheek as they caressed her cheek over and over… and then once more as if amazed by the smooth unwrinkled skin. Her hand slowly fell back to her lap and disappeared into her frayed shawl. "My grand-children were murdered against that wall behind you— executed…in front of me…their parents were taken away first…then the children…why?"

Tears streamed down her face…a clear fluid ran freely from her nose. "I have cried a river of tears! The great Euphrates overflows its banks… it is my fault…now, my days are numbered and I sit here all alone."

Once again, the woman scanned the members of the youthful entourage carefully before replying. "Be careful as you draw near that city. There are many Turks arriving daily. They show contempt toward anyone who is not Muslim, and Armenians especially suffer at their hands." She looked down at her wooden leg. She waved them away with a sweeping gesture signaling that was all she had to say, but before they left, she offered one more helpful suggestion. "Follow this road and you will find a large building. You may find the answers you seek there."

"Thank you ancient one—bless you." Diana bowed her head slightly and walked away. "It is not safe here for us," Diana said as she turned toward the others. "Let us keep moving."

They walked another 10 kilometers before seeing a large building. It was teeming with children. They entered the grounds cautiously and were soon approached by a nurse in a white uniform and an official from The League of Nations—Red Cross unit.

"May we help you?" said the official. "What is this place? Why are all these Armenian children here?" Diana pointed toward the children.

"Come friend, sit with us, and we will explain."

The nurse provided the history of the orphanage and told them many more of these places were needed to house the Armenian children now without parents. The experienced nurse knew she was most likely talking to survivors of the attempted genocide and proceeded to offer food to Diana and the others. The family accepted and filled their empty stomachs.

Diana thanked the two for their work and asked if they would answer a few questions. "We are on our way to Musa Dagh to try and gain passage to another country—perhaps America. What can you tell us?"

The official looked at the nurse—then back to Diana, "There is growing Armenian resistance in Musa Dagh. Many Armenians are convinced that the Turks are planning to arrest and deport them or worse. These Armenians say they will fight; however, I do not know how well armed or how many will join such a movement. We do know that thousands of Armenian children, especially girls, were taken as slaves and given to the Turkish elite. These children were quickly turkified and were forced to forget their past and only worship Allah.

We have also heard of convoys of Armenians headed to Aleppo under guard of Turkish gendarmes. In one specific case, a witness told us that she was part of a group of more than 10,000—but only 150 arrived. They say some of the women hid money in their hair and mouths when they were stripped of everything. They used this money to survive. Most of the girls were stolen by Kurds who came out of their mountain homes with the encouragement of the Turks. Most were sold and were forced to lead lives of prostitution. Others were used as slaves and servants.

Diana felt her body flush with heat at the idea of a resistance movement. The others looked at each other. Diana took out a gold coin and handed it to the nurse. A look of disbelief spread across their faces.

"Take this as a gift for your efforts on behalf of our people; we thank you for doing God's work."

The group watched the tiny children at play for a moment before they left. Their innocent naïveté allowed them the freedom to play with one another despite the calamity that had befallen them. One girl, fearless enough to step closer, smiled at Diana as she lightly touched and inspected the older girl's raiment, bow, quiver, and arrows. Diana smiled down at the young girl—knelt beside her and placed her finger in her mouth. Next, she planted a wet, soon to be invisible fingerprint on the child's forehead.

"In you, I see me. Someday, you will remember the strangely dressed girl wearing weapons who placed her finger on your young forehead and blessed you with the saliva of the Hye." Diana reached into her satchel and produced a smoothly honed piece of green glass into the girl's tiny palm. Diana stood, turned, and walked away. After several steps, she stopped and looked back at the little girl and smiled to see her fingering the smooth green glass shaped like a heart resting in her palm.

The little girl ran up to the nurse and showed it off proudly. "What is it?" asked the girl quizzically.

The nurse bent down for a closer look. Surprise spread across her face... "Why, I think it is...yes, it is...an arrowhead...of course, what else... an arrowhead."

The two figures (one short, one tall) stood together holding hands as the tall young woman archer disappeared over the hill.

⌒ᴎᴛ

The family of six moved swiftly across the plains. They passed through meadows and mountains cautiously—seeking cover as often as possible.

In a few days, they were near Surach. Their bodies were light from lack of food, so they seemed to cover miles like the wind that pushed at their backs.

The next day, they set up camp outside of Birejek. The Mediterranean could not be far off....

Chapter 48

A RED RIVER RUNS THROUGH IT ~ THE EUPHRATES ~

Brosh and Seda left camp at daylight to hunt for fresh meat. As the sun tried to break through the early morning clouds, sharp-eyed Seda spotted a doe feeding on green leaves. She pointed and Brosh readied an arrow. Only bow and arrows were used for hunting now as the group neared the more populated areas. The swift arrow flew true and brought down the doe, but the small deer struggled back to her feet and began to run off with Seda and Brosh in pursuit. The two lost sight of their prey but were able to follow the trail of blood; the wounded animal wouldn't last much longer.

A while later, they spread some branches before them and jumped back at the sight. Two wolves were helping themselves to the deer as two others paced back and forth waiting their turn.

"Shall we try to scare them away?"

Brosh shook his head, "They could turn on us. Better we leave and look for other game."

Before they took a few steps, a muffled roar arrested their progress. The two turned to look from a safe distance. A deep growl and bellow caught the hungry wolves' attention as the bushes parted and a huge brown bear lunged forward threatening the gorging wolves as it stood on its hind legs with sharp claws raking the air in front of it. The ravenous wolves had torn free the hind portion of the deer and now dragged it in the opposite direction not wanting any part of this hunger-driven bear. One could tell these wild creatures had tangled over food in the past; without further resistance, the determined bear soon laid claim to the rest of the mangled deer.

Seda's eyes were saucers in her head as Brosh gently guided her away from the grisly scene. Putting distance between them, Brosh spoke up, "We are fortunate that the wolves found the deer before us, or the bear could've surprised us. We will look for other food, but let us head back to camp."

No other animals were spotted, so the two found their way back to camp carrying only a story to tell.

That evening, Sofi and Lusine fared better while hunting and brought back two rabbits and some dry wood. The group ate well and slept soundly.

Before breaking camp the next morning, the group met together and agreed to make Aleppo their goal.

The next day, the small family broke camp early and steadily moved southwest. The group could hear movement and noise when they approached the road. As practiced, family members camouflaged themselves and waited for the troops to pass. Hundreds of Turkish soldiers were heading toward Aleppo.

Diana watched closely and wondered… *Could they be on their way to Musa Dagh as well?*

As the six blended into the forest, Diana thought about the Armenian resistance. *I know my own heart tells me to join the fight, but I am not sure what the others will choose to do.* She did not have much time to ponder as the terrain began to change and the group could smell and hear a difference in the environment—water! The Euphrates River snaked out in front of them like a blue-brown arterial snake slithering between banks and reeds heading south to its point of origin.

Diana stared at the far bank; it appeared farther than she originally thought. When she glanced at the others, their expressions were the same as hers.

Chapter 49

CROSSING IN THE RAIN ~

The main crossing presented itself upriver, but remained entrenched with Turks. The family of six remembered being told of gruesome scenes involving the drowning and killing of thousands of Armenians in the river. Women were shoved into the river and bayoneted or shot. The river ran red and held many dark memories for Armenians.

The group sat solemnly on the banks as they looked outward and considered their options. They could try and swim, but they would have to leave most of their heavy weapons behind. They could chance a crossing on a ferry, but the risk of discovery remained high.

Finally, they decided to build a raft and float across. They surmised the current would take them miles south, but it would be the safest way to get across without being noticed. Plus, heavy items could be lashed on top of the flotilla. The plan would entail each of them being submerged in the water to prevent being spotted. The raft would be disguised as pieces of driftwood stuck together slowly floating downriver.

They began work on building a crude raft lashed together with bits of rope, rags, and reeds. By the end of the day, the task was complete. All was set to cast off in the morning.

However, the next morning the skies opened and rain poured down. The Lord, in his infinite wisdom, provided cover for the small family's endeavor as it would be more difficult for anyone to recognize a human's presence while raindrops agitated the surface of the river.

Brosh and Lusine pulled while the others pushed the raft into the water with gear on top covered by branches and leaves. Only dark heads bobbed above the surface. Water found open mouths as they bobbed up and down. Each person scissored legs trying to move the wood across the river, yet the progress was slow and hardly noticeable. Tired legs threatened to cramp, water-logged skin tore easily, and the current pushed the six towards the middle of the river where the current was strongest.

After several miles of drifting south, the river turned sharply around one bank and grew narrow and deep. The shore was almost within reach when Diana struck out thrashing at the water—a rope tied at her waist. She almost made it but was swept back to the middle. Alisia grabbed the same rope and tried once more. As she neared the bank, a fallen tree offered a branch to her and she grabbed on tightly. She secured the rope to the branch just as the weight of the raft tested the strength of the rope—it held, but for how long?

One by one, the members traversed the rope to the tree and in a joined effort pulled the raft toward them. Exhausted, the group collapsed on the sand out of breath and strength. As they crawled away from the water, they looked up to see hundreds of dead bodies. Swollen and cut to pieces. The stench caused Seda to wretch as the others tried to look away from the mutilated corpses of all ages and sizes.

"Let us leave this place," stated Brosh as he began to gather his things from the raft. The others followed his example as they half ran and half crawled into the brush safely away from the river.

Chapter 50

GERMAN FRIENDS ~ AND ~ A BAD-DRAGON

May 21, 1915—Wet, tired, and too exposed by the river, the soaked clan forced itself to keep moving southwest until they found cover and a place to make camp.

Brosh gathered stones as Sofi found small, dead twigs and branches. Diana produced a few dry matches from a tiny waterproof container. Alisia made a small, struggling fire by using a tightly stretched skirt slanted at an angle to shed the rain. A low hanging canopy provided porous shelter. The smoke from the fire dissipated in the precipitation, so any risk of discovery was mitigated by the double-edged sword of sudden rain. Besides, cold bodies needed warmth; clothes needed to be dried, and tea helped to fuel weary bodies forward.

Diana spoke as she nudged a stray twig into the fire, "Death moves west with us. Let us be alert. Keep the fire low and smokeless. Let us sleep and rest. Tomorrow we will reassess our goals. Tonight, our thanks go to God for helping us cross the terrible river. Special thanks to our sister Alisia for her courageous efforts on our behalf."

The group cheerfully slapped Alisia on the back and on her wet shoulders as she smiled sheepishly. "Praise be to God."

The next morning brought clear skies. While some clothes were still wet, they would dry during the hike. The weather soon turned warm and the group covered much ground without many words being shared.

Diana came upon a recently used path, yet it was so narrow only one person could navigate it at a time. "Let us follow this path for a while. It may offer us some kind of cover."

The winding trail led mostly west and led to an open field which revealed a small cabin. A corral bordered it on the left and a small out-building sat leaning on its right. A small boy played with a stick he'd made into a rifle on the front steps to the cabin.

"Wait here—Alisia and I will see who these people are and if they are friendly."

As they approached, the boy ran inside as the girls strode forward and waited a few meters from the porch. A man and his wife stepped onto the porch. The man carried a shotgun and the woman stood behind him.

Diana opened her arms, palms upward, "We mean you no harm; we are hungry and tired and hoped you would share some water and food with us. There are six of us altogether. If this is a burden, we will leave you in peace. If you can help us, we can pay you for your trouble."

The bearded man's head was covered in light-colored, almost yellow hair with a beard to match. His wife stood behind him wringing her hands in a grey dish towel. He cautiously stepped forward for a closer look and squinted hard at both girls. He took a few more steps closer and said, "Are you Armenians?"

Diana hesitated...looked somberly at the man and stared at his wife for a moment. "Yes... yes, we are."

"Are the others, the ones hanging back, your friends?"

"They are the rest of our family; we are travelers and have already walked many miles." Diana and Alisia waited for the couple's response.

The man looked at his wife. Her eyes looked up into his before she reluctantly nodded her head. He spoke in a deep voice, "Come inside and bring your family." The man left the door open and the woman began tending the stove and searching the open shelves... a variety of food items began to appear on the table.

Once seated, they learned that the man was German and a teacher in Aleppo. He and his wife had been there many years and learned to speak Armenian. Many Armenians came to him for help last month, but as hard as he tried, he could not stop the cruelty he witnessed.

"What did you see? Please tell us," asked Diana.

"Minister Talaat, an evil man, ordered the extermination of all Armenians in Aleppo. Even babes in the cradle were not to be spared. Neighboring Arabs and Kurds were invited to rape and plunder the Armenians while sordid Turks raped pretty Armenian girls right in the streets—even in front of foreign visitors. They had no fear of reprisals because of the deadly decree issued from Talaat. Even when the Armenians were able to bribe some of the more moderate Turks, the orders came that no Armenians could be protected, and the penalties would be harsh for anyone disobeying the decree. I tried my best to stop the slaughter, but I was threatened with death for myself and my family. The Armenians were rounded up and placed behind barbed wire—no water, no food. They withered away and in a few weeks...soon died of thirst and disease.

Despite the pleas of Europe and the United States—and even the Pope, the killing continued.

"Did any Armenians survive?" asked Diana.

"The only Armenians who managed to survive were the ones who fled toward Musa Dagh. Some say there are thousands of Armenians there who (learning of the Turks' plans for them) resist by fighting and killing the Turks who enter their city and attempted to disarm them.

Many Turks have been killed there, but they continue to come in great numbers. We heard the Armenians battle bravely, but I fear they will soon be overwhelmed. Armenians in the surrounding areas, of all ages, are going to join the fight, but the Turk's numbers seem to only grow. That is what I have been told.

The man's wife placed bread, fruit, milk, and nuts on the table. Hot soup was ladled into large bowls with chunks of hard bread on the bottom. Diana led the prayers as the German family watched....

"Dear Father above who protects and looks after us, we thank you for this blessing you have bestowed upon your lowly servants. Please bless this family for their kindness and hospitality, and now guide us to our destiny in Musa Dagh, for we know that all our strength and courage stems from you—our Lord, our God. Amen.

The group ate heartily.

"You can stay here in the outbuilding for a little while and gain your strength, but we cannot protect you after that—I am sorry."

"Your kindness will be repaid in heaven. We thank you, but we will be on our way tomorrow to join our brothers and sisters in Musa Dagh in life or death."

That night, the family of six shared their thoughts with one another.

Diana spoke first, "Let us speak freely now, for the German teacher has provided us with new information for us to consider. Who wants to speak first?"

Sofi signaled with her hand, "I will follow my family anywhere, so my thoughts are with you. If we go to Musa Dagh, we will die fighting for our right to be free of tyranny and persecution. I can not think of a better way to die."

Lusine followed, "I agree. Musa Dagh—it is our destiny to help with our arrows and bullets to kill as many Turks as we can before we meet our Maker in heaven."

Brosh nodded, "Musa Dagh. Yes, it is right for us."

Alisia spoke softly, "I do not wish to die; I wish to live, love, marry, bear children—my sadness knows no boundaries, but I see no other way. However, if we make it to Musa Dagh, and by some miracle, we find passage out of this cursed land, I want to take my chances in another country."

The others nodded their heads vigorously.

Seda smiled in agreement and scurried across the small room to hug Alisia.

Diana spoke last, "I agree with my sister; her wisdom speaks well beyond her years. Let us begin our journey to Musa Dagh tomorrow. We will skirt around Aleppo and avoid confrontation there. Sleep well, for we have miles to go before we will sleep again. Faces were washed, teeth were brushed, and blankets were rolled out. Before the moon silhouetted the filigreed curtain of leaves and needles, the small band of weary travelers were already asleep.

After a few hours, Brosh made his way outside. As he opened his pants, the cool air blew over his penis, and he relieved himself of the tea he drank earlier. He heard some leaves rustle behind him. Diana brushed past him and squatted by the nearest tree—her left hand braced against the trunk as she followed his example—a slight sigh left her lips. The lack of modesty between brother and sister allowed them to whisper openly in the moonlight.

"I dreamed a strange vision before I came out here," he said over his shoulder as he fastened his pants.

"What did you dream?" asked Diana as she stared up at the full moon.

"I dreamed of a Bad-Dragon that displayed magical powers of kindness and wisdom. This Bad-Dragon knew my story, and he pointed me in the right direction and bestowed upon me courage and wisdom. He said nothing, but I understood him clearly. His fierce looks did not scare me, for I knew he was my friend. Does that sound crazy?"

"I don't think so, but why do you call him 'Bad'?"

"I guess bad can sometimes mean good—you know, like cool. Brosh smiled.

Diana stood up straight, pulled up her pants and turned toward Brosh. Her lithe body glowed with an aura of moonlight and mist. "I always wondered where you gained such wisdom and courage; now, I know. Say hi to that Bad-Dragon for me. I could use some of his magical wisdom right now." They both laughed.

Before they entered the out-building, Diana stepped in front of the young man, placed her hands on Brosh's shoulders, and gently rested her forehead against his as she whispered softly into his face. Her moist breath covered his eyes, nose, and cheeks with soft puffs of her inner warmth. "Dragons possess many magical features, so this Bad-Dragon's timing is perfect. Besides, magic is afoot for those of us who believe in spirituality and God's power. I believe there remains much we do not understand, but by being true to our hearts and fighting the good fight…well, there are forces beyond our imaginations ready to help us in our time of need. Does _that_ sound crazy?" She smiled as she placed her arm around his shoulder. Simon returned the gesture. They quietly walked up the stairs together—brother and sister.

Chapter 51

CLIMB ~ EAT, SLEEP, AND PRAY

Once tired bodies now moved energetically southward around Aleppo in an effort to avoid the influx of Turks entering from the north. Deeper into the terrain, the family took time to hunt, sleep, and replenish their bodies. Day followed day with upward progress on sore feet only relieved by breathtaking views of multi-colored mountains celebrating the late rains of spring. The rocky paths offered only rugged passage through the mountain range, and the altitude thinned the precious oxygen as they trudged along. Nevertheless, no one complained as all thoughts were focused on Musa Dagh and the prospect of joining Armenian brothers and sisters who refused to go silently into the dark destiny deviously designed by the Turkish leadership.

A flat ledge before the next precipice seemed to invite the fatigued family as they looked at one another's dog-tired faces.

"Let us rest here tonight, and tomorrow we will climb and eventually began our descent," spoke Diana as she set down her pack. The others readily rested on their belongings as well. The sun's rays had weakened as it neared the receding western hills.

"We climbed all day today," said Seda as she set down her pack and sat on it. "Look how high we are!" She pointed at the super-terrestrial vista. The others let their minds expand as well. "We must be close to heaven! I bet I can touch an angel from up here."

Brosh laughed and tackled her, they rolled a bit and Seda ended up sitting on his chest. He looked up at her cloud-draped head, "Don't you know you've already been touched by an angel? How do you think you came to have a brother like me?" She laughed heartily as the two continued to wrestle much to the others' enjoyment.

Sofi sat beside Lusine (who often sat alone since Isgouhi's passing). "I would hope we made the most of today because here is a motto I now live by." Sofi rested her head on Lusine's shoulder…. "What you do each day is important because you gave up one day of your life for it." Lusine smiled looking up into the sublime sky.

The family had all night to think about what they would see tomorrow.

Time now to eat, sleep, and pray.

Chapter 52

ANTIOCH (Անտիոք) ~ THE CRADLE OF CHRISTIANITY

June 2, 1915—The family approached the ancient city of Antioch. Towering palm trees and time-worn Roman buildings offered the weary walkers a brief respite. The volatile and unstable ground continued to reveal its scars as it tried its best to recover from a 7.0 earthquake in 1914, the previous year.

Despite recent tremors, the fertile valley in all its historic significance lay out before the family of six like a green-brown sea of waving grasses and wheat stalks bordered by foot-trod tawny, tough turf. This was the sacred land where Barnabus (born Joseph) and Paul labored on God's behalf with such fervent spiritual passion that Christianity flowered and won the souls and minds of ordinary people throughout the land. They were now traversing upon hallowed ground where the Crusaders showed their lion-hearted bravery by heroically defending the Christian Church against the Muslim invaders.

Antioch's history included its great patron goddess and civic symbol, the Tyche (Fortune) — a majestic seated figure, crowned with the ramparts of Antioch's walls and holding wheat stalks in her right hand, with the river Orontes symbolized as a youth swimming under her feet. According to one historian, the Tyche of Antioch was originally a young virgin sacrificed at the time of the founding of the city to ensure its continued prosperity and good fortune.

But that was then...and this is now.... Today, the minarets of Islam are ten times more numerous than the church belfries of Christianity. Today, the once populous city of ancient Syria is now a major town of south-central Turkey near the mouth of the Orontes River. Yes, Turkey now dominates the lion's share of the Middle-East, but oh, how decadent was the land grab, how inhumane the slaughter, and how lowly the regard for human life. **Such infamy shall never be forgotten by Armenians around the world.**

～᠀～

As the family moved warily toward the city, Diana spotted two older women whom she believed were Armenian. Soon, she struck up a conversation. Sofi and Diana asked many questions and learned how the men of this village were expert wood-carvers, and how the chief occupations were the the culture of silk worms for producing raw silk. The silk would be weaved into colorful handkerchiefs and scarves using large wooden looms. She told them how the American Missionaries opened schools and taught the children to read. The women pointed out Armenian homes surrounded by mulberry trees and healthy orchards covered by terraced slopes to the south and west. The venerable ladies referred to the mountain range of Musa Dagh as "Mount Moses" and told the girls that most Armenians knew the beloved mountain and its trails and gorges like the backs of their hands.

At this point, the oldest lady beckoned the girls closer and whispered, "We heard the Turks are planning to exterminate our race, so be careful and watch your backs. They are merciless, mean, and...stupid. Kill them with your intellect and imagination, for they have neither." The toothless woman leaned forward and continued in a whisper as she glanced one way and then another, "One popular priest told his flock to go with the Turks and he would try to lessen the harshness of their deportation, so they followed their spiritual leader's advice. Sadly, no man, woman, or child from his flock was ever seen again. Mercy is a stranger to the Turks. As we speak, most Armenians are retreating up into the mountain because they know there is no chance to defend the lower villages in the foothills against the numerous Turkish troops that are certain to follow.

"We would go with you, but we are too old to climb mountains. No, we will stay and fight them here on our own land...and on our own terms. Besides, we are old now, our lives are behind us. We look forward to our next life—one of everlasting peace and contentment."

Sofi hugged the ladies and kissed each one on the cheek. As she did, she looked over the elder's brightly colored shawl in the direction of the mountain. A large hawk appeared out of nowhere and effortlessly rode an updraft not ten yards away. It's aquiline profile offered a piercing eye that stared directly into Diana's soul—her breath left her body! In that moment, the airborne messenger banked hard to the left and headed for the safety of the mountain. Diana accepted its appearance and direction as positive signs.

Thank you Mother—you still guide me from your perch in heaven. May I make you proud in the near future, for I feel I shall be tested...please grant me the strength to overcome my enemies while helping my friends and the wisdom to know the difference between the two.

Diana's family skirted the historic city, but they did not linger long on the city's fringes. Their goal lay ahead, so they leaned forward and headed west. The mountain grew larger....

Musa Dagh seemed to cast a mystical spell on the group as they moved northwest toward the coast. The small family trekked over the countryside, and the earth rose before them until it crested at the top of a smaller, yet no less formidable mountain range.

"We will take the trail through the mountains and drop down into Musa Dagh and gently place a finger on the pulse of the town," stated Diana. "We will discuss our options afterwards."

Sofi threw her arm over Diana's shoulder and smiled into her sister's eyes. As their foreheads touched, a silent message passed from one sister to the other. Within that transference, Diana "heard" her sister as clearly as if she had spoken in her ear—*We are almost there my sister. Lead the way, and we will follow."*

Chapter 53

TO MOUNT MOSES ~ AND A LAST STAND

June 17, 1915 As the group of six descended into Musa Dagh, they could hardly believe its transformation. The natural beauty of the mountain range gave way to the helter-skelter actions of the people below who appeared like ants from the family's high-altitude perspective. As they quickly followed an ancient path down into the city, the family was aghast to find Armenians of all ages in distress. Warily, they looked for some form of Armenian leadership to offer their services. The city was in a state of confusion and chaos and no order could be found until Diana noticed a grizzled man of middle-age whose posture and countenance projected leadership. Amid decisive gesticulations, it was clear—he was one of the leaders. She strode forward confidently with the others right behind her. She placed a strong hand on his shoulder, and with her face close to his, she spoke directly, "I am Diana. My family has traveled many miles to be here. We are armed and ready to fight and offer our service to help protect our people."

He stared at her for a moment, looked at the others standing behind her. He noted their bows, rifles, and pistols—the salt and pepper beard slowly moved upward as he smiled slightly, "Are you by any chance the **Angel Archers of Death** whose deeds are sung and told widely?"

Diana's blood rose quickly to her cheeks. The others just smiled. Seda beamed, "Now, we are the <u>Angel</u> Archers of Death! Hooray! I love angels!"

The Armenian leader looked past Diana and smiled at Seda's outburst. "You are them! Good fortune has finally come upon us! You are a Godsend—we need fighters and prayed you would come and help us in our time of need."

He pointed toward Mount Moses— "We are headed up the mountain where we can fight with an advantage that will be needed to overcome such overwhelming odds—more Turks come as we speak. We welcome our sisters and brothers of the Hye; we need your arrows, guns, and unflinching hearts." He bowed his head and ran off to tell others of the great news.

Other Armenian leaders and priests soon came into view. "They are so young." said one person from the surrounding crowd. "Yes, but God often works his miracles through the arms and hearts of our youth, for they carry the future upon their shoulders."

The leaders decided to gather a large food supply, so they instructed the people to gather their flocks of sheep and goats and move them up the mountainside. Weapons were also collected and included a few modern rifles but more were old flint-lock rifles and horse-pistols. While hundreds of weapons soon appeared, more than half of the men had only knives, hoes, axes, or shovels.

Diana instructed her family to stay together as they began the arduous climb into a different part of the mountain—one they had never seen. Meanwhile, their Armenian brothers and sisters zigzagged up the familiar rocky path as it twisted and turned deeper into the mountain's inner sanctum.

The first night brought rain which caught the thousand or so families off-guard. Thinking ahead, the men and women made sure the powder for the rifles remained dry and protected. Once the people were in position, trenches were dug, and when the mountain offered only hard-pan dirt—rocks were rolled together to form walls of protection from which the rifles could be stabilized and fired accurately. The best sharp-shooters were stationed strategically on this high ground.

During the next few days, the Turks acquired a thousand men. When the attack came, it was led by two hundred regular Turkish soldiers and a boastful general who announced to everyone he would clear the mountain of Armenians in one day.

The next day, he told the five thousand Armenians to surrender immediately—or die. The Armenians refused. Instead, they shouted down at the arrogant general, "Come on Mohammed, come on, we are not afraid of you!" Such insults infuriated the the Turk commander, and he took the bait. In a fit of rage, the red-faced general angrily ordered his soldiers into a frontal attack. Recklessly, the infuriated Turks rushed forward screaming into the slow moving fog.

Thanks to those already in Heaven, the Armenians were blessed with low clouds and fog that covered the top of the mountain where the Armenian sharpshooters were positioned—they could see the Turks, but the Turks could not see them clearly through the mist. These sharpshooters took careful aim—no bullets were wasted as the screams of assault were gradually silenced until a hush spread over the mountain now obscenely baptized in Turkish blood.

The Turks suffered so many casualties and deaths they were stunned. Meanwhile, the fortified Armenians were barely scratched. The Armenian positions remained steadfast and morale was high after the first battle.

As night after night passed, many brave women, some just teens, used the moonless nights to sneak back down into the village and find more food and water to feed the under-nourished and thirsty families. These intrepid children crept into the Armenian churches (which were slated to be burned and destroyed by the Turks) and saved the crosses, relics, paintings, and anything else they could carry. When they brought them up the mountain, the men rejoiced, and a frenzy of inspiration heated their blood—they were replenished spiritually and ready to fight again!

On July 21, more soldiers advanced on the higher position. This time they brought with them a rapid-fire field gun. Such heavy weaponry was unknown to the Armenians. Once the heavy gun zeroed in on the Armenian strongholds, it ripped apart lookout stations and man-made barriers. Several Armenians guarding the front line lost their lives—many more were severely wounded. The rapid-fire repeating machine gun's range was much farther than the Armenians' older guns could shoot; the Armenian leaders were at a loss on how to proceed.

Before long, Diana heard some talk that one of the young men volunteered to break through the Turk's defenses and sabotage the deadly field gun. The eleventh-hour do-or-die endeavor seemed to be a suicide mission, but the fate of the remaining Armenian families hung in the balance. What else could one do?

As the young man readied himself, a priest approached him. "Are you fearful my son?" The youth fastened a dagger to his belt and faced the priest. "Father, I welcome your blessing and kneel before you, but I fear not failure—my only fear was that I would not try."

"Well said my son, now take this holy blessing into the Valley of Death knowing that God smiles down upon your stouthearted courage." Many Armenians laid hands on the young man's head and shoulders. He who offered his life to be their champion bowed his head as the many hands touched his shoulders and more hands touched those shoulders that touched other shoulders as the crowd flowed outward until hundreds and hundreds of hands touched shoulders sending ethereal energy outward and inward towards its center like a flowering metaphysical force absorbing and releasing sacred power to be channeled Christ-like into its chosen source.

Diana could not see over the heads of those crowding around the youth.

The sharp-shooters were instructed to provide cover for the brave young man. Soon, the great flower opened and the young Adonis appeared in the open for all to see. He carried only a spear and a dagger as he leaped over rocks and dodged bullets fired in his direction.

Diana and Alisia were perched on a small ridge when Diana suddenly grabbed Alisia's arm and pointed toward the running figure. She had not spent but a day with him, yet by the way he moved, she knew it was him. Diana looked back at Alisia in amazement. **"Aram? Is that Aram?"**

Alisia nodded her head, "Yes, I believe it is—Oh my God. It is Aram!"

The two sisters leaned forward, straining their eyes to see more. Had he brought his father and the Freedom Fighters? How could he be here?

They watched him appear and disappear with startling speed and reckless abandon as the athletic leaps and slides took him ever closer to the rapid-fire popping of the machine gun poised on the ledge of a brush-covered cliff.

With great skill and stealth, Aram slithered through the brush and belly-crawled over rocks as he neared the gun's location. A few moments elapsed before he spied a red glow against the dark background of the mountain. All was quiet, but only for a moment; the silence broke with the staccato explosions of the field gun firing repeatedly as it sat heavily on a large flat rock; its barrel smoldering angrily as it sang out its ear-shattering death song.

Aram was well within range of the soldier behind the gun. He could hear the uniformed men talking as they loaded the gun with fresh bullets. The gun's barrel burned orange-red as the men hoisted up more ammo. He waited for the right moment. Finally, one of the gunners stood up to pass the fresh bullets to another Turk. Aram stood quickly, stepped forward as he flung his spear swiftly in the direction of the unsuspecting target—a dull thud sounded as the long spear smashed into the man's upper chest knocking him backwards into the other Turk. The long clip of bullets clattered on the rocks. Aram immediately jumped forward with only a knife in hand and with savage ferocity slew the other soldiers guarding the heavy gun.

As other witnessing Turks scrambled to reach the ledge, Aram stood behind the gun and used his bloody hands and young man's back to push with all his might until the monster machine began to inch reluctantly toward the edge of the cliff. Another soldier scrambled on to the ledge and took aim at Aram, but in that instant, the agile warrior pirouetted—his arm a blur as deadly dagger sped toward the armed soldier cutting through his left cheek and knocking him off balance. One more Herculean shove sent the machine gun menace to the edge of the cliff—teetering. Bullets rang out around Aram as he dove behind the boulder, but now he was unarmed and unable to make it back to the teetering machine gun. More Turks assembled strategically daring the Armenian hero to show himself. **The young Armenian hero was trapped!**

Yet, when one is down to nothing—God is up to something! Diana and Alisia suddenly appeared behind the Turks like angels of death and rained down arrows upon the unsuspecting soldiers threatening Aram. In the confusion, the soldiers turned their guns toward the women archers. Seeing his chance, Aram pulled himself up and threw his weight against the tottering machine gun. Young man and machine flew over the cliff's edge.

⌇⌇⌇

Diana's scream pierced the fog and echoed forth through the mountain. When Lusine, Sofi, Brosh, and Seda heard her cry, they flew down the mountainside to where she and Alisia were pinned down by soldiers.

Like bolts of lightning, arrows began to fly from everywhere. Soldiers' bodies became pin cushions with arrows jutting fatally from their bodies. Many soldiers dropped their weapons and retreated as hundreds of screaming Armenians, men and women, boys and girls, answered Diana's cry and descended from the mountain carrying swords, shovels, hoes, and knives in an inspired effort to rescue their hero.

Diana zig-zagged her way down to the cliff's edge with Alisia close behind. "Aram!" she screamed. *Please God, not Aram, not now, don't take him from me."*

From her knees, she suddenly spotted a bloody hand, and then another trying to claw its way up the cliff. Afraid to hope, Diana threw herself spread-eagled onto the smooth rock as Alisia grabbed her legs. Hands found hands, interlocked, and pulling with every fiber in her being...a familiar face appeared! Aram scrambled up the rock's face with Diana's help and the three dove for cover as more soldiers pushed up the mountain. The sisters ran towards their family members while Aram brought up the rear. As the others pulled their sisters to safety, Aram stumbled on the broken rocks and fell hard rolling into a crack in the mountain. When he tried to jump up and out, bullets ricocheted dangerously close to his head. More soldiers had secured the position; he was trapped once again. He looked for another way out and saw one opening to his left. He climbed furiously as the advancing Turks continued to fire wildly at the fleeing figure. Twisting away from the whizzing bullets, Aram fell and landed hard against a wall of granite; breathlessly, he assessed his wretched situation—a dead end! If he scaled the wall, he would be shot easily by the many pursuing Turks, but if he stayed, his fate would surely be sealed by the relentless enemy.

In that moment of uncertainty, he heard his name called out by a voice he knew from his dreams despite only hearing a few hundred of her words in real time—still, when he heard her voice—-he knew his prayers had been answered.

"Aram! Aram...up here...look up here!"

He looked up and saw Diana with her bow at the ready. The sun had broken through the clouds and enshrined her svelte body making it glow with dangerous beauty as she aimed her arrow seemingly at Aram's head. He froze for a moment and stared at the sun-blocked figure. Her steady hands raised the bow slightly higher and let loose an arrow that sailed just over his head and directly into the armed soldier taking aim behind him.

When Aram looked up again, five other archers stood behind Diana. The Angel Archers of Death, impressive and formidable, appeared in fighting stances with weapons at the ready and fire in their eyes. As more Turks scrambled over the ridge toward Aram, arrows suddenly whizzed repeatedly over the trapped youth's head, and one after another of the surprised Turks cried out in pain as their hot pursuit met a flurry of arrows and one carefully aimed bullet.

"**Now, come now**!," shouted Diana as Aram leaped up onto the rock face… after a struggle, he climbed upward and grasped a waiting hand. Diana pulled with all her strength as Aram leaped into the arms of the two sisters. Arrows continued to fly toward the pursuing Turks who now ducked for cover.

Together, Diana, Aram, and the others weaved between trees, crags, and brush as they made their way up the mountain to safety. The sun blinded the Turks' eyes as they tried to aim their weapons at the fleeing figures. In a few moments, the Archers of Death disappeared into Nature's haven.

Chapter 54

FIND A FRIEND ~ SAVE A LOVE ~

When Diana and Aram found a safe place between the crags of the mountain, they both began to speak at the same time until Aram held up his hand. "I know you have many burning questions, and I will answer them all, but first, thank you...thank you my Guardian Angel." His eyes searched hers for understanding...no other words were needed.

Diana held back as long as she could before asking, "Why...how? I don't understand. Your father? The Freedom Fighters? Are they all here?" Diana's florid face radiated elation and joy.

Aram drew in a long breath, "Okay, after you left...I could not get you out of my thoughts. Your words...simple questions...truthful answers...haunted me. What you said about a new country...a new life in a place not filled with hate and death...I knew you were right, but at the time, I could not explain my feelings. Such feelings were too new and confusing—my tongue lost its ability to speak, and I... I lost my chance to be with you.

After several restless nights, I spoke to my father, he completely understood; I was not expecting his agreeable response, but I underestimated my father's great wisdom once again. He then held my head in his hands, looked deep into my eyes, and told me to go and find you, so I have been searching everywhere. I heard tales of mythological proportion about women warriors with magical poison-tipped arrows and a passion for killing Turkish soldiers and police. I wasn't sure, but I remembered what you said about the coast, so I came here. When my efforts to find you in Musa Dagh proved futile, I lost hope. Yet, here, on this mountain, with thousands of Armenian men, women, and children ready to die for their right to live and worship freely—well, what better way to die than to die fighting for my brothers and sisters. Had I not came upon this righteous cause and took up arms with my brothers and sisters...I don't know what I would have done.

"So, you recklessly risk your life like a crazy man?"

Aram laughed at Diana's concerned inquiry. "Yes, a little like a crazy woman I know who runs screaming at a wild lion." Aram pulled her in close to him. "Seriously, I thought my life was over...so I had nothing to lose. My heart broken, but still beating— what would you have done?"

"I...well...I don't know, but you...your life could have been lost.... I was afraid you would be killed...I thought I'd lost you... Diana's face flushed with emotion as she remained bewildered at Aram's daring journey...alone...for her? All this way...for her?

"The Freedom Fighters and my father still fight the good fight near Van, but I had to try and find you— Again, you came to my rescue. I owe you... and your family...   my life...thank you. Thank you all."

With that said, Aram leaned over and softly kissed Diana on her lips. Once their lips touched, both felt their blood rush to different parts of their bodies, and their hearts began to beat as one.

Diana placed her hand on Aram's chest and slightly pushed him away. "I've never felt like this."

"Nor I," said Aram earnestly. "I know now I was destined to find you."

"We are so young, at least...I am. I do not know about such things," she said as she bowed her head.

"We will learn together. My heart soars to the stars now that I have found you...or you have found me...saved me."

The others came over and slapped Aram on the back and kissed his cheek.

"We missed you," said Brosh. "I was getting tired of being the only man in this family."

Such momentary joy...despite the misery surrounding them... brought much relief.

Brosh smiled...finally, an older brother.

Chapter 55

MOUNT MOSES' MIRACLE ~

The five thousand Armenians trapped on Mount Moses consisted of about eleven hundred men and fourteen hundred women — the rest were boys, girls, and babies. The Turks held the mountain under siege, and after thirty days of fierce fighting, the Armenians' food and ammunition were almost gone. The odds seemed overwhelming, so they prayed to God for a sign…or…a miracle.

The Armenian leaders realized their best hope for survival lie with the Allied ships patrolling the Mediterranean Coast. In a desperate attempt, two huge white banners (made out of bedsheets with a large cross painted in red) were hoisted up—

Help! Christians in Distress! Need Rescue!

A passing French warship on patrol came fairly close to the shoreline. The ship's captain saw the large red cross on the banner and commanded the ship to stop its progress while he investigated the situation. The Armenians prayed with renewed hope.

The best Armenian swimmer was sent out to deliver a note written in French by one of the reverends stating that thousands of Armenian Christians were about to be slaughtered if the Allies did not rescue them. The note was safely sealed in a small tight box hung from a chain around the swimmer's neck. The warship's captain stared through binoculars as he witnessed the heroic effort made by the young Armenian swimmer. Before long, the French sailors were helping the exhausted swimmer on board. Once on deck, he made the sign of the cross several times, so they would know he was a Christian, for he could not speak French.

The French Captain read the message and wrote back asking the Armenians to hold on for eight more days. In that time, the captain relayed the situation to his government. Soon, the French and the other allied powers made the decision to rescue the Armenians. The fighting intensified, but the Armenians fought with renewed hope and even more vigor.

Diana and the others used their learned skills to help rebuff the Turks' desperate measures to wipe out the resistance before the allied ships could rescue the trapped Armenians. Diana and her family watched with pride as women of all ages took up the fight as well and fought right along side the men. More men, women, and children died during the last battles as the Turks tried repeatedly to defeat the Armenians.

Sofi and Lusine were both wounded, and Brosh was knocked unconscious when a bullet grazed his head. The fighting finally broke when the ships' captains witnessed what the Turks were trying to do. The ships' big guns began a barrage of bombardments that cleared a wide area allowing the Armenians a passage down the mountain and on to smaller ships waiting to transport the refugees. Ladders were then lowered and the refugees climbed aboard the huge warships.

Diana, her family, and the resistance fighters bravely held the Turks at bay while the refugees were evacuated. Eventually, the mission was successful with most of the refugees safe on board and headed to Egypt.

When the ships began arriving at a safe port, an accurate census was taken of the survivors:

427 Babies and children under four years of age, 508 girls from 4—14 years of age, 628 boys from 4—14 years of age, 1441 women above 14 years of age, 1,054 men above age 14.

Total: 4,058 men, women, and children were rescued.

These Armenians of Musa Dagh survived fifty-three days on Mount Moses. They were taken by ship to Port Said in Egypt and placed in refugee camps provided by the British Government until the end of World War I. The Armenian Red Cross and other countries' medical teams tended the sick and wounded.

Refugee life in Egypt's Port Said presented many problems, but the hospitality of Egypt and the help provided by the British and French will never be forgotten.

Eventually, many Armenians returned to their native villages after the war, but many more sought and found passage to several other welcoming countries throughout the world. One of these countries was a young country in need of more people, so it readily welcomed immigrants from all over the world. The growing United States of America opened its arms and welcomed thousands of immigrants during this time period. The vast variety of skills, perspectives, cultures, and knowledge these determined people brought to the North America shores propelled this young country toward recognizable world status in a relatively short period of time.

As time passed, Diana and her family (including Aram) found passage on a ship carrying immigrants to America. The money for passage depleted most of their funds, but they accomplished their goal—passage to a new country and a chance at a new life.

Chapter 56

TWENTY-NINE DAYS AT SEA ~ A BLUE BABY BOY

Diana describes the boat trip to America.

The boat's compartments were full to overflowing, but we managed to squeeze into a small corner of the ship. There were many people, children, crying babies, and much confusion. Different languages rang out all around me as I walked the length of the ship to stretch my legs. Later, Aram offered his shoulder for me to sleep on, but the rough seas rocked the boat violently and my my stomach became uneasy. We seemed to take turns joining many others who also leaned over the side of the ship to empty sour stomachs on white-capped waves.

The seas remained rough and soon many more people were sick and vomiting over the side of the boat—if they could make it there. My family and I tried to sleep and save our strength for the long voyage. We had little food. Some bread and water was made available every day, sometimes rice—simple sustenance. Still, as the days passed, more people became seriously sick with different diseases. We stayed close together and tried to separate ourselves from those people who were coughing and vomiting. It was hard to sleep, to breathe, to wash…oh, how I missed being able to bathe myself.

One young woman with a swollen belly experienced severe pains one night. An Armenian nurse provided much needed help when the time came to deliver the baby, but the little boy was born blue—and despite desperate attempts, he never took a breath in this world. The mother was inconsolable.

Preparations were made and a small service was held on deck. Brosh helped one of the craftsmen, and they constructed a simple wooden coffin to protect the newborn infant now wrapped in an embroidered white scarf bordered in delicate filigree.

After prayers, the tiny box was sealed tight and slid overboard as the large boat rocked to and fro. The grieving mother could only look on helplessly as her son's coffin splashed lightly into the welcoming sea. However, the sealed box did not sink; instead, it began bobbing in the waves. Still, as the sun set in the horizon, we all bowed our heads in respectful sorrow.

The next day, I heard crying and screaming at daybreak. Aram and I made our way along the undulating deck and there at the back of the boat, standing with arms outstretched over the rail toward the ocean— stood the distraught young mother reaching out desperately to the wide blue ocean. I approached the woman hoping to console her when I suddenly saw her source of great distress.

There below the back of the massive ship floated the miniature coffin. Somehow, the tiny coffin with the little blue boy inside remained entrenched in the huge ship's continuing wake and bobbed up and down as it relentlessly followed our ship as if reluctant to be separated from its wailing mother.

The sad scene brought many to the back of the boat, but as much as we tried, we failed to comfort the mother or remove her from her wave-tossed watch.

Chapter 57

AMERICA'S COPPER LADY ~MOTHER OF EXILES

Diana describes the harbor entrance of the United States' Eastern Seaboard.

Sofi and Lusine both recovered quickly from their wounds, and Brosh laughed when we teased him about how his head must be made of hard wood to be able to ricochet a speeding bullet off his skull. It left a rather striking two-inch scar along the left side of his scalp. Sofi and Lusine compared their wounds with Alisia's healed leg scar.

When we first heard people yelling that they saw land, we ran to the rails looking over the waves and through the wisps of fog and spray. Soon, we were surprised to see a giant green-colored lady statue cradling a book in one hand and a flame in her other raised right hand. There were spikes coming out of her head, and she looked so strong that my breath stopped as I stared in disbelief. How could anyone build such a gigantic statue? She was majestic, with a determined gaze and serious brow, yet welcoming as her upraised arm held out its huge torch—a beacon of light to show us the way to Ellis Island. Someone said she was a copper goddess given to America by the French for their help in defeating the Germans. They said this woman was called "The Mother of Exiles", and that the seven spikes in her crown represented the seven continents and the seven seas—and all were welcomed to her shores. A strong woman who symbolized America's willingness to help others in distress. As we drew closer, the poetic inscription engraved upon it was translated for us. It read (in part) as follows:

Give me your tired, your poor,

Your huddled masses, yearning to breath free, The wretched refuse of your teeming shore, Send these, the homeless, tempest tost to me, I lift my lamp beside the golden door.

Emma Lazarus   (Died November 19th, 1887)

My heart melted and my eyes wept when those words were translated for me.

Our bodies tingled with excitement when we finally were asked to disembark. Before we knew it, huge buildings surrounding us jutting up into the bright blue sky. I almost fell over backward trying to take in the dizzying height of each edifice.

The American officials directed us into a great hall with high rounded ceilings covered with beautiful tiles. Archways led to different rooms, and the building seemed to hold countless compartments and sections. This is where we had to get into line and wait...and wait....and...wait.

First, I was given a medical exam. When I passed that, I was moved to another area and again had to wait to take an oral test. An older official set me down and asked me an important question—"What is your name?" I understood and told him. Interpreters helped us communicate, and my treatment continued in a fair and professional manner.

One after another, we each passed our tests and were led to a doorway. The next thing we knew, we were outside. The sunlight blinded me for a moment, but in the very next moment, our group was being led out of the building and onto the busy streets of New York. Only then did we realize we were strangers—in a strange land. We just stared, mouths agape—we truly made it to this new and wonderful country.

Now what do we do?

Chapter 58

FACTORY WORK...
UNLEAVENED BREAD...

"The buildings are so tall they hurt my neck. I almost fell over backwards trying to see to the top of them. Which one are we going to live in?" Seda spun in a circle trying to see all the skyscrapers at once.

The small family had no sense of where to go, but one Armenian older gentleman who had fought bravely alongside them on the Mountain of Moses (and joined them on their pilgrimage across the stormy sea) saw the group's bewilderment and offered them his help.

"You might be able to find factory work here in New York, but the competition is fierce, and the wages are low. Come with us; my family and I are leaving for a place called Worcester. It is not far from here in a place called Massachusetts. I have a brother who is there, and he says the factories are hiring Armenians and other immigrants."

Diana talked it over with the group and returned to the man in a few moments. "Thank you for your kindness. We have a little money left, so we will follow your counsel and try to find work in Worcester."

Diana continues her narration after arriving in Worcester.

"We used most of the remaining money we had to travel to Massachusetts by train. Looking out the window, the rolling hills were covered with so many trees I could not see the ground. Upon entering Worcester, I saw many buildings made from red bricks. They were long and sturdy structures with many windows. We found simple quarters for reasonable rent, and began working at one of the glass factories. The factory managers trained us well and soon we were making glass windows, doors, car windows, aquariums, and other items completely new to us. The hours were long, but the pay was enough, so we earned our own money for rent and food, and the foreman said we were good workers.

～٦️ベ٦️～

"As the months turned into years, Aram and I married and rented our own modest home on the third floor of what our neighbors called a triple-decker. The two families below us were immigrant families as well, and we were soon sharing amenities like we did with our neighbors in Armenia.

Alisia started a small leather shop (father's influence) and will soon leave the factory when her business begins to make more money. She met a friendly Armenian young man by the name of Armen Kustigian. They are hopelessly in love and dating regularly. She remains my "twin", my best friend, and my "Sun".

Sofi will be married soon to a large Irish man with a grin as wide as his shoulders. His name is James Robert O'Doud whom she met in the factory, and although he has no neck (all chest and head), he showed her gentle kindness, and she soon fell in love. The two of them complete each other.

Brosh left the factory, rented an aged barn, and became a craftsman working wonders with wood. Some of his pieces include finely crafted bows, arrows, tables, chairs, picture frames, and bookshelves. His items are becoming widely known and in demand. Being blessed, Brosh inherited several acres of land in the country from an old man who bought a table from him. He and Brosh became friends when the older man's wife died a year ago and the work on the ranch became too much for the frail elder. Brosh offered to help the man with chores on the property and cared diligently for the old man's two horses. When the lonely man died, he left Brosh the small ranch.

Lusine found a modest home that she shares with three other women. It has a fine kitchen with a large oven/stove. The entire neighborhood opens its doors and windows when she bakes, and soon she has plenty of visitors ready to sample her culinary creations. Last month, she used her small savings to open a small bakery. Already, it is quite popular and offers "Armenian bread" (unleavened bread). The Americans call it cracker bread. We visit her regularly for her freshly baked delights as they are the best in Worcester.

Seda spends her free time with Brosh and helped him set up his home. They continue to laugh and tease each other as their love for each other continues to blossom and evolve. For now, Seda is staying with Aram and myself. She helps me with chores around the house and loves to cook. She looks forward to helping us with our baby which we expect next year—his name will be Simon. Seda's natural beauty is only eclipsed by her inner thirst for knowledge, and she has enrolled in a local public school. Her English improves rapidly which helps all of us as she serves as a translator and interpreter for us whenever we need her.

She likes to join us for our weekly walks in the park. We live near Elm Park which offers walking trails, a tranquil pond, and a variety of trees that shade the peaceful park and invites people of all nationalities and from all walks of life to come and enjoy its charming gifts.

Our growing Armenian-American family comes together every Thanksgiving and Christmas to share our blessings and thank God for his providence. We also offer up a special blessing for our family members now gone. Yes, Thanksgiving is a wonderful American holiday we have enthusiastically embraced along with other cultural traditions that help expand our horizons and enhance our vision.

Our lives here continue to change, and despite the language barrier, new opportunities open up every day. America opened her arms to us, and we hope to be worthy of her great generosity. Nevertheless, we shall *always* remember our own country we left behind, and our loving relatives both here on Earth and in Heaven."

God bless and godspeed to all struggling immigrants of the past, present, and future who seek only better lives for themselves and their families.

The End

ABOUT THE AUTHOR

Bruce Badrigian grew up in Worcester, Massachusetts. He left the East Coast for the West Coast in 1971 with his dad's military duffel bag and a small hand-made sign that simply read WEST. After hitch-hiking for 2 1/2 weeks (perhaps another story), he made it to California. He soon settled in a small beach town called Cayucos where he would coach Little League baseball, serve on the Cayucos Advisory Council, serve on the Cayucos School Board, and live happily for the next twenty years.

After graduating from Cuesta College and Cal Poly University in San Luis Obispo County, he put his B.A. in English and teaching credential to its best use and began teaching at Mission College Prep in San Luis Obispo. After a year, he accepted a teaching position at Morro Bay High School where he would teach English and Reading for 33 years. After completing his Senior Project at Cal Poly on a little known program called Advanced Placement (AP), he started teaching the first AP classes on the Central Coast. Later, he would be hired by Nat Allyn (Western Regional Director of the College Board) to train new AP English teachers throughout California. He also created a reading program for his struggling students called Bad-Dragon Reading.

After receiving his Masters in Education and a Reading Specialist Credential, he taught English and Reading to graduate students, student teachers, and current teachers at the University of La Verne (5 years). After he semi-retired, he became a university supervisor of student teachers in language arts at Cal Poly University in San Luis Obispo (2 years). He also served six years as president of the San Luis Coastal Teachers' Association and has been a member of the Curriculum Study Commission for twenty-seven years. Currently, he teaches English part-time for Cuesta College (18 years).

He enjoys spending time with his wife and three children, writing, playing Pickleball, kayak fishing for trout in McCloud, CA and golfing in and around Morro Bay and McCloud.

He and his wife divide most of their time between Morro Bay and McCloud. Mr. Badrigian also travels back to Worcester, MA to visit family and old friends. This novel is his first historical fiction piece.

62056910R00177

Made in the USA
Charleston, SC
30 September 2016